DEAD MESSENGER

By Tim Mahoney

First Edition
Copyright © 2015 Tim Mahoney
www.tpmahoney.com
Cover design: Zoe Shtorm
Proofreader: Kathleen Lewinski

Other books by this author:

Dead Like Lazarus
Dead a Long Time
If the Dead Could Speak
Secret Partners
Jack's Boy
We're Not Here
Halloran's World War

ISBN: 978-0-9908974-3-9

This book is dedicated to my brother and sisters,
good souls all of them:
Dennis
Maureen
Kevin
Susan
Kathleen
Ellen
Billy
Jim
. . . .

NOTE

This novel is based closely on the true gangster history of the Public Enemies era.

The Barker-Karpis Gang, as presented here, were revealed mostly by information given the FBI by three underworld sources: Bess Green of Saint Paul, Byron Bolton of Chicago, and Volney Davis, who grew up with the Barker brothers in Oklahoma.

During the early 1930s, Saint Paul was denounced as "the poison spot of American crime," on the floor of the U.S. Senate. Since the turn of the century, the city had been home to a protection racket that allowed criminals to purchase immunity from prosecution. Aided by a profoundly corrupt police department, gangsters based in Saint Paul roamed the Midwest, pulling off bank robberies, kidnappings and murders.

Most of the notorious criminals of the Public Enemies era had connections to Saint Paul's underworld.

CHAPTER ONE

JANUARY, 1934
EAGLE RIVER, WISCONSIN

The week after New Years, the phone calls began. Afraid it
might be the sheriff, I didn't pick up.

Being a wanted man preys on your mind, ceaseless. You never
know when they'll come for you: just as you finish dinner, in the
middle of your restless sleep, when you've just stepped into the
bath. I was isolated, deep in the forest that winter, and anyone who
motored down the driveway would only be trouble: Burglars, the
sheriff, or, worst case, the friends of Swede Fanlund.

So for days, I let the phone ring. It wasn't out of the question,
here in rube country, that the sheriff would phone and ask me to
turn myself in. The would save him the trouble of driving through
snow drifts.

One cloudy, cold afternoon I could stand the ringing no more.
"Hello?"

Silence. It was not a hang-up, but I could get no response. After
several shouts I slammed the earpiece into its cradle.

I thought of dialing O and asking questions, but the telephone exchange was downtown, next to the jail. Deputies were in the telephone office flirting with the operators day and night.

Every day I took the dogs for a long walk in the snow-packed woods. They were enjoying Eagle River, I was not. Snowflake was fluffy, white, and loved to roll in the snowdrifts. Hula Girl, a black Border Collie, amused herself by sniffing mouse trails underneath the snow.

We climbed the hill behind the cottage, me on snowshoes, and stomped into a pine forest. A path followed the single strand of overhead power line, and led to the burned ruins of my aunt Doris's farm. Those ruined acres belonged to my sisters and I now, but weren't worth much, having been torched by Swede Fanlund. Our charred potato farm was almost surrounded by Cousin Cindy's 120 acres of forest, lakefront and swamp.

One mild day, when we returned to the cabin after a walk, I made coffee in a French press and sat with the dogs near the big roaring brick fireplace. I had become quite the reader in my isolation. I'd just finished *The Thin Man* and was beginning Dorothy Sayers' *Murder Must Advertise*. I was imagining London when the phone rang.

I picked it up. I listened. Someone was breathing into the other end.

"Hello?"

No answer.

"Who are you? Why are you calling here?"

Nothing. No hang-up, no voice, no more breathing.

I put down the phone, unnerved.

Last summer, in a surge of guilt, I had thrown my weapons into the Mississippi, a decision I now regretted.

On the lake side of the cottage was a porch that doubled as a spare bedroom. I walked into it and stared out the windows and up the snowy driveway. Nobody could drive down it without me hearing the crunching of tires. There were times this winter when nobody could drive down it all, without a snowplow. Still my guilty mind whispered that they would come for me on foot, on snowshoes, on skis through the woods. Swede's men or the sheriff, it didn't matter much anymore. I had lost the means, or even the will, to resist.

This kind of isolation gets to you. Although it was prison I feared, up here I was living in jail of my own, with a view of an ice-bound lake. The radio, the books, the dogs were my only friends. And the radio station, beamed from Rhinelander, came in garbled. I dared not go into town except on grocery and hardware dashes, and only when the stores were busy. I had the urge, somehow, to attend Mass, but didn't want to risk being seen, a stranger in a small congregation. So I visited Saint Peter The Fisherman at off times, lighting a candle for the good departed souls: Mom, Dad, nutty Uncle Joe, cranky Aunt Doris. Since Swede Fanlund's specialty had been arson, I lit one for him too.

The phone woke me the next morning, and the calls came, two or three a day, all week. I answered every time now, sometimes raging into the phone, sometimes silent with contempt, but the caller's routine never varied. Was it a child playing a prank? A lunatic in an asylum? I considered cutting the wire, but that phone, and a trusty Essex Terraplane, were my only connections to the warmer world.

On Tuesday, January 16th, the phone rang all day it seemed, and I let it ring except for that last call, deep into the night.

"Nice of you to think of me," I said. "Call back when you have something to say."

On Wednesday the phone didn't ring at all. That afternoon, I heard a car in the forest, slipping and grinding down the long driveway.

The dogs were howling for blood and my hair stood on end when I saw Swede's blue Pontiac slaloming down the hill. For a spooky moment I believed in ghosts but then realized it must be Swede's friends coming to kill me. I had the instinct to run for the kitchen door, open it, and at least let the dogs escape. But they were both herding dogs, bred to stick with the shepherd, and I rehearsed a plea: Let the dogs live, they've done nothing wrong. I saw in a flash that a gangland death wouldn't be so bad. Clean, efficient, painless. There were rules to our game, and torture was out of bounds.

As the car rolled to a stop in a snowdrift between cottage and lake, I experienced a pulse of pure madness. Swede was dead, right? The Gates of Hell had not opened. The laws of physics had not been suspended. My heart was pounding as if that big pale bully, resurrected, might actually step out of the car. The dogs by now were insane with fury.

The Pontiac's passenger door opened. Around the long blue hood strode Alvin Karpis.

He wore a brown fedora and a tweed overcoat, and his oxfords, polished, disappeared in the snow. I saw no weapon, but that did not ease my panic. Karpis and Swede were connected, although I did not know how deep their fellowship had been.

Karpis mounted the stone stairway.

I had no feelings now. I was watching myself from Heaven, a place of peace and indifference to these ridiculous, puny Earthlings.

I opened the door.

"Well," Karpis said, "aren't you going to invite me in?"

I stepped back. That Pontiac behind him was idling, all doors closed, huffing smoke into the pure piney air. Men were inside that car, but looking over Karpis' shoulder at frosty windows, I could not tell how many.

I stepped back. Uninvited, Karpis unbuttoned his coat. He threw it on the couch, and topped it with his fedora. His outerwear gave the impression of a bank president, but underneath he wore a hunting outfit: plaid shirt and rough wool trousers. He did not seem to be carrying a pistol. He had lost weight since I'd last seen him, in summer. Even then he'd barely weighed 120 pounds.

"Nice," Karpis said, looking around like he was considering buying the place. "Stylish."

Cindy's place was elegant, for a lake cabin. It had hardwood floors in the living room, a big picture window framing Snipe Lake, an impressive brick fireplace, plush furniture, brass floor lamps, and a grand piano.

"They said we'd find you here," said Karpis.

"Who said?"

"Can you put a couple of old friends up until the weekend?"

With Karpis in the house, the dogs had calmed down, circling and sniffing him with reluctant acceptance. I too began to recover my nerve and said:

"Who are these old friends?"

But I knew he meant Fred and Doc Barker.

"You know them all right," Karpis said. "And more important, they know you."

I stammered. "There's only one bedroom," I lied.

"We're hardy," said Karpis. "We'll sleep on the floor."

He peered into the kitchen, then stepped over to the parlor's windows for a view of the snowy backyard. "Powers, I hate to intrude on an old friendship, but we're in a situation."

He unbuttoned his padded shirt, stood in front of the fireplace.

"Nice and warm," he said.

"Well, I came out here to get away," I said. "You know, from things. Peace and quiet. I like that."

"Maybe you were a little quick on the draw," he said. "But I had no use for the Swede."

"I have no idea what you're talking about."

Karpis clapped me on the shoulder. "That's the spirit."

"How many are you and how long do you want to stay?"

Karpis, removing his leather driving gloves, held up four fingers.

"Four. Four of us. Just until the weekend, at most. We'll probably be gone by Friday. We'll take care of the groceries and the booze, and we'll leave money for the house."

He lit a Chesterfield, stepped over to the ashtray, an amber glass dish held up by a brass stand. It was next to Cindy's piano. Upon that piano was a framed photo of a young girl.

"Cute," said Karpis.

"The owner," I said. "Long time ago." Cindy had played a haunting piano before the disease struck her. She's bitter now, and living in a sanitarium in Milwaukee. Angry and proud, she tolerates no visitors. Nobody was to see her in her ruined, crippled state, but remember her always as a beautiful, promising child.

"Powers, don't give me that blank look," Karpis said. "You're a hunted man. We know what it's like. Guys like us stick together or they pick us off one by one."

I began to realize I had nothing to lose by letting them stay. If the state of Minnesota had its way, I'd be locked up for a lifetime at Stillwater. Harboring gangsters wouldn't be the worst of my crimes. Like most people who knew him, I had come to loathe Karpis. A greedy opportunist with no conscience or feeling, he was cavalier about destroying whoever and whatever stood in his way. I feared what he might do if I shut him out. I certainly couldn't call the sheriff. If I refused to host this gang, they might move in here anyway. They'd shoot me and the dogs, and let our corpses freeze in the woods, to be devoured by raccoons and wolves. If I was busted for harboring gangsters, so what? Those charges would be dropped as I stood trial for two murders I did commit, both in front of witnesses.

Karpis blew smoke.

"Until the weekend," I said. "That's it, though. No longer. This place is really too small for houseguests."

"You won't even know we're here," said Karpis.

Karpis opened the front door, waved, and shut it quick against the cold. I stepped over to the windows that framed a view of the lake. Three bundled men struggled out of Swede's Pontiac. Two wore hats and one had a bloody white rag tied around his head. The bloody man's eyes were covered with dark goggles. He was a easily a foot taller than his escorts. They hustled him up the stairway and I recognized him the moment they pushed him blind through the door.

This was Ricky Alt, millionaire son of the Saint Paul brewer.

I had never said more than hello to him, but had seen him often around Saint Paul. He stood a rugged six-foot-three. About seven years ago, he had been on the Notre Dame football squad. He'd been a second-stringer and played only a few downs under Coach Rockne. But those fleeting moments of Fighting Irish glory made him a minor celebrity. He'd come back from college to learn the brewing trade. But he had a princely arrogance, and had alienated Altwasser's brew-master. Papa Alt, who couldn't brew a cup of tea himself, bowed to the brew-master and banished his only son from the works. Ricky'd been sent downtown to be president of the family bank.

And here he stood, a giant among these jockey-sized guys who made up the Barker Gang. Karpis was the tallest, at five-five. The brothers Doc and Fred barely hit five-and-a-couple inches tall.

The Barker brothers steered Ricky to the couch. Karpis lifted the dark-glass goggles from Ricky's eyes, ripped the bloody t-shirt from his head, dropped it to my polished floor. Ricky's head was a mess of dried blood. He seemed doped or dazed, his eyes registering nothing.

"What do you have in the way of bandages?" Karpis asked me.

I backed toward the bathroom.

"What do you want?" Fred asked the dazed man. Unbuttoning his own cashmere coat, Fred asked: "Can we get you tea?"

"And crumpets," said Doc.

Ricky sat on the couch, blinking, his eyes adjusting to the light.

"What do you got to eat?" Fred asked me.

"Uh ah," I stammered from the bathroom doorway.

"The man's famished," said Fred.

"I ah roasted a turkey a couple of days ago."

"Well carve it up, man," barked Doc.

"And tea," said Fred. "He's a tea man. Aren't you, Ricky?"

I detoured into the kitchen. If I could have joined my dogs cowering under the table, I would have. It was electricity that made it bearable to live here year-round. A refrigerator and toaster were plugged, in their turn, into the kitchen's single electric outlet. The main occupier of that fridge was a small roast turkey, which had been feeding me and the dogs for breakfast, lunch and dinner. I pulled it, draped in aluminum foil, out of the fridge and set it on the pink Formica-topped kitchen table. That brought the dogs out from their hiding places and got them standing on hind legs.

Fred appeared at the kitchen door.

"Pardon us for barging in," he said.

He stepped into the kitchen.

"We was raised with manners but..." he shrugged. "Business is business. It took us a couple of weeks to find you."

"That's good, I guess."

I carved turkey breast with a long, sharp knife. Through the doorway I had a framed view of Doc, hustling in two rifles, and a shotgun and tommygun. This knife was the weapon I'd mentally reserved in case of intruders. As a weapon, it was now about as useful as a ping-pong paddle.

With the wood cook stove always burning, it was a hot kitchen, but I got the shivers when I realized these gangsters would make a stand in this cottage, if they had to. I pictured it. The woods full of deputies and G-men, ferocious firefight, bullets ripping through windows and walls. These guys did not fear police but seemed to relish the chance to fight them. Every copper could be outwitted, bribed, or shot down, that was the Barker view of the world.

Fred stepped into the kitchen, picked off a slice of turkey, popped it into his mouth. He had a severe hairdo, thick and greasy red on top, shaved on the sides. It was a haircut for hard times, as the buzz-shaved styled would minimize trips to the barber. And barber shops were not only expensive. With all those detective magazines lying around, they were dangerous places for a wanted man.

Fred salted a turkey slice using Mr. and Mrs. Happy Pig, the salt and pepper shakers Cindy had won at the Vilas County Fair.

Fred tossed turkey bits to the dogs.

"How did he get hurt?" I asked.

"Aw it's nothing," said Fred. "Head wound."

"Lot of blood," I said.

"Couldn't be helped. He's a fighter."

In the parlor, Nurse Karpis was ripping one of my t-shirts into a bandage.

"We couldn't figure you was living alone or not," said Fred. "Looks like you are. No signs of a woman."

He stared through the kitchen windows. "How's the deer hunting?"

"Season's over."

"Hell, season's don't matter. Where's your nearest neighbor?"

Snipe Lake lay between us and anyone to the West, and those cottages across the lake were half a mile away. To the east, you'd have to trudge past Aunt Doris' burned acres, down Sunset Road and around the bend just to come upon two abandoned homesteads. To the north lay a swamp. And to the south, a bunch of snow-bound cottages without heat or occupants this time of year. But the less Fred knew about Snipe Lake geography, the better, so I shrugged and said:

"Down the road apiece."

"Then there's nobody to know if we're hunting, is there? Doc," Fred shouted into the living room. "Deer a plenty."

"No hunting, no shots, no noise," warned Karpis from the living room.

Karpis seemed to know the layout of the house, and led Ricky stumbling through the kitchen toward the back bedroom, a child's room. Ricky hadn't uttered a sound, and walked like a drunk.

"Rough on the kid," I said after they passed.

"Nah," said Fred. "Don't worry, he can take it. He's a football player, right? It's nothing worse than a tackle."

On the tabletop I set five fluted white dinner plates and silverware. I ladled onto them cold, cooked-down cranberries. On the stove I set a cast iron frying pan, filled it with gravy and sliced turkey. Into the oven went a steel platter mounded with cold mashed potatoes. I opened the fire door, glowing logs in there.

"Where's a liquor store in these here woods?" asked Doc, picking meat off the turkey carcass.

I told him how he could find one. But I warned him: "You noticed my car at the head of the driveway."

"Yeah, almost on the road," said Doc.

"I don't park down here," I said, "because you can get snowed in. If it snows heavy tonight, your car could be stuck down here for days. Hard to get up that hill if it ices over."

"Bah," said Doc.

"I park up there and snowshoe down."

"Carrying groceries?" Doc asked.

"There's a sled out back."

"Well ain't you rustic." He turned to Fred. "Freddy, he's a son-of-a-bitching Eskimo."

"Mind your manners," said Fred. "He's our host. You're a houseguest."

Doc smirked. He teased the dogs, holding a turkey leg above their snapping jaws.

"Go asshole," said Fred.

"Who you calling asshole?" said Doc.

But Doc worked into a fisherman's jacket and left, slamming the front door so hard it rattled the dishes in the china cabinet. He sped up the driveway, tires spinning, and I could hear that Pontiac's engine whine even after it reached Sunset Road.

With our meal warming up, I followed Fred into the living room. I looked around for those weapons, but they had been stowed, maybe in a closet or under a bed. Karpis was sitting on the couch, smoking a cigarette, leafing through a copy of Startling Detective Adventures.

"I should ask," I said. "Just out of curiosity."

Karpis looked up, blank.

"Can I ask?" I said.

Karpis shrugged.

"How much?" I asked.

Fred looked at Karpis and they both laughed.

"Double," said Karpis.

"Twice as nice," said Fred.

CHAPTER TWO

WEDNESDAY EVENING,
JANUARY 16, 1934

Rick's soft moaning wafted like a musical wail from Cindy's childhood bedroom. We, his captors, played poker in front of the flaming fireplace. The dogs snoozed, turkey-stuffed and content under the card table. I played a losing game, distracted, imagining myself on trial for kidnapping. No juror would believe I was innocent of the original conspiracy.

My fear came in waves. In between I was calmed somewhat by recalling the result of the William Hamm kidnapping trial. A disastrous federal prosecution had targeted the wrong gang, even as the Barker-Karpis boys celebrated in Reno, blowing the ransom in high gangster style. There was no reason to believe the G-men had gotten smarter in the two months since the Hamm trial went sour.

It was Doc's turn to sit with Rick in the little bedroom. At the poker table, Karpis, bored with a nickel-ante game, yawned and pushed back his chair. Fred, on a lucky streak, stacked coins. I walked to the picture window and looked out, pure darkness. Not a light in the cabins across the lake, all stars obscured by a cloudy sky.

Fred stood beside me, swirling bourbon in a squat glass.

"Ever been ice fishing?" he asked.

"Nope," I said.

"I'd like to go ice fishing."

"Now? I mean, tomorrow?"

"No, you know," he said and drank. "Someday. What's to catch?"

"Don't know. Not much of a fisherman."

"What? You live on a lake and you don't…" He turned toward Karpis. "Hey, Ray he…"

"I heard," said Karpis. "The man doesn't fish. So what?"

"A man don't fish, he's wasting his life," said Fred.

Karpis wandered over to join us, put a hand on my shoulder. "George likes this man."

"Fuck George," said Fred, "and fuck his college education and fuck his hundred-dollar suits."

"Now now," said Karpis, "we're all in this together, George too."

"I don't mean no offense to you, personally, Powers," said Fred. "It's George is a little high-falutin for us simple hill folk."

"You're not simple and I'm not a hillbilly," said Karpis.

Maybe there's some strange psychic connection between all human beings, something beyond understanding, I don't know, but we'd hardly finished talking about George when the phone rang.

"Get it, Powers," said Karpis.

It was a female voice: "Person to person, long distance for Mister Ray."

"Just a moment, operator."

I held the black candlestick phone toward Karpis. He snatched the base in one hand and the earpiece in the other and snarled: "This is Mister Ray, I accept."

Then he listened. With every moment his face grew darker, angrier.

"I've heard enough," he barked. "Don't call again. We'll send someone to see you."

He slammed the earpiece onto the table so hard the phone's bells rang.

"Well?" said Fred.

"They're giving us the stall," said Ray.

"What kind of stall?"

"Blood in the cab," Karpis said.

"So?"

"Papa Alt thinks his kid is dead. I told Doc and I told Weaver: Don't get rough."

"So what's the old bastard saying?"

"He wants proof," Karpis said, "that Lord Fauntleroy's alive."

"Who was on the phone?" Doc asked from the kitchen doorway.

"Shotgun George," said Karpis.

"They got the dough ready?" asked Doc.

"Not even close," said Karpis. He swept into the kitchen, returned with a carving knife and severed the phone line.

"What the hell!" I said.

"Precautions," said Karpis.

"The sneaky pricks got wiretaps," said Fred.

"Federal sons of bitches," said Doc.

Karpis said: "We end up making five, ten calls a day between here and Saint Paul, how long before the operators notice?"

"Nosy cunts," said Doc.

"I imagined he was calling with good news," said Karpis.

"Good news? George?" said Fred. "He lectures you to death."

"What are we going to do?" said Doc. He approached the poker table, swigged from the bourbon bottle.

"Use a glass, pig," said Fred.

"Afraid of my cooties?" said Doc. "Too late. You had the Barker cooties since you was a kid. I say we kill the son-of-a-bitch and snatch another one. You'll see how fast they pay up after that."

"My genius brother," said Fred.

"Enough bickering," said Karpis. "We've got to think our way out of this one."

"Now that you boys cut the phone line," I said, "how the hell are you going to know the ransom's delivered?"

Karpis looked at the ceiling, impatient.

"Look, it's already arranged," he said. "Doc goes to a certain tavern down in the town. What is it, Doc?"

"Lone Buck."

"He's there every day at five," Karpis said. "Like he's just got off of work, wanting a quick beer. When the ransom dough comes in, the tavern gets a call at five exactly. Asking for Mister Red if something's gone wrong, asking for Mister Green if the money's okay."

"They pour a good beer in this state," said Doc.

"Never mind that," said Fred. "Papa Alt wants… what does he want?"

"He thinks his kid is dead," said Karpis.

"So what?" said Fred. "We're supposed to take a photo of his kid holding today's newspaper?"

"With what camera?" said Doc, "the one we ain't got?"

"Buy a cheap one," said Fred.

"No no no," said Karpis. "A town this small, a stranger buys a camera, these people have nothing to do but gossip about small events. Somebody will put two and two together."

"Mick's known in town," suggested Doc. "He could buy it."

"No I'm not," I said. "I keep a low profile, deliberate."

"Well ain't that the shits," said Doc.

"What time do the Chicago papers get here?" asked Karpis.

CHAPTER THREE

WEDNESDAY NIGHT/
THURSDAY MORNING

That night was the coldest of my life. There weren't enough
blankets and quilts for five people. The cottage was steam-heated
from a basement coal furnace, but the porch/guest-bedroom had
no radiator. It was about ten degrees outside that night, the cold
leaking in around the windows. It got into my bones. I slept only in
snatches. I dreamed of Swede Fanlund. He was falling off the roof
of my apartment building, endlessly falling, screaming in agony.
Although in the actual horrible event, he went silent to his death
over the wall.

I dreamed of being arrested for his murder. I saw delight in the
sadistic faces of Inspector Crumley and his partner The Bulldog. I
dreamed they beat me, bruised me, and worse they mocked me as I
was tied to a chair in the basement of the police station.

Somewhere in the middle of that long night I begged my patron
saint, the Archangel Michael, for relief, for warmth and sleep. Just
before dawn, he delivered.

By 11 a.m. I was in town, at Bonson's Cash and Carry, buying
potatoes, eggs, sausage and onions. Fred and Karpis knew I would
return. Although nobody said it out loud, the Barker-Karpis gang
was holding my dogs hostage.

With the clarity of morning thought, I realized why they had chosen me. I had worked well with Shotgun George during the Hamm snatch. I lived on an isolated property. I could not go to the police under any circumstances. Once the gang had decided on using me, they only needed to know that I was out here, and alone, which explained all those phone calls.

Bagged groceries in the car, I sat with its engine and heater running. I watched through frosty windows as the Eagle River flowed out of the lake. Here it ran fast and open, despite the bitter cold. Bald eagles circled, master predators, swooping over the water. One of them snatched up a big catch. Too big. With that fish in its talons it could hardly fly, and had to drop it writhing and bloody into the bay.

The train from Chicago delivered the newspapers at 11:35, only one bundle. It was lugged away on a sled by the son of Beatrice, the widow who owned Eagle River World of News. Unfortunately, she did know me. There was no choice here. Eagle River was a town of 1,200 hardy souls, and two blocks of downtown shops. If you wanted reading material of any kind, you had to patronize Beatrice's narrow dark store. She trapped patrons at the cash register, regaling them with stories of every malady she'd suffered.

And she'd suffered plenty.

I bought the Chicago Tribune, along with a few local papers for camouflage. Beatrice took my quarter, complaining that her hands were so arthritic now she had to trust the customers to pick out their own change. She was a sweet-natured, but tormented plump old lady with blue eyes and a curly cloud of platinum hair.

She asked after my cousin Cindy.

"It's the polio, ain't it?" said Beatrice.

"Multiple sclerosis," I said.

"That's not so bad," said Beatrice.

"She's in a wheelchair now. Carton of Chesterfields, please."

"Lord," said Beatrice. "That's where I'm heading. A wheelchair."

"Oh, I hope not."

"You smoke Chesterfields now?"

"Switching from my pipe," I said. "They say Chesterfields are easier on the throat."

"My knees got no car-ludge left," Beatrice said. "So the doctors tell me. They're a pack of bald-faced liars. I keep telling them I'm going to die any day now. I can't stand on these weak knees. My head throbs day and night, and my blood pressure could drive a locomotive. If I'm dead before sundown, I won't be surprised. Jimmy," she said, nodding toward her son, who was browsing the girlie magazines, "he'll be off before I'm cold in the ground. Off for Chicago."

The Alt Kidnapping did not make the front page of the Chicago papers, and the Saint Paul papers arrived, at best, a day late. There was a story on Page Three of the Chicago Tribune, though, four-paragraphs jammed in, bottom of the page. Sketchy in the extreme, the story said Richard Alt, president of the River State Bank, was last seen getting into a taxi outside his office in Downtown Saint Paul. The taxi was discovered at the edge of the Highland Golf Course, its driver half-frozen in the trunk. The rear seat of the taxi was spattered in blood. Police and the Alt family had gotten a telephone message from the abductors, but would not publicly disclose its contents.

I drove back to the woodsy intersection of Sunset Road and Cindy's driveway. I parked in a snow rut, hauled groceries, cigarettes and newspapers to the cottage on a Flexible Flyer, its red runners gliding beautiful over the sparkling snow. Hula Girl and Snowflake trotted up the hill to greet me, tails wagging. Hula Girl stuck her snout into the grocery bag. Snowflake ran ahead. If dogs know anything, they know breakfast.

Bags in my gloved hands, I struggled through the kitchen door. Karpis and Fred were leaning over the kitchen table, reading from a yellow legal pad. I set the groceries on the table.

"Ask Powers," said Fred.

"Read it," said Karpis, and handed me the pad.

It was block-printed in a nervous hand:

Pa:

I am quite alive thank you for your concern and they are treating me well. Please do as they ask for these are serious men of business. I am comfortable but it won't be long before they loose patience. Give a hug to Minnie and my love to Marie, and I hope to soon be back in the embrace of our family.

Richard

"Well?" Karpis demanded.

"Comma after ask," I said.

"The hell with commas," Karpis said. "Is it spelled okay?"

"Lose," I said, "not loose."

"To hell with spelling," Fred said and snatched the pad from me. "I'm looking for secret messages."

Karpis rolled his eyes.

"We make the Chicago papers?" Doc called from the bedroom.

"Page three," I called back.

"Son of a bitch," said Doc.

"You see any secret messages in what he wrote?" Fred asked me.

"Like…"

"Code. Trying to give away where we're at."

"I… don't see it."

Karpis grabbed the carton of Chesterfields. He set it on the dusty shelf above the stove, alongside tin pots and a ceramic cookie jar that looked like a gigantic apple.

"I'll take that newspaper," Karpis said.

"Make it big and bold," said Fred.

"Big as his bankroll," said Karpis, and walked into Cindy's little bedroom.

He returned a minute later with the top of the newspaper ripped off. The signature RICHARD WILHELM ALT was scrawled underneath the printed words: CHICAGO TRIBUNE. Karpis had torn that newspaper header off just below the date, Thursday, January 18, 1934. He wrapped that signed newspaper header and the letter into a thick envelope, which he licked and sealed.

"Well," Karpis set the letter atop the flour bin. "Who's cooking breakfast." He clapped his hands.

I had mentally prepared for this battle on the drive back. These guys were prison-hardened. They were always probing for soft spots in the people around them. If you showed too much weakness, they were ruthless enough to conclude that, ultimately, you didn't deserve to live. Maybe once you had served your purpose, they'd do the world a favor and bump you off.

"Not me," I said, "I went for the groceries."

"Well, I can't fry an egg," said Fred.

"Don't look at me," said Doc in the doorway.

"Well somebody's got to cook," said Karpis.

"Let the college boy cook his own breakfast," said Fred.

"Low card draw," said Doc, shuffling cards.

Doc lost. Standing at the cook-stove, wearing a sleeveless t-shirt that exposed his ugly prison tattoos, Doc dumped sausage into a cast-iron pan. He refused to cook potatoes, claiming they had no part in a good Southern breakfast.

In self defense, I made coffee in the French press. Cup of fresh coffee in hand, with Doc cursing, clattering and cooking behind me, I stared out the kitchen window. I saw forest, but my mind envisioned my Saint Paul penthouse. I remembered another winter night, when I awoke with a headache after a hellish nightmare, looked out to see a fire on the river docks. Those flames turned out to be the funeral pyre of Sadie and Rose. They were bad girls, but not evil, and no justice would ever avenge their deaths now. I could not forget that their fatal mistake had been to snitch on the Barker gang.

"Chow's ready," called Doc, and banged the cast iron pan with an egg-turner. By the time we sat for breakfast, the kitchen was sweating hot. I cracked a window to let in some winter air.

"Who's going to take pretty boy his breakfast?" asked Fred.

"Your turn," said Doc.

We piled our own plates greasy with fat sausages and scorched eggs. Karpis, not a coffee man, drank milk. Doc bitched that I forgot to buy oranges. Fred ate in the bedroom with the prisoner. When we had wolfed down the breakfast, Doc swigged whiskey from his pocket flask and said: "I ain't cleaning up. I ain't your mother."

Doc glared at me. In those eyes I saw it was Doc against the world, and he hated all of us.

"Powers will be leaving us," Karpis said.

"We need a son-of-a-bitching maid, then" Doc said.

"Mick," Karpis said, "George is waiting for you at the Hotel Saint Paul, room 914. It's seven knocks exactly or he won't open the door. Give him this envelope, and await instructions."

"How long we going to be trapped in this son-of-a-bitching forest?" Doc groused.

Karpis handed me the sealed envelope, ransom note inside.

"You should leave now," he said. "What's time's sunset?"

CHAPTER FOUR

SAINT PAUL, MINNESOTA
THURSDAY NIGHT
JANUARY 18, 1934

Weeks back, I had arrived at my Eagle River hideout in a Chevy coupe. It was a get-away car stolen by one of Tom Filben's minions in Saint Paul. I soon traded that Chevy in at a Rhinelander dealer for a 1933 Essex Terraplane K. This was a two-door sedan which itself had been traded in after skidding sideways into a tree. The passenger-side running board was crushed, and the dented door was stuck shut, but that damage made it affordable. Just as important, it was a fast car, capable of 80 mph. It was almost as fast as an airplane, and had the endorsement of Amelia Earhart. It could outrun the four-cylinder jalopies used by most coppers.

So cruising behind six powerful Terraplane cylinders, I made Saint Paul an hour after dark. The city was winter-quiet, snow-frosted, weeknight dull. I parked on the dark side of the Library, sneaked across Rice Park, and slipped into the service entrance of the Hotel Saint Paul. It was chilly in the stairwell. I was desperate for warmth after hours in a car that leaked air through its wounded passenger door. In my inside overcoat pocket was a letter that would send me to Alcatraz for life if the G-men across the street got their mitts on me.

I huffed and puffed up the stairwell to the fourth floor, and took the elevator from there to the 9th. I slipped into the warm, plush carpeted hallway, and knocked seven times exactly at room 914.

The door opened a cautious crack, then was flung wide by Shotgun George Ziegler.

He wore underwear and a loosely-tied bathrobe. His boxer shorts depicted red-faced, cheerful Santas. The bathrobe was hotel-issued, a deep blue emblazoned with gold royal crest.

He shut the door, discreet, behind me. He latched the security chain. The room was lit only by a single lamp near the windows.

"What have you got?" he whispered, hoarse.

His hair was combed straight back and wet, as if he'd just showered. His big blue eyes searched mine for signs of betrayal. My leather-gloved hand trembled as I handed him the ransom envelope.

He sniffed it.

"What am I to do with this?" he said.

"I thought you'd know," I said.

"I don't deliver messages, Powers, I author them."

He tapped the envelope twice to the side of his head, then slipped it into a desk drawer.

"I have made my one and only call to the Bavarian mansion," he said. "They are aware of the price we demand. They also know that we require them to name three potential emissaries, from which list we will make our choice."

He retrieved the envelope. "On second thought," he said, "I have lost all trust in that simpleton from Missouri."

Who he meant, I had no idea.

"So congratulations, Powers."

He handed the envelope toward me.

"You performed so splendidly in our last adventure," he said.

I stared at the envelope.

"Go on, take it," he said.

He dropped it into my overcoat pocket.

"Powers, God gave you an imagination, use it."

"Hey, that's not my role, George, I…"

"Well it is now. Would you like a quick drink?"

He stepped toward the bar. "I had a veritable lifetime's worth of liquor delivered yesterday." He raised a bottle from the bar.

"Martell Cognac," he said. "Just off the boat from Hong Kong. It's going to be a while before the very best liquor makes it here from the civilized world. Prohibition. What on earth were we thinking?"

He poured generously into two gleaming snifters.

"Legal at last. I like to imagine all the world's ships, loaded with booze, headed for our fair Republic." He handed me a glass. "You do know that we're a Republic and not a Democracy."

"Hadn't thought much about it," I said.

He offered a toast: "To the Alt tribe, and their ill-gotten fortune."

I clinked. I sipped. I felt myself slipping into a cold, dark nowhere. I threw myself a lifeline.

"I'm not your delivery boy," I said.

"Well you see, Powers," he said, sipping, "there simply is no one else. The simpleton from Missouri is a psychological basket case. I have no idea why our friends dragged him up here, but it was a dreadful mistake. And Handsome Curly is in charge of herding the women." He shrugged. "So you see, it's just you and me, and I, according to the master plan, am not to budge from this over-priced dungeon. Strict orders from the hillbilly hierarchy, you see."

He held his glass toward me and said: "We don't want to disappoint the boys, do we?"

I had never met either Curly or this simpleton from Missouri. I
worried that the Barker-Karpis gang kept getting bigger. More men
in the gang meant more potential snitches.

George said: "We've got to send the hillbillies an answer, they're
deaf, dumb and blind without us, Powers. We're their eyes and ears
in Saint Paul. So I recommend you secure accommodations,
although definitely not…" he waved the snifter … "within sight of
this hotel."

He dug into his bathrobe pocket, brought out a pack of Camels,
offered me one. I declined. He slipped his cigarette into an ivory
holder, and held it bobbing in his lips.

"How was the drive?"

"Cold," I said.

"We'll all be enjoying a warmer climate soon," he said.

Yes, Hell, I thought. I removed my gloves, unbuttoned my
overcoat, as if I already could feel the heat of Satan's realm.

"Powers, were you a paper boy in your youth?"

"Who wasn't?" I said.

"Oh, I wasn't," he said. "Mother would not permit it. She never
allowed me to get my hands dirty. I was college-bound from birth,
you see. My admission to the University of Illinois was a grave
disappointment to the old woman. She had her heart set on
Harvard or Yale or at the very worst Northwestern. The family
traces its noble lineage back to the Holy Roman Empire. *Reichsritter*,
you see. The noble heritage of *junker*. But for the unfortunate
events of 1848 …" he waved that cigarette-and-holder. "As a lad,
you threw the newspapers, did you?"

I wasn't quite following that, having just been taken back to the
Holy Roman Empire.

"Pardon?"

"You threw newspapers on people's porches. From a filthy sack,
carried around your boyish shoulders."

"Something like that."

"Well, you already know how to make the delivery."

"Look here, George," I said. "I never used those tickets."

"Tickets?"

"To the Barber of Seville."

"I'm not quite following you."

"The last time you and I had a working agreement," I said, "you paid me with two tickets to the opera."

"Oh, that," George said, and slapped his head. "Strictly an oversight, I assure you."

"Even half a share would have been a couple of thousand dollars."

"Well I doubt we were talking quite half a share, in any event. That would have been extravagant."

"Some amount of cash was expected, can we agree on that?"

"You see my man," said George, and put his arm around me like he was my uncle, "the hillbillies had an extraordinarily difficult time cleaning up the money. They are, after all, sixth grade dropouts. They hopped the train to Reno, you see, but their friends out there thought the money was too hot. They finally found an agent in San Francisco who used it to purchase a shipload of bootleg booze. So you see, it was absolutely months after the event in question that clean money was available. And by then, unfortunately, you and I had simply lost touch."

He reached for his wallet.

"Keep it George. I'm out of this."

"I'm afraid you're very much in."

He held out a $100 bill.

"Expense money," he said. "To be followed by many more of its brethren."

"No thanks," I said. "I'm known here. If I spend a bill that big, tongues will wag."

That was my excuse, but actually, I was already preparing for the inevitable trial. The Barker-Karpis Gang, whether they knew it or not, had snatched the son of a man whose father had a friend in the White House. During the Presidential campaign, when Franklin Roosevelt stepped off the train at Saint Paul's Union Depot, it was Papa Alt first in line to greet him. They were natural allies, and had become personal friends. FDR campaigned to bring back beer, and that rang the money bell in Papa Alt's mansion. The Barker gang might have been blind to it, but I knew the federal heat in this case was going to make Hell seem like the North Pole. Sure, the Feds blew the Hamm prosecution, but I had the feeling this kidnapping case was going to be different.

I wanted to be able to say: Your Honor, I did it under threat, and did not take a dime.

"I'm a patient man," I told George, "I'll wait for my share."

"Then let us create," he said, "a masterpiece of the genre."

At a roll top desk sat a Corona portable typewriter and a stack of heavy bond paper. It was letterhead paper featuring the big bold word Blackstone and the silhouette of a hotel. I sat before the typewriter. I rolled in a sheet of this letterhead as George hovered over my shoulder.

"Powers, there will be a thousand hoaxers, lunatics and charlatans calling the family and the police over the next few days. I have advised the Alts that genuine communications will be delivered on this letterhead. Also, any telephonic messages will include the key word Blackstone."

"Blackstone," I said.

"Ready for dictation?" he said. "We have enclosed proof that your son is alive and well. You are to place in the window of your son's office the blue eagle sticker of the National Recovery Administration. By this sign we will be apprised that the money is ready for delivery. Once that sign is appropriately posted, you will be notified of the necessary steps to deliver the money to us and thereby procure your son's release."

I finished typing and said: "That's all?"

"My man," he clapped me on the shoulder, "Brevity is the very soul of communication."

As I slunk down the hotel's back stairway, I knew George was right about one thing: I was in. I would never get the Barker Gang out of my cottage unless I delivered their message.

George's plan, however, was flawed. He imagined I would steal a newsboy's sack of newspapers, walk down the boulevard delivering them, and casually throw a paper on the Alt's porch. But it was nearing 7 p.m. and the Evening Dispatch and Daily News had long since been delivered. Any paperboy out now would raise questions in the minds of whoever saw him. I modified George's idea and bought just one copy of the Dispatch in a downtown drugstore. Its screaming half-page block of headlines said:

RICHARD ALT KIDNAPPED
$200,000 RANSOM ASKED

It was a spooky feeling, to hold both that newspaper and the ransom note. In my idling Terraplane, I read in the news columns that the family had named three go-betweens, as the kidnappers had demanded via telephone. They were: R.L Pearson, a real estate consultant; Father McCarthy O'Sullivan, family priest; and Andrew Stockwell, an executive at Altwasser Brewery.

I knew them all. The Dispatch had committed its usual sins of omission. R.L. Pearson was known around Saint Paul as Serious Bobby. For years he'd been the city's top underworld diplomat. He had been the chosen go-between in last summer's kidnapping of

William Hamm, and was now a "consultant" to the Hamm
Brewery. His "consulting," had nothing to do with real estate.

Father McCarthy O'Sullivan, an honest man as far as I knew,
was Cathedral Provost. He was the Archbishop's tough guy and
emissary to the underworld.

Andrew Stockwell had, for the last years of Prohibition, been
manager of Alt-backed speakeasies all over town, which also meant
he was in charge of bribery.

When I finished reading between the lines, I gave the Dispatch a
newsboy fold and slipped the ransom envelope in tight.

The Alt Mansion stood on a side street just across from the
Altwasser Brewery. A more grandiose beer baron would have lived
up on Summit Hill, but Papa Alt, apparently, liked to keep an eye
on the shop. His mansion, on the banks of the Mississippi,
overlooked both river and brewery. I parked a block away, behind
the concrete loading dock of a machine shop.

I watched.

The brewery's iron gates were locked against the night, the great
works vibrating, throwing off the stench of rotten vegetables. The
hum of its machinery echoed all over the neighborhood. With beer
legal now, bricklayers were half-finished a building that would
double down on Papa Alt's plan to inebriate the Northwest. I
studied the Alt's white stone mansion for a while. There were many
cars parked on either side of the street, and the home glowed with
lights intense from every room.

Some of those cars belonged to G-men, since kidnapping was
now against the federal law. It was only a couple of months ago
that J. Edgar Hoover had slammed Machine Gun Kelly into
Alcatraz on a kidnapping rap. This new island prison was escape-
proof, the feds boasted. Kidnappers especially were warned of
harsh discipline, shark-infested waters, and damp, cold cells.

A car circled the block. It revealed itself underneath each streetlamp, first as a luxury car with a hood five feet long. Then as a dark red sedan with white sidewalls. Then as a brand new Cadillac-LaSalle. On its second time around it settled for far-off parking. It was such a flashy, extravagant car I figured it belonged to a very important man, perhaps a representative of the governor or state's attorney general. As it sat idling, lights ablaze, I memorized the license number.

Then its engine shut off and out got two men. One was a giant, the other a mere mortal carrying a doctor's black bag. Under-dressed in only a dark suit, the doctor hustled toward the Alt Mansion, climbed the steps and into the porch's light. Behind him, that giant was revealed to be Father McCarthy O'Sullivan.

A doctor and a priest. Desperate medical measures and Extreme Unction? Maybe old Otto Alt was having a heart attack. Great. Worries galloped like a panicked horse through my mind. Add a second-degree murder charge to the kidnapping.

What if I walked into Roland Heater's office and told all I knew? Well, the feds were as bloodthirsty as the gangsters. J. Edgar was eager to prove his college boys could slug it out with tommygunners. A few hours after I turned rat, G-men, the Wisconsin State Patrol, and sheriff's deputies would assemble in the forest outside Cindy's cottage. A horseshoe-shaped ambush would trap the gangsters against the lakeshore. A gun battle would leave several cops dead and wounded. And hell, half of them would be deputies, just farmers picking up part time dough by carrying a badge. The firefight would kill Snowflake, Hula Girl and Ricky Alt, as well as the three gangsters. Karpis might surrender if he were the last one left alive. But the Barker brothers would rather burn in Hell than rot in Alcatraz.

On the other hand, if I delivered this message, Papa Alt would pay $200,000, which he could well afford. Hell, he had donated more than that to the Roosevelt campaign. Ricky would be let go unharmed, as William Hamm was. The Barker Gang's kidnap victims were let go because the ransom was almost beside the point. The kidnappings were a dramatic warning to these brewers, that they should bring their gangster friends along into the profitable future.

So I had a big decision to make, me, a lowly gangland messenger, sitting in a banged-up car on a frosty night in an industrial parking lot. Death and destruction on a terrible scale, or clipping off a piece of a fat-cat's fortune.

A woman in hooded parka walked a sweater-wrapped dog down a lamp lit street. She glanced at me, suspicious, a dark figure in an idling car. I shut the engine and wondered if just freezing to death would be my best option. But my dogs! I imagined Doc Barker shooting them because they barked too much. That vision got me going. I started the car again, rolled down the window. When the dog-walking-lady was out of sight, I sped past the Alt Mansion, heaved the newspaper over the iron fence, and it bounced off the bottom step. I made a vicious right turn at the river road, slid sideways, banged against the curb. The car tilted as if it might roll into the Mississippi, then righted. It stalled. With frantic looks in the mirror I started it and zoomed toward the better part of town.

Up on Grand Avenue I parked, thrilled by my escape, shuddering with relief. I popped out of the car behind the Barking Dog Tavern. I sneaked around to the back entrance, where a long dark hallway led to the restrooms and a bank of three public telephones. I grabbed a receiver, dropped a nickel, dialed the number George had given me. A female answered, maybe one of Ricky's sisters, maybe a maid. After a glance over my shoulder for eavesdroppers I choked out: "Newspaper. Porch. Message."

As I was about to hang up I remembered to blurt out: "Blackstone."

I hustled out the door and down the back alley.

It was a couple of icy blocks to Myrtle's luxury apartment. The lights were blazing, but the shades were down on her alley windows. Those lights about broke my heart, something warm flooding me after all this cold and frantic fear. Myrtle! In my winter's isolation I realized I missed the woman, I probably loved her, bad girl that she was.

I mounted the stairs, breathless. From inside her apartment I heard chirping parakeets. I rapped lightly on the door.

"Go away you bum," said Myrtle. "I'm not home."

"Myrtle," I said, trying to whisper through the door. "It's Powers."

The door cracked open as far as the security chain would allow.

The door closed and then swung wide. Myrtle grabbed the lapel of my overcoat and dragged me in.

"Get in here, are you crazy?"

"Somebody looking for me?"

"Everybody's looking for you."

"Well, it's nice to be wanted," I said and shrugged off my coat. I embraced her, kissed her, held her away. She wore a Chinese bathrobe, black, red and gold. Her breath smelled heavy of booze.

"Hey," I said.

"It's nothing," she said.

I held her chin in my hands. She looked like she'd gone a couple of rounds with a heavyweight palooka. Her cheek was bruised, her eye socket swollen, black and blue, her eyelid half shut over the damage.

"Who the hell did that to you?"

She pushed my hand away. "Nobody, Mick, it's nothing. What do you want to drink?"

The room, now that I got a look at it, might have been the scene left by wild animals. A rose-painted glass lamp was shattered, lying on the hardwood floor near the radiator. Unruffled, though, were Charles and Amelia, chirping merry in their tall golden cage.

"I ain't got around to cleaning up yet," she said. "It's the maid's year off."

A framed drawing of Japanese lovers in erotic positions hung crooked on the wall. The telephone had been torn away from its moorings and lay at the leg of an easy chair. A coffee table stood legs up on a Persian rug.

"I just got home myself," she said.

"Where from?"

"Loretta's."

I threw my overcoat on the telephone table, took a long look around and said: "Who's the mug?"

"Forget it, Mick, I got drunk and fell down the stairs."

"Right," I said.

"You know how it is."

"I certainly do. Now give me his name."

"What are you going to do, tough guy? You spit on the sidewalk, they'll send you to Stillwater."

"I know some guys."

"Mick, butt out. I can handle it."

"Apparently not."

Her face darkened with anger. "You too? You're going to humiliate me too? I thought we were old friends. Let's have a drink like we were old friends. Old friends don't tell each other what to do. Old friends are kind to each other. Because they're old and because they're friends, and because this life is killing them little by little. Don't judge me, Mick, I been in courtrooms, and if there's anything I hate it's a rotten, smug-face judge."

"Okay, but if you need a tough guy to square this up…"

"I know, thanks, Mick, now I'm dying for a drink."

We walked into the kitchen, where the booze was. The Myrtle I once knew had an antiseptic kitchen, because she never cooked. But this kitchen was piled with greasy pots. The sink was a monument to unwashed plates. Every burner on the stove hosted a crusty pan. Silverware, stolen from the best hotels, lay scattered and soiled on the drain board.

Myrtle opened a cupboard to reveal a selection of booze that could stock a tavern. She had never been much of a home drinker, doing her boozing in public, preferably with an orchestra in the background and a squire paying the tab.

"Canadian Club, Four Roses, Crab Orchard?"

"Crab," I said.

"Soda, ginger, straight?"

"Soda," I said.

She nudged aside a pile of dishes and fixed me a drink, knocking ice out of an aluminum tray she fetched from the tiny frost-crusted freezer.

"I'm looking for a place to stay," I said.

"Don't look here."

"I've been spending a lot of time alone," I said.

"I'm not in the mood for company. Ever again if I can help it. I'm through with your kind, Mick. I hate you all. Except you. And a couple of others. A million men in this city and only six of them got any heart."

We clinked glasses.

"So what are you doing in town?" she asked.

I sighed. "That, I can't tell you."

"Huh," said Myrtle. "I'll bet."

"I missed you, kid."

"Oh cut the baloney." She turned away and set her glass on the stained white porcelain sink. "I'm used up Mick." She lifted the shade and stared into the dark alley. "Victor died you know. Christmas Day."

The glass in her hand shook, ice cubes rattled. I lay both hands, gentle on her shoulders.

"I heard."

To spare Myrtle's feelings, I wasn't going to say that I knew how. "Professor Banks," as he was known all over gangland, was found hanged in his cell at the state prison in Waupun, Wisconsin. He'd played prison Santa on Christmas Eve, then hanged himself with the big black belt.

"No funeral," she muttered. "He didn't want one."

And now she began to cry, huge tears running down her cheeks, I could see her reflection in the dark window.

"My Professor," she sniffled. "He taught me everything."

She wiped tears.

"And he never laid a hand on me. A gentleman. Where am I going to find a gentleman, Mick, I'm so old and fat."

"And enticing," I said.

"You always were Mister Flattery."

"I'm sorry about the Professor," I said.

"Thanks, I guess," she said, and picked up soiled napkin and wiped her tears, snuffling. "I shouldn't cry, what's to cry about, bad news, it oughta make you happy, it just proves what a rotten world we live in."

"There's a big mess going on, all right."

"Mick, I'm not asking, because look, I know the answer. The Alt kid gets snatched and all of a sudden you show up like a ghost. I hope junior's all right but even if he is, I'm afraid, Mick. I'm afraid they're going to drag you down into darkness."

"Aw, Myrtle, what are you talking about?"

"I heard them Mick. They were right here. Right in that living room. I was in here, penned up with their women, and the boys were out there talking, and you know Gladys' little daughter had to go to the bathroom and I walked her out to it and I heard them. Fred and Doc and Ray, sitting with Harry, and they got a pop-in visit from Big Ryan too."

"Harry's the finger-man?" I asked.

"It's Harry's job, so now you know what you're mixed up in."

"I'm mixed up in nothing," I said.

"I can see right through you, Mick, you always was a terrible liar, you got the mug of a disappointed altar boy."

"Harry," I said.

"The mastermind," she said, "with the usual assistance of the Saint Paul Police."

 She drained her drink.

"Is the junior banker okay?" she asked.

"How would I know?"

"Just wink if he's okay."

"Got something in my eye," I said.

"Thanks, you're quite the blabbermouth."

"Myrtle, you could be an accessory if you knew too much."

"Are you listening to me, or do my words pass right through you? They planned it," and these last two words she shouted: "*right here.*"

"Okay, but that doesn't have to come out in the Saturday Evening Post."

"If them federals crack one acorn, Mick, the whole tree comes down. Come on, drink up, sugar, I can't afford to have you here."

CHAPTER FIVE

COMMODORE HOTEL
SAINT PAUL, MINNESOTA

I checked in at my favorite hideout, the Commodore. On the front desk were stacked the evening papers, Dispatch and Daily News. I bought a copy of each to bring upstairs.

BLOODY ALT TAXI

FEDERAL AGENTS GRILL CABBIE

According to the stories, Bank President Richard Alt had gotten into a cab outside the bank just before noon yesterday. Passersby had noted that the cab contained a second man up front, assumed to be a driver in training. Police had discovered that taxi an hour later at the Highland Golf Course, the shivering cabbie trapped in the trunk. The back seat of the cab was bloody. Otto "Papa" Alt had a brief phone conversation with someone claiming to represent the kidnappers. They had demanded that the family name three go-betweens and prepare a $200,000 ransom. Other than empty boasts and idle threats from various authorities, that was pretty much all the story said.

But I was electrified by the sidebar. It was a tepid rundown of the shady history of Saint Paul kidnappings. But the byline shocked me.

By Janie Vetter
United Press

Only when she and her baby left Saint Paul for her parents' farm could I admit I was half in love with Janie, although she was far too young for me. Maybe it wasn't Janie herself, maybe it was youth and innocence I pined for. There is a point in your youth when you still have options. That was long gone for me, but Janie had a future, and my feelings for her were a mixture of admiration and envy.

I stared out into the dark courtyard. The radio blared so many bulletins that there was scarcely time for music. J. Edgar Hoover was thumping his chest like a Washington gorilla. Squads of G-men were headed to Saint Paul by car, by train, by airplane. Reporters and newsreel men were pouring in from all over the nation. Something crazy was eating at me, everything was eating at me, I worked into my overcoat and gloves and ran down the Commodore's back stairs.

I caught a taxi to downtown, grateful that the doorman was off shift for the evening. It was approaching ten at night but the morning papers had a midnight deadline and Janie might be working right up to it. I counted on my fingers: Her baby Dane was now seven months old. Was the baby okay? Why had Janie returned to Saint Paul?

A sick feeling settled into me, like it would never leave. The Hamm Kidnapping had been over quick, and had never become a world-wide story. The Alt Kidnapping, maybe because of the

family's White House connections, was news in Washington, was
news in Paris, for all I knew it was on the radio in Peking.

The Barker Gang had blundered into deep, deep water.

At the Daily News building I found a bundled-up kid running a
broom over the loading dock. I asked him where the United Press
office was. Usually, he said, the UP reporter worked out of a
cubbyhole behind the press room, but there were so many
reporters in town now, they'd rented a room at the Hotel Saint
Paul.

I hustled up there, through dark icy streets lit only by tavern
signs, four dark blocks over the streetcar tracks up a gentle rise to
the Hotel Saint Paul. I slipped in the back way. The office suites
were on the third floor: R.G. Tietz, Dentist. Graf and Graf
accountants. The Saint Paul Protective Association. All those
offices were dark. On the other side of the gilded elevators, the
clattering of a teletype machine, along with cigarette smoke, drifted
out of an open transom.

I backed into a dark alcove and listened: Muffled voices. Soft
curses coming over the transom. A young harried man opened the
door and I glimpsed Janie, working like she was chained to the
teletype, bent over it, intent, sweaty, typing. She seemed older, she
looked awful in that harsh light.

The harried man closed the door and rang for the elevator. I,
ghost in the darkness, waited him out. I slipped out the back door
of the hotel and walked, leaning into the brutal wind. It was below-
zero cold but I could not risk hailing a cab in the gangster part of
town. At the Commodore I slunk into my room. The arctic wind
rattled the windows. The radio played the National Anthem and
faded to static. I went to bed, rolled up in itchy wool covers. I
expected a miserable night and that's what I got.

No warmth, no refuge, no love, no sleep.

CHAPTER SIX

DOWNTOWN SAINT PAUL

Papa Alt's River State Bank was a bunker built for the future, an Art-Deco edifice of glass and stone, four stories high, across from Rice Park and in the shadow of the Federal Building. Two huge windows looked in on the bank lobby. Smaller windows were meant to give passersby a side view of the handsome young bank president. Richard Alt worked in a modest, sensible office, American flag and framed photo of FDR in the background. It was all so reassuring.

And mostly a lie.

What you couldn't see through that window was the bank's dark dealings. Laundering the Denver Mint loot had been the bank's founding fortune. Bootlegger money had boosted its bottom line. Money laundering became a profitable side business. Gangsters, bootleggers, con-men, gamblers and bank robbers needed banking services like everyone else. The Alts, the Northwest's richest bootleggers, saw no need to shoo gangsters away from the teller's window.

Since Rice Park and surroundings were the soul of downtown Saint Paul, thousands of shoppers and workers walked past Papa's bank every working day. When I hustled by to check that window, I would be just another face in the crowd.

That Friday morning I didn't so much as wake up as I stirred myself from the chair where I sat out the night. Since I was up anyway, I drove to the Cathedral for 6 a.m. Mass. The crowd consisted of fourteen elderly people, myself, a priest I didn't know, and a sleepy altar boy. I figured my attendance would slice a year off my sentence in Purgatory. I said a prayer for the safety of my dogs, for Richard Alt, even for the kidnappers. Let the Barker gang escape, Oh Lord, spend their money, be happy with it this time, and let people alone.

No furnace ever built could heat that massive Cathedral, and I was stiff with cold, and feeling weak, tired and afraid when I caught the streetcar downtown. I sat in the last seat, face deliberately turned to the frosty window. I resented each stop, as the doors opened and icy drafts blew in. Damn these bundled people, the winter-scrunched faces, the streetcar's floor wet with melted snow, the clanging, the lurching. I wondered if I would get to Rice Park before leaping from my seat and screaming like a banshee.

I stumbled off the car at Rice Park. Hunched into my collar, fedora slouched low, scarf covering everything but my eyes, I walked the wide sidewalk between the Federal Building and the Hamm Building, glanced at the River State bank's window as I passed.

I wasn't quite sure what I saw. I was looking for the blue eagle sticker of the National Recovery Administration and thought I had seen it, sort of. I felt a bump of optimism at first, followed by doubt. In the Hamm Arcade it was wet and warm and a sundry shop sold coffee, candy and donuts. Beneath the rows of Charleston Chews, Mary Janes and Chunkys, the morning newspapers were propped up, all with screaming headlines.

KIDNAP MYSTERY DEEPENS

HOOVER SENDS TOP AIDES FROM D.C.

Coffee shaking in my hand, donut lumping in my swollen throat, I stood aside on checkerboard tiles as people whirled in the revolving door. I watched out the big window as the crowds picked their way along the slippery streets.

I decided to make another go of it.

I tossed coffee and donut into a stainless steel garbage tube. In boots that felt lead-heavy, I walked past the windows again and saw, quite clearly, an NRA sticker cut in half. Half an eagle. Half an answer.

I kept walking, squaring the park, past the Wilder Charity Building and toward the Library. Nobody sat or lay on the frozen benches, so I cut through the park, dodged taxis, and sneaked into the service entrance of the Hotel Saint Paul. I took three flights of fire stairs, then used the elevator, then rapped seven times on the door of room 914.

George did not answer.

I stepped back. I walked down the hall to the elevators, then back and knocked again. I thought this guy wasn't going to budge from his room?

Not wanting to look like a bandit, I removed the scarf from my face, tucked it into my coat pocket and stomped down the stairs for a tour of the lobby. The desk clerk just had to throw me a cheerful "Good morning, sir!" on the day when I least wanted to be noticed.

Gentlemen of business were reading sensational headlines in the plush chairs of the lobby. A couple of wise guys gamblers were conning a bar porter, who was cleaning up last night's liquor spills. A bellhop pushed an enormous cart of suitcases along a deep plush carpet, railroad tags fluttering from their handles.

No George anywhere.

I hustled down one flight of stairs to the basement's Uptown Café. It was the only eatery in the hotel open now. Nothing so pedestrian as breakfast could be served in the haughty Grill Room.

There sat George, alone at a small corner table, his tan fedora resting on a white tablecloth set with silverware. He cradled a white mug of coffee in one hand, while the other turned the pages of the Pioneer Press.

I took the seat opposite him, slung my damp overcoat over the back of the chair.

"Are you hungry, Powers? Should I signal the waitress?"

"No."

I picked up a plate that held the yolky remains of his breakfast, set it on the table behind me.

"Have you seen it?" I asked.

"Have I seen what?"

I whispered: "The eagle sticker."

George sat back, perturbed. "I thought that was your affair."

"Yes it is my affair and guess what? The bastard posted half an eagle."

"Which half?"

"The top, does it matter?"

"Well I wonder what on earth that means."

"It means they're half ready?" Our table was against the wall, isolated, but still I whispered. "It means they only have half the stuff ready? It means they're only willing to pay half? I have no goddamn idea what it means."

"Powers, we live in an age of communication. Take my investments, for example. I can wire my man at the Board of Trade, and poof," he waggled one hand, "fortunes in wheat, bought and sold instantaneously."

He leaned forward, confidential.

"But if I were you I'd avoid the markets, notoriously fickle. For my own investments I have a man on the inside. He can see many moves ahead. He can sense the rise and fall of markets like an old sea captain can read the ocean."

"Okay, but…"

"We likewise have a man on the inside in this affair, don't we?"

He put a hand on my arm and engaged me with a sincere gaze. "The copper."

"You're saying…"

"The next obvious move is to get an explanation of the half eagle, and that will require a communication with our inside man."

"How the hell am I supposed to do that?"

"Oh, Powers, you're a resourceful fellow." He turned, raised his hand at the waitress and said: "Check here please."

I crossed Wabasha to the Western Union, which stood flanked by Midwest Bail Bonds, and Downtown Dutch's Pawn Paradise. Upstairs from all these was H.H. Kruk chiropractor and Grace's Modern Dance studio. I stood in the dancer/doctor alcove for five minutes, to look for anyone who might be tailing me. Then in the Western Union I filled out a telegraph slip, in code.

The doctor who had called at the Alt mansion had driven a Cadillac with the license plate number 71364. The simple gangster code was to add five to the number, and drop the 1 if the result was double digits. So the doctor's license plate number translated to 26819. I wrote down those numbers and the coded word RNSS. I handed that slip into the clerk's window along with a dime, and watched him telegraph that message to Filben.

Then I circled the block, checking again to be sure no one was shadowing me, and cut through the Hotel Saint Paul's lobby. There I stood gazing through the enormous windows at the steps of the Federal Building. People skittered up and down the stairs as a Post

Office minion in red earmuffs cleared snow with a coal shovel. Most of those people were going for routine mail transactions but some were G-men, reporters, lawyers, Saint Paul detectives. I realized George was right, only one man could interpret that half eagle.

Big Joe Ryan had been a Saint Paul detective for more than 20 years. Until his recent demotion in favor of Tom Dahill, he'd been chief for a decade. I had taken a beating from the sadistic bastard, as had hundreds of people in this city. But Ryan's stationhouse beatings were more than pure sadism. They were encouragement to contribute to the payoff system he had built. Those who paid got off easy. Those who didn't were beaten and jailed. And so what looked to some like mere brutality had an economic purpose.

A photo deep inside the newspaper showed that cops were sleeping at headquarters, in bunks, on 24-hour call until Richard Alt's return. Big Ryan probably wasn't among them. As captain of the kidnap detail, he was more likely at the Alt Mansion, but I dared not approach it in daylight.

I tried the easy way. I called Ryan's home from a pay phone. His wife said he was very busy, who was calling and I hung up.

So I drove down Seventh Street, parked in an alley two blocks from the brewery and the Alt Mansion. I waited, car wedged between a brick grammar school and the Czech-American Club. I turned the engine on and off for heat. I had been in Big Ryan's armored black Plymouth once. It was slow, thick-skinned and heavy, like the man himself. I figured I could tail it and if he spotted me, so much the better. As I waited, bundled, schoolchildren burst out for recess, hardy Minnesotans in training, braving the 17-degree morning.

After I had sat through two hours' surveillance, that big black Plymouth rumbled around the corner, turned on Seventh, headed downtown. Amid buses and streetcars, coal trucks and taxis, I tailed him. I flashed my lights. Tapped my horn. It was unmistakable, the Big Fella was driving and alone. As we neared downtown he turned off, down a block to the river, and parked near the river docks in front of Martinucci's, a popular spaghetti joint. This was the dock where Sadie and Rose had been burned, almost two years ago now.

I waited a moment to see if any other car would join us.

As the Plymouth idled, I yanked the hand brake, jumped out, and let myself in to Big Ryan's car. I was overwhelmed with the fear that he would arrest me for the murder of Swede Fanlund. I was shaking and hoped he didn't notice.

"You're up early," said Big Ryan, bruiser hands on the wheel. The heater was blasting hot in here, Ryan dressed only in a suit.

"What's the message?" I asked.

Big Ryan spread his arms on the back of the seat.

"You do know, Powers, who you're talking to."

"I think so."

"All right, then," he said, "who are you supposed to be?"

"I'm the guy."

"What guy?"

"The messenger."

He slipped a big black pistol out from under his striped suit-jacket.

"Dead messenger," he said.

He cocked the hammer. "If you ever flag me down in public again …"

Big Ryan, as I knew well, had left bodies in dark alleys. I had a vision, very brief, of God. He was scruffy, with dirty hair and tangled beard, like a hobo who's been out of work too long. I looked down the barrel of that pistol, like it was a tunnel leading to a dark eternity. Only part of me was frightened now. The other part, exhausted, surrendered.

He let the hammer down easy, but with the barrel pointing danger at my face. He holstered the pistol.

"We meet at the eagle statue," he said. "At midnight precisely. Maybe I don't show but if I do, you get out of your car and into mine. If you're not there, I keep going, and you don't want me to keep going. If you show up in any car but your own, you're finished. If you show up in the company of anyone at all, you will not live to see the sun rise."

"Understood," I said.

"Now ask."

"What does it mean that they cut the NRA sticker in half?"

"It means they're willing to pay half, obviously."

"Does the family have the cash ready?"

"There's a great deal of confusion," he said. "The answer is maybe. Otto went deep into debt expanding that brewery. He shoveled a ton of cash to the bastard FDR." He sighed. "In a way, Otto caused his own problems. We had a system here. It was working."

"Does he have the cash?"

"Otto's brewery is deep in debt, and his bank isn't solvent either. There have been hijinks and cooked books in both places. If he can get even half the money, it will come from his friends on Wall Street. So let's put it this way, against my advice, he's made his half-ass offer and awaits an answer. So? Will the boys take half?"

"The gang is going to ask: What do the Federals know?"

"The college boys are scrambling," he said. "They are chasing phantom leads all over the country."

He looked at me pointedly, hazel eyes behind schoolteacher's thin eyeglasses and said: "Anything else?"

I slipped out of his car and slouched toward my own. Ryan's big armored Plymouth made a U-turn and headed for Downtown. I let myself in to my Terraplane. The treachery of it began to sink in.

Ryan, a longtime friend of the Alt Family, was playing birddog for the kidnappers. He was undermining the G-men even as he pretended to be their ally. He had been in this kidnapping from the beginning, as proven by his presence in Myrtle's apartment on the night the gang met for the final planning.

That's what we had been dealing with in Saint Paul all along, a city run by treacherous gangsters with badges, gangsters in the prosecutor's office, gangsters on the bench and on the city council, a city of shadows, of the double-cross and the triple-cross, a city whose bright boulevards were really dark alleys lit by greed, a frigid little city without morals, conscience or justice.

It was coming up on 11 in the morning. The thought of a six-hour drive made me realize how hungry I was, and in Martinucci's, somebody was baking bread, frying meatballs, stirring sauce. I had a deep longing for something good, something homey, something comfortable, a plain, honest meatball sandwich followed by a long nap and maybe I would wake up and find that the last few years were only a sick dream, and it was 1929 again, and Peggy and I were living in a penthouse, overlooking the city lights, enjoying the rowdy nightlife while I supported us easily with a couple of monthly runs to Winnipeg. I could hold that picture in my mind a long lovely time, but not forever, because it ended with the night that Peggy, lips quivering, face cast to the floor, said: "Mick, I can't live this life anymore."

"I'll quit drinking," I said.

"That's not it," she said.

I waited until Martinucci's opened and bought a meatball sandwich to eat in the car as I drove toward Wisconsin. Six hours, a couple of tomato sauce spatters, and two stops for gas later, I rounded that curve where Highway 70 hugs the Wisconsin River, running under ice now, shallow, rocks appearing here and there. I turned onto Sunset Road feeling both optimistic and worried. I fought visions of bad, bloody things that might have happened to Ricky Alt and my dogs. I had to suck up courage just to get out of the car and trudge down the hill through the dark forest. Only the last pink hint of sun was left on the western horizon, the most brilliant stars beginning to pop out into a deep purple sky.

Even in the dark I could tell by the tire ruts in the snowy driveway that the boys had been reckless, coming and going. As I reached the top of the hill and started down toward the cabin, I could smell the wood smoke. When the dogs started barking I felt such relief that if I hadn't been posing as a tough guy, I would have cried like a scared little boy.

Somebody let the dogs out and they ran up through the snow, greeting me as if I were the savior. They ran in circles, they rolled in the snow, Hula Girl won the race to the house, while Snowflake sat on the porch, panting frosty breath.

It was about 85 degrees in that parlor. Someone had brought in a huge load of firewood from the shed, dropped it on the parlor floor and made a blazing fire. Karpis was wearing a thermal undershirt, sleeves rolled up. Doc wore a white cotton sleeveless undershirt that exposed his whirling crazy tattoos: a horse, a cross, a demon, a snake, no color but blue. Beer bottles were scattered throughout the parlor, and plates had been set on the floor and licked clean by the dogs. It was so hot I just about ripped off my overcoat.

Fred, arms crossed, wore an Army sweatshirt with the arms hacked off, and was leaning into the kitchen doorway. The whole place stank overwhelming of sweat, cigarettes and beer.

"Hey, Tarzan, how was the jungle?" said Doc, and handed me a beer. He was lurching drunk.

"Well did we crack the vault?" asked Karpis.

"Kind of," I said.

Fred, sensing bad news, gave a cynical smirk.

"They want to pay half," I said.

Karpis stuck a Chesterfield into his chapped lips. "Why, that German chiseler."

Fred gave me a two-handed shove that send me staggering back toward the fire.

"Half?" Fred shouted. "What'd you tell that kraut bastard?"

"Nothing," I said. "They cut the eagle in half. I talked to our copper. That's it. They can pay half. The Alt's are broke."

"Then they get half their kid back," growled Doc, waving his beer.

"Shut up," Fred said, and cornered me near the book shelf. "What did you say when they said half?"

"I never talked to them. I'm the messenger that's all. They're waiting for your answer."

He flipped me the middle finger. "There's your answer."

"Hey," I said, "I'm not the enemy."

"He's right," said Karpis. "Be reasonable, Freddy."

"My little brother," said Doc with a rueful laugh. "Reasonable?"

Fred walked a circle over the parlor rug and then turned to face me. "You drive back there. You tell them no way. You tell them Ricky's on the clock here."

"Hell, we could blow up their son of a bitching brewery," said Doc.

"Calm down," said Karpis. "Think."

"Think?" shouted Doc. "I been trapped in this house three days now." He leaned over the dining room table. He was a little guy, but a powerhouse, built like a wrestler, top heavy and tough with prison muscles. "I say we take an ear."

"No, no, no," said Karpis.

"Just a slice," said Doc. "Message loud and clear."

Fred crossed his arms over his chest. "I say we raise the ransom. To $250,000."

Doc pointed at Fred. "Genius," he said. "And it goes up fifty grand for every day he stalls."

"No body parts," said Karpis. "This is a professional outfit."

"Raise the ransom, then," said Fred.

This set off alarm bells for me. The higher the ransom, the greater the likelihood it wouldn't be paid, and then would come the shootout I feared. If that shootout happened tonight, or any night I was here, I'd be among the dead because the Barker brothers would plug me if I didn't engage the cops in battle.

"Fellas," I said, "I really believe 'em. I believe the Alts are broke."

"Oh, you do?" said Fred.

"It makes sense. He's building onto that brewery. He's put every dime into it. Money's tight. He gave a ton of cash to FDR. His crappy little bank is wobbly. You can be rich and low on cash."

"Listen to this son of a bitch," said Doc, "you can be rich and low on cash. Now what the hell kind of double talking bullshit is that?"

"We give them three days," I suggested.

Nobody said anything for a moment. Fred shook his head, a disgusted look on his face. Karpis allowed curlicues of smoke to escape from his mouth. Doc scratched manic at his hair.

"Cooties," Doc said.

I shed my suit-jacket, loosened my tie. "All this dry heat, it's bad for the piano," I said. "That's why we have steam radiators, that's why we have coal. You're not supposed to heat this house with the fireplace."

"The piano," said Fred, "we've got a hostage in there and this guy's talking about the piano."

"It's a $2,000 instrument and it doesn't belong to me."

I ran my hand across its polished ebony. After a glance at Cindy's pictures, I imagined her raging from her wheelchair.

"Let's talk about the three days," said Karpis. "Why three days? What's magic about three days?"

Well, there was nothing magic, it was just a stall. But I had to say something.

"Gives them until Monday to collect the cash," I said. "Come on, the bank's got to be open for this to work. It's hard to raise that much cash on a weekend. Monday's the deal. We're all gone by Tuesday night, fat and happy."

"Hmm," said Karpis.

I focused on Karpis, the only one of these guys driven by reason. "It's fair and square, Ray," I said. "You're a fair man. You've got to give 'em a chance. The Alts are strapped. We caught them at a bad moment. Whoever fingered this job should have known it."

"What about the G-men?" said Fred.

"They don't have a clue. Nobody has any idea where we are, we could stay here a month."

I immediately regretted saying that.

"But we won't have to," I said. "Give 'em three days to deliver the full ransom."

"And then?" Karpis said.

"They'll deliver," I said. "How's the kid doing?"

"The *kid*," spat Karpis, "has a wife and family and is president of a bank. He's no more a kid than any of us."

"I'm the oldest here," said Doc, for no apparent reason, and despite the fact that I had him by ten years.

"So don't go soft on us, Powers," said Karpis.

I said, "Our best chance to collect, Ray, is to give them a few days."

"Fuck it, he's right," said Fred.

"He already give me the cooties," said Doc, scratching his scalp.

"Who gave you the cooties?" asked Fred.

"President Alt," Doc said.

Karpis backed to the mantel, where he had a glass of milk set next to a scotch bottle. He whirled the last inch of milk cocktail and drank it off.

"So what do we do, boys," he said. "What's the strategy?"

Doc said: "We send Barney Oldfield back to Saint Paul with a bloody envelope."

"Ignore my brother," said Fred.

"Deer blood," said Doc.

"Not a bad idea," said Karpis.

I said: "Better yet, Ricky writes a letter to Pops pleading for his life. Claims he's miserable and frightened and begs his Pa to hurry. Heartfelt, see. That last letter was too … breezy. Too folksy. We need urgent."

"I'll scare the shit out El Presidente and that son of a bitch will write us a good letter," said Doc. He produced a blue revolver from his trouser pocket.

"No need to be crude," said Karpis.

"Who you calling crude?" said Doc.

Karpis ignored that.

"Ray, who you calling crude?" Doc advanced on him.

Karpis, hands up like he was being mugged in an alley, retreated toward the fireplace.

"Calm down, Doc."

"Calm down?" said Doc, tremor in his voice. "I'm trapped here."

"We all are," said Karpis. "Next week, we'll be in Florida, fishing in Florida, imagine that, Doc, all of us on a boat."

"Yeah, okay I guess" said Doc. "You're the brains, Ray." He sat on a wooden chair at the dining room table where he had laid out his roll-your-own kit. He began filtering tobacco out of a leather tie-pouch.

"I like duck huntin better than fishin anyway," Doc muttered.

"Well imagine duck hunting then, in Florida, on a quiet lake, a calm morning, the water like glass." Karpis tapped his head. "Keep a good outlook."

"Good outlook," grumped Doc, rolling that cigarette. "Three more days of this cabin fever shit, and the man wants a good outlook."

"This cabin fever shit," said Fred, "is going to make us rich."

"That's what you said last time."

"And you was rich," Fred reminded him "until you started playing cards."

"Son of a bitching casino," muttered Doc, "they had it fixed crooked."

"They're all crooked," said Fred, and patted his brother's tattooed shoulder. "Just remember that. Hang on to your money this time. Let Ma keep it for you."

"Ma," snorted Doc.

"Well, let's get a night's sleep," said Karpis. "We can't do anything until morning."

Sleep was becoming a foreign concept, and my insomnia was made worse by the overheated house. I was glad for once to occupy the coldest room. Snowflake and Hula Girl, forced by Nature to wear fur coats, preferred to hide in this porch/bedroom, under the bed, next to the cold wall. I puffed up clouds of pipe smoke. I badly wanted a drink but Master Gout said no. I tried to read *Murder Must Advertise* but could not concentrate on the story. Apparently some fellow in London died falling down the stairs. That seemed like nothing compared to what was going on in this cottage, and I couldn't latch on to a polite London mystery.

I dozed in jumpy snatches, waking every hour or so. The dogs first slept with me, atop the rough wool blanket, but then abandoned that, probably due to my squirming and thrashing. They seemed well-fed and did not cower like they would if they'd been badly abused in my absence. This part of my Cathedral prayers, at least, had come true. A pet dog is the last innocent on earth, and unlike humans, no longer needs to rely on vicious instinct. I leaned over the bed to talk comfort to them deep in the night.

"I'm going to take you both to Cuba when this is over," I promised them.

As snow began to gently drift through the pines I watched the moonlight over the silver lake, and it all seemed so beautiful. There was something very sad about that winter beauty. I watched that gentle snowfall until the pink fringes of dawn showed up, and then soft-footed into the kitchen. The radiators had grown silent and nobody had gone downstairs to tend the furnace, so the house had gone from desert heat to bitter cold. I stepped into wool trousers, wrapped in a hunting shirt, and trudged down to the basement, worked the grate, shoveled coal over the few warm embers, shut the door, opened the slots for maximum oxygen. Above I heard rustling feet. Someone opened the kitchen door, let the dogs into the yard. Despite my restless night, I felt confident. Papa Alt would pay in full. Only a matter of time.

Upstairs it was Doc at the kitchen door, his back to it, as if guarding against any escape. Despite the mess in the parlor and dining room, the kitchen was in good order. Only one greasy pan was left on the stove top, the sink drainer was piled precarious with washed dishes and pans.

I stocked the cook-stove's firebox with kindling.

"You run a good kitchen, Doc," I said.

"It's President Alt," he said. "He was restless. He wanted to do something. I put him on kitchen duty."

I lit the kindling with a foot-long match, laid a single split log across its flames.

"Good," I said. "Good for him to be busy."

"You know, Powers, you ain't such a bad guy. It's gossiped that you ain't got the spine of a level guy, but I don't know."

"Spine, is that what they say?"

Doc pulled the curtain away from the door glass, peeked out. "I heard you knocked off a guy named Swede. I heard he had it coming."

Now I was trapped. If I admitted shooting Swede Fanlund, it might turn out that Doc was his friend. On the other hand, if Doc wasn't his friend, a righteous killing would gain me the respect I needed to deal with this gang.

"Swede Fanlund," I said, "was he a friend of yours?"

"Huh," said. "I couldn't stand the son of a bitch."

Still wary of a trap, I only said: "Me neither."

"Them dogs of yours is a hoot," Doc said. "The white one, he's a circus dog, right? Rescued from a circus? I taught him how to somersault, you should see it."

He crossed in front of me, stinking of booze, pistol heavy in one trouser pocket.

"Let's get El Presidente up," he said, and banged on the bedroom door. "Reveille, asshole," he said.

Then he stepped back and laughed. "He ain't used to being called asshole. He's used to being called Yes Sir."

Richard Alt cautiously cracked open the bedroom door.

"Come on out, Mister President," said Doc. "Walter here is making us coffee, ain't you, Walter?"

I, aka Walter, filled the tea kettle. "It'll be a while," I said. "Got to get that stove fire going."

Richard, groggy, was dressed in my pajamas, bursting out of them, since he was bigger than me by four inches and twenty pounds. He attempted a grin, grimaced, his hand went to his head. It was crudely bandaged but no longer bloody and not, I noticed with relief, oozing with infection.

"Bathroom," Richard muttered.

"Go ahead," said Doc, and stepped aside.

When the bathroom door closed, Doc said: "He's tougher than we thought."

"Football player," I said.

"Yeah?"

"Don't you guys do your homework?" I asked.

"What the hell does that mean?" Doc said.

"Uh, you know, you're going to snatch the guy, I figured ..."

"What's this shit about homework?" Doc said and advanced a step on me. "What are you, some kind of schoolteacher?"

I backed off.

He thumped my chest with his forefinger.

"Where do you, Shaky Powers, get off telling me, Doc Barker, to do my fucking homework?"

"I asked, that's all."

"Well don't ask," he said.

"Be calm."

"Don't tell me to be calm!"

"Okay, Doc, what do you want for breakfast?"

The red angry glow began to fade.

"We got one thing," he said. "Sausages and eggs."

"Okay," I said, and opened the fridge, "let's get it out."

"Ma had a stove like that. It took all son-of-a-bitching day to heat up."

"Not these modern babies," I said, and patted the cold stove. "Twenty minutes, tops." I set a tray of eggs and a lump of something bloody wrapped in butcher paper atop the boiler.

Richard wandered out of the bedroom, entered the kitchen like we weren't there, sat at the table, put his head in his hands, as if in abject misery. Doc approached him from behind and put a hand on each shoulder.

"Your old man's negotiatin," said Doc. "He thinks you're only worth half."

"I'm surprised," Richard said into his hands. "I wondered if Pop would give anything for me at all."

"Yeah," said Doc, and patted the big man's shoulders. "He will, he will."

"We never got along," said Richard.

"Hell," said Doc, "I hated my old man like a cat hates water. But you know what? Now we're best friends. He seen the light."

"Ah," Richard said, skeptical. "You don't know my Pop."

Fred appeared in the doorway. "What's for breakfast?"

"Sausage and eggs," said Doc.

"What a surprise," muttered Richard.

"You shut up," said Fred.

"El Presidente is a good kid," said Doc. "Be nice, brother."

"Where's the coffee?" asked Fred. "My mouth tastes like I slept in dirt."

"Brush your teeth more than once a year," suggested Doc.

"Quit using my toothbrush, asshole. Yours is green."

Fred slipped into the bathroom and began gargling, loud and rude.

Karpis walked in from the living room wearing a silk robe. His hair was greased like he meant to keep a date with a wedding photographer.

"Somebody light a fire in this joint," Karpis said.

"I just did," I said.

"Ricky," said Karpis. He sat down opposite Richard. Karpis' back was turned on the rising sun over pine trees.

"We need your help," said Karpis.

"He knows," said Doc. "I told him. I told him about the half."

"Now your old man needs to see reason," said Karpis. "He's got plenty of dough and only one son, see, so it's a simple equation. We need you to help us convince your Pa."

He looked over Richard's head at me. "Who's cooking breakfast?"

"I am," said Doc. "You think I learned nothing in the joint? I can crack five hundred eggs an hour."

"We've got to get this fellow some breakfast," Karpis said, as if he were a man of deep empathy. "Richard, we need a … we need you to write a very convincing letter. If you exaggerate a little, there's no harm. See, if you tell your Pa you are suffering greatly, that you are in mortal terror, that your life is a living hell, why, that will speed the whole thing up. We'll go back to California and you can go home to your wife and little girl. We'll all be happy."

"Except your Pa," said Doc.

"Doc, please be quiet and let me finish," said Karpis. "So that's all we need from you, Richard, a little extra drama in the letter, but we need it to come from you, to sound like you. You need to sound wounded and scared, terrified that you'll never see your loved ones again. Can you do that for us, Rick?"

Maybe Richard moved his lips in response, I don't know, because all I could see was the back of his head, hair still blood-matted.

"Now you know, and I know," said Karpis, "that no harm will come to you, as long as you don't try to escape. Whether we get the money or not, we will release you unharmed. Remember Billy Hamm. Where is he now? Sitting pretty in his office. So if your Pa doesn't come through, we set you free in the woods and try our luck elsewhere. But you can speed it all up if you're convincing with Pa. You've got to write us a letter of pure fear. If you do that for

us, we'll get Shaky here to deliver that letter to your Pa this
morning."

CHAPTER SEVEN

THE HOTEL SAINT PAUL

So after a meal of burnt sausages and runny eggs, without bread and only weak coffee, I said goodbye to Snowflake and Hula Girl and trudged up the hilly driveway to my Terraplane for another long icy drive into Saint Paul. Tucked into my inside jacket pocket was a wax-sealed letter.

Just as I pulled out onto Sunset Road, it began to snow.

It wasn't much of a snowstorm, but it added a seventh hour of white-knuckle driving along Federal 8. In Saint Paul, I parked on the street that ran along the river bluff, where Ramsey County was building its new jail, all concrete block now, construction suspended by winter. I walked to the Hotel Saint Paul, sneaked up to the 9th floor. I heard music coming from behind the door as I rapped in the prescribed rhythm: One two three, one two three, one.

An eye came to the peephole. The door swung open, no George in sight, but the music got louder.

Hiding behind the door, George pushed it shut. An unlit Camel in an ivory holder bobbed in his lips. He wore a gold chain around his neck, ending in a crucifix twisting on his bare hairless chest. A pair of blue golfing trousers was cinched by a white belt at his waist.

"I should have guessed you were a classical music fan," I said.

The music was coming from a record player set on a mirrored dresser. The record player looked like a small wooden suitcase, complete with handle. It was plugged into the wall, its top flung open, a black disk wobbling under the needle arm.

"Mozart amuses me. It's one of his more trivial operas, but I rather enjoy it."

"Oh it's opera? How come they're not singing?"

"My man, you're listening to the overture."

"Sure, I get it."

George lifted the record player's arm, replaced the record from a stack of disks on the dresser. Scratchy orchestra music began blaring. Another overture? From a wide extravagant closet, George chose a pink shirt and an undershirt that had been pressed and bagged at the hotel's dry cleaner. As he donned those shirts, the player's tiny speaker squeaked with a high-voiced woman singing in earnest. George, getting dressed, sang along.

"I guess opera's easier to like if you understand Italian," I said.

George closed his eyes as if in awful pain.

"It's German. They're singing in German." He inserted gold cufflinks in that eye-popping shirt. "Mozart's genius virtually created the modern German state out of three dozen squabbling duchies. It was pride in that music that brought the German-speaking peoples together. But Powers, you didn't come here for lessons in high culture."

I unbuttoned my overcoat, reached into my suit-jacket pocket for the note, handed it at him.

He backed off, hands up in horror, as if I'd shoved a hand grenade in his face.

"Powers, there are these things nowadays called fingerprints."

"It's sealed anyway," I said. "I can just tell you what's in there."

"Do!"

With a huff of irritation, he smashed his cigarette into a glass ashtray, lifted the needle arm. The opera stopped, replaced only by the whistling of the radiator.

"They asked him to pour it on a little bit," I said.

"And what is that supposed to mean?"

"Exaggerate, you know, so his old man … give some urgency to it, I guess."

"And how is our young hero holding up?"

I shrugged. "He's walking around."

"He's walking around? You said he's walking around? My God, he is supposed to be bound, gagged and blindfolded." He kicked the dresser so hard, the pile of records shifted. "Those stupid, ignorant hillbillies." He turned on me. Pointed at me. "They assured me …"

At the frosty windows, he leaned in, rested his forehead against the glass, as if desperately seeking a clear view of anything.

"He knows what you all look like?" he asked over his shoulder.

"I would say so."

"I have half a mind to abandon this foolish enterprise immediately."

At a roll top desk stood a bonded bottle of Courvoisier, alongside a green portable Corona typewriter. He poured himself a drink into a snifter.

"So now, young Alt will be able to point to all of them in a court room."

He downed the brandy.

"Well isn't that just … Powers, what we have here is an amateur production."

He poured a snifter half full, handed it to me.

"You're going to need that drink," he said, "Unfortunately." He sat, turned the chair around so he could lean into the back of it.

"Powers, I mis-timed my assets."

I nodded.

He said: "Wheat futures, you see, are boom and bust."

"So you made a bad bet."

"In crude terms, that is correct. You see, Powers, I live a rather extravagant lifestyle. My background and culture virtually demand it."

He poured himself another drink. "Deluded fools," he said.

I slipped the ransom note into my pocket, sat in a red velvet chair that looked like it been built for European royalty.

"Melvin Purvis," he said. "Absurd name for a copper, don't you think?

I knew that name from the newspapers as Chicago's top G-man.

"An unknowing pawn of the Chicago police," George said. "You see, the little pipsqueak has no street knowledge whatsoever. His last combat, his only combat, was with his law school professor. He was tricked and manipulated in the Hamm prosecution by a demon Illinois cop named Tubbo. Never mind the details. It all goes back to Louie..."

"Louie?"

"Code name for a certain nationally known figure. You see Powers, there were only twelve on the draw. Four Italians, eight of us. You might call the eight of us, the American boys, you might call us vice presidents, or junior executives. You had to be Italian to be among the big four, you see. The entire pie was sliced every month, and we received a hefty stipend. The big four, the chief executives, got 12 percent, and the rest of us got 6 percent each. I'm talking now about the entire profits of South Side bootlegging. It was like being on salary at J.P. Morgan, only without the drudgery of work."

He drank.

"And very few meetings," he added. "In fact we avoided meetings assiduously. I miss those days. It's not easy being the communications man for a gang of hillbillies that is bound to come to ruin. If you're wise, Powers, you'll skip town when this is over."

He drained his glass.

"Maybe skip the country entirely," he said. "Let's get to work, shall we?"

He nodded at the Corona typewriter.

"They didn't have these typewriters when I went to college, not this kind, sleek and portable."

He reached out to pat the machine, thought better of that, withdrew his hand.

"So we need a note to go along with our young hero's plea, a note that lights a fire under Papa Alt's derriere. I do have a ransom delivery plan, Powers, tell me what you think of it."

I sat back in that royal red chair, filled my pipe. Despite not wanting to be involved at all, I was intrigued by the game of gangsters versus rich guys and cops.

George said: "A man we choose from among Papa Alt's inner circle gets on a public bus. He is carrying two suitcases full of cash. The bus heads into the countryside. At some place of our choosing, we light a signal flare. Papa Alt's man suddenly claims to be ill, insists on being let off at the next intersection. Brilliant, you see?"

I lit a bowl of Havana Gold, puffed a cloud of rum-and-chocolate dreams.

"Our Mister Moneybags gets off the bus alone," George said, "or it's no deal. Who shall we choose, Powers, advise me? You are quite familiar with this snowbound excuse for a city."

"Well, if it's all small bills packed in two suitcases, how much do they weigh?"

"I've done my calculations quite carefully, Powers, and it's in excess of 30 pounds each."

"The priest, then. He's six-foot-six and built like a grizzly bear. A former prize-fighter. He could lug a hundred pounds off that bus. At his size, he's unmistakable, they can't possibly trick us with a substitute. And he surely won't be armed. He's a, what do you call those guys, pacifist."

"All right, the man of God. Perhaps his selection will please the Almighty. Certainly it will amuse the press. So, when our priest does alight, he sets his burden down, walks away, and we swoop in. The authorities cannot possibly prepare a trap at all points along the bus route."

"Might work."

"Might work? Powers it is a plan of sheer genius. Simple and foolproof."

I blew smoke toward him.

"Wouldn't you agree?" he asked.

"I'm a horseplayer," I said. "There are no sure things."

George, angry, stepped aside and said: "Man the typewriter."

I stood at the desk, had a side glance into the mirror. No denying this was me, Michael Patrick Powers, kidnapper.

Doomed kidnapper.

At the roll top I removed my suit-jacket, rolled up my sleeves.

"We shall work in stages," George said behind me.

I slipped in a piece of Blackstone Hotel stationery and started typing.

"No no no I wasn't dictating."

I ripped the letterhead out, rolled a new one in.

"We shall work in stages so as not to tip our hand," George said. "The first stage is to get them to prepare and package the money, and send a signal when they are ready."

"Okay," I said.

George cleared his throat.

"You are hereby declared," he dictated, "in a very desperate undertaking. You are to gather $200,000 ..." he waited as my typing caught up ... "in fives, tens and twenties. When this is ready for delivery ... you are to place an advertisement ... in the Daily News personals section ... which says "Come home. All is forgiven. Richard."

He waved away the smoke from my pipe.

"Very nice, Powers," he said. "Excellent accuracy and punctuation. My congratulations to the nuns who schooled you."

He cleared his throat and said, "Line space, please. New paragraph ... Ready? Type: As emissary we select... make that have selected ... your friend the priest.

"Do not stall, do not delay. Do not involve any police agency, or there will be further... not farther now, it's f-u-r ... trouble.

"Be assured that your son is unharmed, as proven in the accompanying documents ... and that we intend to strictly honor our side of the deal as you would expect from true gentlemen."

He paced, came back to examine the sheet in the typewriter and said: "What do you think, Powers, do we need a Complimentary Close?"

"A what?"

"You know, sincerely yours, something like that."

'Well it is a business letter, I guess, but we're not going to sign it, are we?"

"Good point."

George walked to the window and stared out. "Somewhere in this vast metropolis..." his voice lowered, "I'm speaking facetiously, Powers, this is a cow town. But somewhere out there a man with far too much money is about to meet with cosmic justice. Doesn't it give you a thrill, Powers, to be the very agent of justice?"

"I never thought about it that way."

"That's your trouble, Powers, you haven't been trained to think. You see that's what they teach in college, the power of thought and communication. Thought is meaningless without communication.

Now I'm depending on you Powers, to once again get this message to the beer-addled Bavarians in their frosty mansion."

"One thing," I said, and knocked ashes from my pipe into that glass ashtray. "Who's going to handle the ransom cash? Not me. No way. I'm not touching it. Don't ask."

George waved me off.

"We already have a stooge. A simpleton. Lap they call him."

"Lap?"

"It's some kind of hillbilly name. Don't worry, just deliver your message and we'll be far, far away before Melvin Purvis knows we were here."

Billy McAmbly was ironing his uniform trousers when I peeked in from the kitchen. Maureen had let me in and run ahead to announce: "Uncle Mick is here."

Billy was standing at the ironing board in his underwear and high dark socks. He stood the iron up on the board and crossed the room with his hand out.

"Well you son of a gun," he said as we shook hands. "Who let you out of jail? Maureen honey, get your Uncle Mick a can of beer."

I sat in the living room in an easy chair that had a crater worn into its seat. A sepia depiction of Jesus with halo hung over it, speared with a frond from last Palm Sunday. Children's coloring books lay on the bare wood floor, one opened to the splendid animals of Africa. Maureen handed me a sweating can of Altwasser and I said, "Thanks, darling, how's the little scholar?"

"Fine," she said.

"Mick and I are going to talk, honey," said her dad.

She scooped up coloring book and crayons and headed for the kitchen.

"Good Jesus," Billy said, "you should be down at headquarters. It's a madhouse. Dahill's lost his mind entirely. He's put Big Ryan in charge of this thing, can you imagine? Fox and the henhouse. I doubt Ryan is fool enough to be mixed up in this, but I guarantee you one thing." He unplugged the iron. "Ryan knows who the snatch team is."

"What do they have you doing?"

"Me? I go nowhere near this thing, Mick. It's a ball of snakes and I don't want to get strangled. What it means to me is overtime, and I get the cash to fix the goddamn radiator in the goddamn car."

He held up the uniform shirt, dark green, brass buttons, his name stitched in black thread over the right pocket.

"Gotta look sharp, though. The place is overrun with big shots. I'm telling you, Mick, federal men from all over the country. And the reporters, Jesus, from New York and California. I'll end up in the newsreels."

"It's a joke," I said, "isn't it?"

"Of course it's a joke. I wouldn't doubt that sly old German set it up himself."

"Papa Alt? Why would he do that?"

"Siphon off that two hundred thousand, that's why."

He sat across from me on a half-collapsed couch, folding his uniform blouse, making room for himself by plowing away a jumble of wooden toy trucks.

He leaned toward me, big red hands on bare hairy legs. "You know the Grand Jury meets in secret, right? But in this town, there are no secrets. Guess who the jury was about to call."

I shrugged.

"Richard Wilhelm Alt."

"In the case of ...

"The case of the swindled horseplayer. Now guess the amount of the swindle? Two hundred thousand dollars, exactly."

"How did it work?"

Billy shrugged his big shoulders. "They're coming up with new swindles all the time, it's amazing, I'll tell you."

"Horse racing …" I muttered.

"Put two and two together, will ya Mick? The old man's building a walled city over there, Christ there must be a hundred grand just in the piping. He needs to triple his fleet of trucks at two-thousand a truck. His bank's wobbly now that all his bootlegger accounts are gone. Now his kid is in the dock in a big-time swindle. Only he's quote unquote kidnapped the day before his date with the Grand Jury. And then there's the ransom amount, exactly the same as the swindle."

He sat back. "Go ahead, Mick, tell me it doesn't stink."

"It stinks," I said.

"And your wily old friend McAmbly is staying a mile away from it. You know I'm eight years from the pension. Jesus," he swigged beer. "I'll end up a bank guard. No wonder Charley Bragg killed himself."

A thunk sounded underneath us. Billy shouted: "Kevin! I heard that!"

He shook his head. The look on his face went through phases: irritation, amusement, pride.

"All winter," he said. "Kid hits fungoes in the basement."

While in the McAmbly home, I had left the ransom notes in the glove compartment of my Terraplane. This avoided the risk, however small, that G-men would bust in and haul McAmbly away with me. But all the time I was visiting with Billy, the ransom notes were like a lead weight in my mind. I had to deliver them, but how?

I had taken enough risk driving past the Alt mansion, and vowed never to do that again. I could imagine the G-men waiting in neighbors' driveways. The Barker gang wasn't expecting me back at the cottage until Monday night or Tuesday morning, so I had time to devise a plan. I drove downtown to Union Depot, rented a locker, and deposited the envelope containing the ransom notes. Then, I couldn't help it, I phoned the United Press and asked for Janie.

Even from a phone booth in the train station's noisy marble cavern, I could hear the clattering of her teletype.

I said, "It's your friend the gangster."

"Who is this?"

"Master of two canines."

"Powers? I heard you were dead or in Cuba."

"They working you hard?"

"I can hardly take a breath," she said.

"You need a break? I'm at the train station."

"I'm in the middle of something."

"What?"

"A story, what else?"

I was desperate to see her, so I baited the hook.

"I've got a tale for you."

"Oh, Powers."

"You want to hear it over a grilled cheese sandwich?"

"I haven't been out of here in two days."

"Well."

"I'll probably smell bad," she said.

"I'll hold my nose."

I waited for her at the depot's lunch counter. A grumpy man in a white tent hat, with deep lines in his narrow face, poured me a cup of coffee. Something resembling motor oil floated on its surface. I pushed it back at him and asked for tea.

"Out of tea," he said. "Coffee. That we got."

"You call this coffee?" I said.

"I don't call it nothing, pal," he said. "I dump the grounds in there, pour in water, this is what comes out. Any complaints, see the management."

A locomotive sounded its deep wailing horn, came hissing along the snowy tracks, like a vision of steam heat in an arctic landscape. That locomotive, bell clanging, send shivers through the building.

"Milk?" I said.

"Went sour," he said.

"Orange juice?"

"This time of year? What do you think this is, Florida?"

"Coca-Cola?"

"Fountain's acting up."

"What do you have?"

"The time of day and coffee."

"It's the time of day then, to complain to the management."

"Right now I am the management."

I sighed.

"You want booze?," he said, and pointed a gray bent finger. "The bar's still open."

"There's going to be a girl comes looking for me," I said. "Red head, freckle face, early 20s. Send her to the bar, will you?"

"Does it say lost and found here, or does it say cafeteria?"

I palmed him a quarter.

"Send the red head," I said, and, coat over my arm, headed for the bar.

Passengers at the bar quickly downed their drinks and headed out for the bright lights and the noisy, huffing train. The locomotive had backed in those new-fangled streamlined cars, a stainless-steel glimpse of the shiny future.

In a moment I had the bar to myself. It had a church atmosphere almost, with stained glass windows, low lamps. The mahogany bar had a gleaming brass rail for footing. I bellied up and the barman, a little round ball of a guy, poured me a ginger ale without the usual smart remarks about was I on the wagon. In five minutes Janie rushed in, snowflakes in her dark wool hat, which she removed along with her coat, and draped on a stool.

"I believe I'll have something hot. An Irish coffee, please."

She gave me a long once-over and said, "Boy, do I need a drink. Powers, good to see you, you look so … pale. Have you seen a ghost?"

"Long winter," I said.

"The dogs? The dogs are okay?"

"They keep asking for you."

She sputtered. "Well, here I am."

"Baby Dane?" I said.

"Eighteen pounds," she said, and smiled. I'd never seen her wearing lipstick before and now I realized she smelled of perfume. "Almost eighteen pounds," she corrected herself. "And trying to sit up."

"Dare I ask? Is he with on the dairy farm with grandma?"

"For the duration," she said.

"For the duration of…"

"My special assignment. The UP is not going to keep me on after this kidnapping is over. If I'm lucky, they'll bring me back for the trial."

"If there is a trial," I said.

"So you're living in, ah…"

"Powers, it's humiliating enough to go home at my age, with a baby, so don't push me, all right? Yes, if you must know, my parents took me in. Okay? Satisfied."

"Sorry," I said.

"What do you know about this mess?" she asked.

The Irish coffee served, she licked at the creamy top.

"Come on," she said, "I thought you wanted to spill."

"Ever hear of a guy named George Ziegler?"

She looked around suspicious, then whispered. "Yes I certainly have. Capone's lord high executioner."

"Come on. Says who?"

"Chicago federal gangster squad. I have a source there now. I'm still working on my gangster book, Powers. Believe it. Shotgun George. His weapon of choice is a double-barreled shotgun. Saint Valentine's Day? He was playing tuba in that band. Some of my sources say he was leading the orchestra."

"We're talking about the same guy? Snappy dresser, late thirties, blond hair?"

"Never met him, never want to. Do you remember Jake Lingle? Every reporter in Chicago remembers him, I guarantee you. Don't get too cozy with gangsters, that was the message there."

She sipped her coffee. "So Powers, how do you know this Chicago master criminal? And where have you been all winter? I hear you've been scarce around town."

She shuddered, lay a hand on my arm. She had yet to remove her red wool gloves.

"I had to tell them, Powers," she whispered. "I swore it was self defense. I said I'd testify that Swede came after us. I don't know. It was Crumley and the Bulldog. They didn't take notes, they didn't even bring me downtown. I think they didn't know what to do with the baby. Anyway, it seems crazy, but I never heard from the cops again, so you tell me."

"Oh, they'll shake me down, don't worry. That's why I'm laying low. What do you know about the Alt snatch?"

She smiled. "Why do I have the feeling you know more than I do?"

"See the thing is," I said, "the snatch is more complicated than it looks. Don't fall for the simple story, Janie, it's got more strands than the transatlantic cable."

"Stretch one out for me."

"Cops," I said. "In on it."

"In what way?"

"From the beginning. Big Ryan. Be careful. Watch for the double cross."

"Come on."

"What more do you want? Hey, the Alts aren't the most innocent victims you've ever met."

"How so?"

"You used to cover the county beat here, you know Irish Kinkead. Go over there and flash him some leg. While he's got a boner, maybe he'll tell you, off the record, what the Grand Jury's hearing. Specifically relates to a guy who lost a bundle in a horse race swindle. That's a big piece of the puzzle."

"That's all you can tell me?"

"That'll keep you busy for a month right there."

"What does a horse race swindle have to do with this kidnapping?"

"Get Irish Kinkead to tell you."

"Powers, I'm a wire service slave now, all I do is feed the teletype. I'm on constant deadline. I can't go traipsing around chasing horse swindles."

I slapped my palm on the bar. "Fine. Then believe all the crap the cops feed you."

"I'm just a reporter, Powers, not the attorney general."

"Forget it," I said. "What did Crumley say, that night?"

"He was pissed that he had to climb the stairs. He said a building of four stories should have an elevator, there ought to be a law. That was most of it. He huffed and he puffed and he looked over the parapet and saw, you know, what there was to see, and he shook his head and said, What do you think, Bulldog, and Bulldog says, I quit thinking in 1925 and Crumley says long way down, and Bulldog says, yep, and that was pretty much it."

"Typical Saint Paul investigation," I said.

"You're lucky, Powers."

"Lucky, that's my middle name," I said. "Take a break from that teletype, kid," I said. "Go over and see Irish Kinkead. Shake it up a little."

I stopped at Snyder's, the late night drug store, for a can of Windex and a bottle of Sal Hepatica. When I tried to slink through the Commodore lobby, the desk clerk waved a telegram at me. I sat in a plush chair by the big roaring fireplace and ripped open the dark yellow envelope. It was from Tom Filben, in code. His man at the motor vehicle bureau had come through. The telegram said: 490 UTXYQESI PTJSNL Which translated to 945 Portland Koenig.

The code was too simple to fool the feds, and maybe easy enough to be cracked by Saint Paul cops. But the gamble was they'd never come across it, and it certainly would foil the snoopy telegraph clerks, who routinely saw messages in code.

I lit my pipe for a contemplative smoke. Papa Alt in desperate need of cash. Richard involved in a big-money horse racing swindle. Why had the Barker gang not bothered to conceal their identities from Richard Alt? Surely Harry and Big Ryan were in on the scheduling, but was Otto Alt the hidden engineer of this train?

That seemed crazy. But something was going on underneath the surface. Harry and Papa and Richard and Chief Ryan were once in a tight business arrangement all having to do with moving illegal beer and cleaning up dark money.

But how could anyone logically figure Shotgun George, Al Capone's hit man, as writer of the ransom notes?

During Prohibition, Big Joe Ryan had been Papa Alt's protection man. Harry had run Papa's beer distribution system. Richard at the River State bank laundered the profits. The Barker gang was working at Harry's direction and under the protection of Big Joe Ryan. What the hell was going on here?

I, pinch-hitter in a ballgame with no rules, had scant idea. But I clearly had a job to do. I borrowed the Saint Paul phone book from the desk clerk. I flipped to see Dr. Mark Koenig, MD, 945 Portland Avenue. Doctor, I said to myself, grab a bat, you're up next.

CHAPTER EIGHT

SATURDAY, JANUARY 20

I didn't actually sleep that night, but merely fought off twisted, wide-awake dreams. Peggy, my long-gone wife, used to say to me: *Mick, you always take the easy way out. But sometimes the easy way isn't the right way.*

I had already thought over the so-called right way to end this, and it led to a murderous gun battle in the woods. In my waking dreams the snowy woods were on fire, a blaze set by an army of pyromaniac Swede Fanlunds, come back to life and dressed in dirty mechanic's uniforms, blow torches in hand.

Deer, porcupines, squirrels, all the innocent creatures, ran for their lives in this nightmare, making tracks in the snow as the flames roared furious toward them, accompanied by the dying howls of Snowflake and Hula Girl and the echo of machine gun fire rattling out over the frozen lake.

I dreamed, too, of my first run down from Winnipeg, just four cases of whiskey in the trunk, meeting Pat Reilly in the alley behind the Green Lantern for the payoff, Reilly just a batboy then, dressed in Saint Paul Saints flannels. I dreamed of the horror on Myrtle's face, like a spotlight shining on it, the night I plugged Rico four times and ran off into the woods. I dreamed of the day I bought drinks for all the gamblers at the Royal after my 100-to1 shot Jim Dandy won the Travers Stakes. I remembered screaming as Swede

Fanlund burned me with a cigarette in the Sacred Heart schoolyard while his bully boys held me down. I dreamed of the year we beat Cretin High, me gloving that last out with the kind of stretch that only lefty first-basemen can manage.

In the morning, stupefied by useless thoughts, I set the envelope containing the ransom notes on the dresser, cleaned it with a rag dipped in Windex. Like a lot of my friends, I was alarmed by fingerprint technology, and imagined the G-men would soon be able to solve every crime ever committed.

Sal Hepatica I had taken sometimes for the gout. But this time I bought it for the bottle. I dumped the Sal Hepatica salts down the sink drain, washed the bottle, dried it. Now I had a wide-mouth bottle, a vessel for a ransom note. I rolled the envelope up so it fit tight, about half of it sticking out of the bottle, like a paper fuse to a bomb.

Out on the streets, it was just me, the milk trucks and the newspaper carriers. I drove my Terraplane a few blocks to Herb's garage. I used a key Filben had given me to let myself into the dark body repair shop, where I swapped my car for a clunky, dark two-door Oldsmobile. It had, I was assured, a reliable engine and stolen plates.

I drove that Oldsmobile up Cathedral hill, then over the quiet dark frigid streets toward Doctor Koenig's house. A block away from it I cut the headlights. Doctor Koenig had a broad front porch to welcome friends and family. Patients used the side door, in shadows now. That door was pebbled glass and marked with a sign: Waiting Room, with an arrow pointing upstairs. I stepped out of the car, and heaved the Sal Hepatica bottle at the side door. My intent was to break the glass, but the bottle bounced off, harmless, and landed spinning on a snow-flecked doormat.

A shoulder high stone wall stood between the doctor's house and the street. I picked up a rock from the top of that wall and heaved it like I was throwing first-to-home. That rock crashed through the cut-glass of the front door. I hustled into the Oldsmobile and drove away, dark car into darkness.

Back at Herb's, I swapped back into my Terraplane and sped down Fort Road to a seedy Sinclair gas station that had a public phone around the side. It was like holding a block of ice to my ear as I dialed Doctor Koenig's home number.

A female voice said: "Hello?"

"Put the doctor on the phone."

"Who ist this?" A female with a German accent. The house maid? "The doctor haf no office hours today."

I said, "Honey, a rock just came smashing through your front door. Didn't you notice?"

"A rock?"

"Put the phone down and go to the front door and come back and tell me what you see."

Apparently all she had to do was turn around. In a heartbeat she said: "Oh mein Gott. Is broken everywhere."

"Tell the doctor there is a message in a bottle at the side door. Get it? Message in a bottle. Side door. Very important. Wake him up. Emergency."

And then I hung up.

On weekends, the Town Talk opened at 6 a.m. Friday and didn't shut down until after they'd served Sunday lunch. Although it was across from the police station, and might seem like the last place for me to go, Opal or Lillian would be on duty, and either could be persuaded to stretch the truth and provide me with an alibi. I sat at the counter where Lillian, flipping eggs in the kitchen, could see me. I blew a kiss at young Opal as she walked by, balancing breakfast platters as she tip-toed to the detective's table. I kept my back turned to the cops, none of whom I knew.

Lillian darted out to refill her coffee mug at the big stainless boiler.

"How's the working girl?" I asked.

"Working," she said.

"What's the latest gossip from HQ?"

"You haven't heard?" She sipped coffee, gave me an intent look from behind those cat eye glasses.

"You know me, soul of ignorance."

"About Mister Pearson?"

"What about him?"

She put one finger to her lips, turned her back and, all gray uniform and white apron, walked through the swinging steel doors and into the kitchen.

I put my hand out to stop Opal as she rushed past.

"What's this about Serious Bobby Pearson?"

"I was told to shut up about it," she whispered and escaped to the opening in the stainless steel wall. There she hung order slips from greasy clips.

She tried to avoid me on her way back to the cop table but I put up my hand and shouted: "Waitress, can you take my order please?"

Opal shrugged, like I was teacher handing out homework and she a reluctant student. She leaned on the counter hands and arms, too tired to stand straight.

"Mick, why do you make trouble? Were you brought up in an orphanage or something?"

"I'm asking about a friend of mine."

"Friend? Not the way I heard it."

She popped pink bubble gum, brushed that Black Irish hair away from her blue eyes.

"Anyway," she said. "He's gone, and I don't mean to Florida."

"You mean he's dead?"

Opal pursed her lips as if talking, patient, to an idiot.
"Seriously dead."
She formed a gun with her hand and shot me with it.
"What'll you have?"

I don't remember ordering. I don't remember who set poached
eggs and toast in front of me on the green Formica counter. I do
remember the newsboy coming through hawking the morning
Pioneer Press. I do remember paging through and seeing not one
word concerning Serious Bobby.

I knifed up my breakfast, but didn't eat much of it. The one guy
who might know about the demise of Serious Bobby, underworld
diplomat, conspirator in the Hamm Kidnapping, was Billy
McAmbly.

Although it was hardly after 6 a.m., I called him from the Town
Talk's hall telephone. Kevin answered, voice husky, and shouted:
"Dad."

"Billy," I said, "you on O.T. today?"
"Every day," he grumped, "until the Alt kid gets back."
"What time you getting in?"
"When my ass gets me there."
"I'll be waiting," I said.
"Could be all day," he said.

There's no better place to count eggs than inside the hen house,
so I slipped out of my overcoat, left it in the car, and walked past
those tall concrete columns and into the madhouse of law
enforcement. The desk sergeant, red faced, sat high like a judge,
underneath a giant brass clock and in front of a microphone as big
around as a softball bat. He threw me a look that said he'd crush
me like an insect if only he cared enough. The hallway benches
were lined with half-asleep men, and a few women, whom I took to

be out-of-town reporters, exhausted on their 24-hour duty. Hands
in my trouser pockets, pretending a casual air I did not feel, I
wandered past smoked-glass doors marked with the names of the
detective divisions: Purity, Bunko, Auto. Without knocking I
opened the door of Homicide.

In there were desks, unmanned, but piled chaotic with case files.
Back by the water cooler, one chair occupied by his ass and another
by bloated bare feet, Inspector James Crumley rested on the closest
thing he could devise to a bed. The ceiling lights were glaring awful.
Crumley's stained gray fedora was tilted over his eyes, a shield
against all illumination.

"Hey, Powers," he said without lifting that fedora. "Which cat
house did you spend the night in?"

"Allergic to cats," I said.

"Do me a favor," he said, and adjusted that hat so he could see
even less. "Bring Ricky Alt back."

"What?"

"His daddy misses him."

"Don't even joke, Jim."

He creaked in the chair.

"You boys got to treat him right now," Crumley said. "Little
Ricky ain't used to no rough stuff. Remember, them college boys is
delicate."

"Be serious, Jim. And speaking of Serious ..."

"Oh yeah, ain't that a shame. Just when things was looking up. I
seen his name in the paper just last week."

"What do you mean?"

"He was going to be made vice president over at the Hamm's.
They're doing good over there. Thousand barrels a day, I hear."

"He got plugged?"

"And Bobby was such a good friend of Big Joe Ryan."

"Where and how? They got any suspects?"

As Crumley was about to answer, Bulldog McMullen bumbled in, wiping his whiskey-red face with a men's room paper towel.

"They got any suspects, Bulldog?"

"In what?"

"Serious Bobby."

"How about this Powers guy?" Bulldog said, and punched me easy in the shoulder. "Can we grab him? He's guilty of something."

"I was just about to cuff him," Crumley said. "For the Ricky Alt snatch."

"Come on guys."

"Good thing we're only homicide cops," Crumley said. "Kidnapping now, we ain't got the smarts to work them complicated crimes. We're just lowly detectives, right, Bulldog?"

"Last I checked," said the Bulldog.

"Well, this Serious Bobby thing, we better get right on it," Crumley said. "The public demands answers."

"Maybe you should interview Big Joe Ryan," I said, "if him and Bobby were so tight. Ryan ought to be working the case, right, the murder of his good friend?"

"Interrogate Ryan yourself, tough guy," said Bulldog. "The big weasel is upstairs right now with Dahill and the G-men."

"Upstairs?" I said.

"Temporary office off the gym," said Crumley. "Secret headquarters of the kidnap squad, now."

"It stinks in there," said McMullen. "That's why I don't exercise."

"Exercise kills," said Crumley. "I know a guy dropped dead skipping rope."

"Action up in the gym this morning," said the Bulldog. "All kinds of ransom rumors. You don't think the brain trust is going to call us in, do you?"

"Hell," Crumley said, "the G-men wouldn't even spit on us, now."

"What about Bobby?" I asked. "Where'd they find him?"

"Can we disclose that information?" asked the Bulldog. "To a civilian who ain't done us a favor all month?"

Crumley lifted his bare feet off the one chair and sat up. He brushed his shirt front as if it was covered in crumbs, and it might have been. A stained white cardboard disk, which had once held a coffee cake, lay at the base of his desk phone.

"Mendota Heights," said Crumley. "Laying like a dog in the ditch."

"Shot four times, twice in the noggin," said Bulldog. "As he was flouncing down the steps of his mother's home. He was the kind of fancy boy visited his mama every week."

"Shame," said Crumley. "You can't even visit your mother in this town."

"Well, it didn't happen in this town, did it Jim?" said the Bulldog. "Mendota Heights, scene of the crime."

"Out of our jurisdiction, now," said Crumley.

"Ain't that a coincidence," said the Bulldog. "What do they got out there, Jim, two traffic cops and a part-time chief?"

"Oh, at best," said Crumley. "That town lives off speeding tickets, now."

"Funny how that happened," said the Bulldog, "Serious got plugged just a couple of yards across the city line. Saint Paul Police can't investigate. I wonder who could have done it, don't you Jim?"

"You don't want to cross no lines, now," said Crumley. "I never leave town myself."

I drove back to the Commodore for a nap. Like the cops, I had been up all night. I checked the pocket watch my old man had given me, it came from his first job out East, the Erie Railroad. It was just after 7 a.m. I assumed that Doctor Koenig had rushed the ransom notes over to the Alt mansion. The ad deadline to make the Saturday Daily News was 9 a.m. The first editions hit the streets some time after 1 p.m.

All I could do was wait. I couldn't sleep so I dialed her.

A gruff male voice answered. An Ozarks voice.

"What do you want?"

"Wrong number?" I said. "I thought I was calling Myrtle."

"Well she ain't coming to the phone. Don't call here no more, pal. I find you I'll kick your ass."

And then he hung up.

I drove over to Myrtle's apartment building, sat and watched and waited. It was a windy, mild, sunny, snow-melting morning, with actual liquid atop the ice on the sidewalks. I bought a cupcake and coffee at the Steinhoff Bakery. About 9 a.m. I saw a tough character sneak out the back way of Myrtle's dark brick building. He was dressed in rough coat, a big yellow scarf he had borrowed from Myrtle and the trousers from a good suit. He crossed the street to the Walgreen's drugs. He could have more easily come out the front way, since Myrtle's apartment looked out on Grand. But no, he had walked all the way down the hallway, circled the apartment from behind as if trying to avoid something.

I went down an alley myself, and into the Barking Dog Tavern. I slipped into the dark hallway and dialed Myrtle.

"Hey, kid," I said, "it's me."

"I can tell by your voice its you."

"I got kind of a rude fella on the phone last time I called."

"Mick, it's better if you stay out of it honey."

"If you don't like this guy, Myrtle, I can take care of him."

"No you can't."

"Don't underestimate me."

"Estimate has nothing to do with it. He's one of the Ozarks boys. The easiest thing is to let them skip town. They'll be gone in a few days, Mick, when this whole thing blows over. Do it the easy way, honey, come see me next week when I'm lonely."

She hung up on me.

The easy way, she said. Hmmm. This Ozarks guy was six foot tall, well built, a decade younger than me, I would need some kind of weapon to take him.

There he was, walking along the sidewalk, tapping a pack of cigarettes. I felt helpless watching this guy cross the street. I had dumped my weapons into the Mississippi last summer, and vowed no more guns. I hated the idea of this thug abusing Myrtle. He slipped into the alcove of the Grand Theater to get out of the wind and light his smoke. I pretended to just stroll by.

"Hey buddy, can you spare a smoke?"

He gave me the stink eye. He had the Daily News and Dispatch under his arm, with their screaming kidnap headlines.

He shook out a Chesterfield. "I suppose you want a light too," he barked.

There was a scar on his chin, made only more visible by his dark stubble. It looked like the scar from a knife fight, a nasty slash. He had dark hair, going thin, and black eyes. I made a study of his face.

"They got any news in those papers?"

"I strictly buy 'em for the funnies," he said.

With a stick match, he lit the cigarette in my lips.

I coughed. The theater poster in back of him trumpeted Bette Davis in "The Big Shakedown." Bette was reclining, resisting a Latin lover.

"So I see by the papers," I said, "rum's officially legal today."

"I don't go by what's in the papers," said the man from the Ozarks.

"I sure wish a fella could get one of those liquor licenses."

He looked me over as if he'd just seen me. "There's too many booze joints in this town already," he said. "I ain't never seen anything like it."

"So you're not from around here."

"Nope."

He blew smoke, thoughtful, at a clear blue sky and asked: "Do I know you from somewhere?"

"I doubt it."

"Well, stranger, I'll see you around."

"Thanks for the smoke," I said.

Where had this mystery man come from? That called for another trip to Bertillion, but not today, I had taken all the chances I wanted to. I began to formulate a plan to get the cops to do my dirty work.

CHAPTER NINE

SATURDAY AFTERNOON

There's never a newspaper around when you need one. I was lurking a half hour at Blind Benny's and the Daily News truck was nowhere in sight.

Seven Corners was as busy as a madhouse during an air raid. The January thaw had brought Minnesota gophers out of their holes. You could actually see their faces, bereft of scarves and ski masks. In the tangled intersection, it was grinding trucks vs. honking cars vs. clanging streetcars vs. scurrying people, and one poor sap of a traffic cop trying to unsnarl it all.

I turned my back to the traffic and browsed the magazines hanging by clips off the wall. *The Ring* featured Teddy Yarosz, dukes up, as if anybody gave a damn about middleweight pugs. *Scribner's* headlined a chapter of *Tender is the Night* by F. Scott Fitzgerald, the magazine sure to sell out in his hometown. *Bedtime Stories* featured a half-dressed, smiling, leggy brunette perched on a bar stool, hands gripping a glass of whiskey.

I turned away from the lurid cover of *Bedtime Stories* to look up at the Cathedral.

"Getting bold, aren't we Benny?"

"We're all getting old."

"Bold," I said. I jerked my thumb at the girly mag. Benny wasn't totally blind, he saw the world in a milky fog. He could always see school boys trying to steal from him.

"If the Archbishop had binoculars …" I said.

"You know what's the trouble, Powers?"

"What's that?"

His wife Gussie bustled behind the counter, giving change, her wool gloves missing the fingertips.

"We come off the gold standard," lamented Blind Benny. He shoved his inky hands into a dirty apron. His red sweatshirt was mottled by newspaper ink. "Used to be we could count on something. Gold. Now it's funny money."

"Is he selling smut licenses?"

"Who?"

"The Archbishop."

I bought a half-frozen Snickers, handed him a nickel.

"Without gold, how do you know a nickel's worth a nickel?" he complained.

I looked around for a Legion of Decency sticker, didn't see one. Catholics weren't supposed to buy at a newsstand that wasn't displaying one of those. Benny, a Jew, may not have cared about the Archbishop's reading preferences, but he'd never defied the Legion, not here in the heart of Catholic Saint Paul.

"I guess the Legion of Decency is going soft," I said.

"Decency in this town? In my next life, I want be a bum. No worries, no taxes, no censors, no bundling up the returns, no late trucks, no winter winds, half my life is bundling up returns."

"He's telling his life story, this one?" said Gussie, tying dated magazines with twine.

The Snickers was like a rock in my teeth. Over the years, Benny had half-enclosed his newsstand and put in kerosene heaters, but any true warmth in here would only come in May.

"The government wants me to get a cash register.," Benny said. "I said what for?"

"Taxes is what for," said Gussie.

A blue truck lurched around the corner and without really stopping, disgorged two bundles of newspapers. They hit the sidewalk and flopped over, the bigger one coming to rest face up, a blank sheet obscuring its headlines.

Benny snipped the bailing wire with a wire-cutter, revealing a headline that took up a half page.

ALT RANSOM NOTE DELIVERED

I pitched two pennies into a coin-filled ashtray. Newspaper under my arm, I pushed into the Mrs. Sippy Tavern, one of a thousand new beer ventures, this one taking over a shoe repair shop. In the big window's light, I paged past the front page news to the real news, the personals. Despite scanning the columns three times, I saw no ad. The ransom money would not be ready, at least not today.

I walked next door to Lee's Chop Suey. It was run by real Chinese now, since Jack Peifer had sold it. His Japanese minions had run it for years, on the theory that nobody in Saint Paul could tell they weren't Chinese. And on the other theory that mushy chop suey was only a side business anyway.

The waitress was a skinny Chinese girl, a wild-eyed child of twelve at most, who was barefoot and wore a sarong. I felt strange giving such a tiny child my order for tea and egg rolls. There were only a few scattered patrons. While awaiting on my tea I read on the front page how Doctor Mark Koenig had reported to police that his door had been smashed with a milk bottle containing the ransom note. The exact ransom demands were not divulged. However, the kidnappers did deliver proof that Richard Alt had survived his abduction, the news account said, and had written a heartfelt letter to his family.

Milk bottle?

It was a Sal Hepatica bottle.

Oh well, I'd long ago lost trust in newspapers.

I wondered about those boys back in Eagle River, cut off from all communication, except what they could make out in the static of the Rhinelander radio station. I hoped they weren't out hunting deer. The season had long passed, and gunshots in the woods just might bring the sheriff.

The Alt kidnapping had pushed all the other crime news inside. Atop Page Three a headline read:

HAMM'S VP SHOT
ON STEPS OF
MOM'S HOME

The murder happened just after ten at night, the story said, as Mister R. L. Pearson was concluding his customary Friday night visit to his sickly mother. There were no direct witnesses, but one neighbor claimed to hear a powerful car roar off immediately after the gunshots. The ambulance left his body for the coroner's truck, and took his mother directly to Anker Hospital with symptoms of a heart attack.

The story claimed, without a hint of irony, that Robert Pearson was a real estate consultant hired to assist the Hamm family with brewery expansion plans. There was, strangely enough, no mention of his being named as a potential courier in the Alt kidnapping. Neither was there a hint of his gangster connections, nor of his underworld nickname. Neighbors were quoted as being shocked by the killing. They claimed that R. L. Pearson was good to his mother, didn't have an enemy in the world, and had a cheerful greeting for all he met.

Homicide Inspector James Crumley assured the press that police were following several promising leads.

So I was in Limbo until ten p.m., when the bulldog edition of the *Sunday Daily News* would hit the streets. I considered hanging around the newspaper loading dock to filch a copy of the want ads as they rolled off the press. But that would have created witnesses in the press room. And I had bigger concerns. I had a midnight meeting with the man I was pretty sure had just snuffed out Serious Bobby.

I headed for the police station and mounted two flights of crowded buzzing stairways to the Bertillion room. Outside the temporary kidnap headquarters, a gaggle of reporters were interviewing some G-man I had never seen. There were more than a hundred G-men in town now, if you believed the *Daily News*.

My mind was racing with the notion that I was the cutout, the disposable man. I had been just that my whole career in the underworld, playing a game of shadows and survival. The cold-eyed killers were the Bishops of this church, the rest of us just altar boys. Serious Bobby, the head altar boy, had served his purpose. Maybe he was getting too close to William Hamm. Maybe his loyalty was suspect for that or another reason. Maybe he knew one too many secrets. Maybe Big Ryan figured Bobby was holding out on him. Maybe Big Ryan plugged him to send a message about the importance of loyalty at this crucial time.

All I knew for sure was that, in the hands of G-men, I was the only stool pigeon who could link Big Ryan to both the Hamm and Alt kidnappings. And tonight I had to get into a car with this murderous cop.

I pushed into the Bertillion room.

McAmbly was asleep on a cot. He wore his uniform jacket sloppy, open on his big belly, his stained white shirt.

I sat on a library stool and shook his shoulder.

"Billy."

His eyes fluttered. He looked at me blank, pushed himself into a sitting position, began hacking with a mean winter cough.

"Serious Bobby," I said.

"What about him? Christ, a guy needs his sleep."

"What happened?"

"He's dead."

"I know he's dead. Who? Why? Come on. The Alt family names him as a potential go-between, and a day later he's dead?"

Lieutenant Tierney burst in. He was a wiry little guy, impeccably dressed, with a sharp thin face, a halo of dark hair underneath a perfectly-creased fedora. He drummed his hands impatient on the counter.

"Gimme the next batch, will ya Billy."

He nodded at me as if I belonged there. Tierney was Big Ryan's partner, and co-leader of the kidnap investigations. He was also tight with Big Ryan's enemy, Tom Dahill, chief of police. What game was being played there? Was Tierney secretly in Big Ryan's pocket? Was he spying on Big Ryan and telling all to Chief Dahill? No wonder Billy stayed out of it.

"Go home and get some real sleep," Tierney advised McAmbly. "We're going to quit after this. Nothing's coming in. It's as quiet as a church basement after Bingo. Who's this?"

"Friend," said Billy.

"Give this man a ride home," Tierney advised me. "He's been up too long."

Tierney pushed out the door into the hubbub. Shadows of policemen and reporters passed on the other side of the smoked glass.

"They got somebody in mind?" I asked Billy.

"For Serious Bobby? Nah. I wouldn't look for it, Mick. These gangland things, they know how to get away. I wonder who he crossed."

"I was wondering the same thing," I said, and pointed toward Big Ryan's office.

"What are you pointing at?" asked Billy. "The North Pole?"

"I think Serious Bobby displeased somebody. I think maybe this somebody didn't want there to be any link between the Hamm kidnapping and the Alt snatch."

"Died of a broken heart, I heard."

"A broken heart?"

"Yeah, poor Bobby, he wanted to make a career out of delivering ransom money."

"Okay, Billy, look, I need a mug," I said.

"I'm exhausted."

"I'll find it."

"Knock yourself out."

The Bertillion system was sorted by measurements taken from arrested men and women. These were characteristics that could not be changed, for instance, the measurement from fingertips to elbows, and the size of the earlobe. It did not rely on names, since every gangster had a dozen of them. Someday, perhaps, Bertillion would take second place to a fingerprint system, but for now cops were stuck with this. Having no idea of any of the measurements of Myrtle's thug, I was reduced to pulling file drawers and flipping cards. What the hell, I had all afternoon, although it occurred to me that I should probably get out of here early and enjoy what might be my last sunset.

I flipped cards as Billy snored, as feet pounded down the hallway, as reporters shouted questions down the stairwells.

After a half hour, I found him.

William Weaver. Aka Lapland Willie.

On probation, Ramsey County. Weapons bust, 1932.

Acquitted of murder, Tulsa, Oklahoma, 1928.

Sentenced to three years in McAlester Prison, Oklahoma for grand larceny, served one year, released 1927. That would have put him in McAlester at the same time as Doc Barker.

His front-facing photo showed clearly the scar on his chin.

Only now did I remember: Back in 1932, when I was chasing down leads in the murder of Sadie and Rose, I talked to a couple of fellows over in Hudson, Wisconsin. Their town had been raided one winter night, and among the raiders was Fred Barker, Alvin Karpis, a man with blond curly hair, and a tall dark man with a knife scar on his chin.

Now I had a name for that guy. Lapland Willie Weaver.

I took the card out into the light and nudged Billy's cot.

"Ah Christ," he said. "I wasn't asleep anyway."

"You were snoring."

"I snore wide awake now," he said.

He reached to the floor for his pack of cigarettes.

"Look at this mug," I said.

"So?"

"Does he do anything for you?"

"Green Lantern," he said.

"What does that mean?"

"He went down at the Green Lantern, summer of 1932, like it says there. Didn't the nuns teach you to read? See, Dahill had just come into office, and Big Ryan was pushed aside. Dahill figured he'd serve notice on gangland. So some of Dahill's boys visit the Lantern, and come back with two heavily armed thugs. Machine guns! What do you boys want those toys for? Charges filed. Thugs in jail. Everything's fine until …

"Until?"

"Papa Alt bails them out."

"Papa Alt?"

"Yep. Five hundred smackers apiece."

"Papa Alt in person?"

"Are you nuts? He sends the butler."

Billy lit the cigarette. "Christ, it leaves a lousy taste in your mouth."

"The cigarette or Papa Alt's bail out?"

"Both. So the machine-gunners hop a train going back to the Ozarks, we issue warrants, you know how that goes."

"Where the hell is Lapland?" I asked.

"Some part of Missouri, I heard," said Billy. "Where it laps over into Arkansas."

"Well, he's in town again," I said.

"Do tell."

"He broke probation, could be nabbed."

"See the sheriff. We're lousy with G-men right now."

I needed a smoke bad, but with Billy already coughing, I decided to smoke downstairs. The whole thing was getting too crazy for me.

I could easily figure one part of it. Lapland Willie went way back with the Barker brothers. Then two years ago he was in that group of land pirates that raided the town of Hudson. Two months after that, he was bailed out on machine gun charges. Now suddenly he shows up in Saint Paul, moves in with Myrtle, just in time for the Ricky Alt kidnapping.

I stood watching the big clock above the admitting desk, lit my pipe and put the last piece of the puzzle together. Lap Weaver was the payoff man. He was the sucker the Barkers had recruited to stand out along the bus route, light a trash fire, pick up the ransom, and drive it to some rendezvous with Barker and Karpis. That's what he was doing in Saint Paul.

The harder piece of the puzzle was why Papa Alt bailed him out in 1932. And if this bail-out was a favor to Harry Sawyer and the Barker Gang, why had they betrayed Papa Alt by kidnapping his son?

I pushed out the heavy door into the cold, brilliant sunshine. For a while there, I couldn't see a thing.

CHAPTER TEN

SATURDAY NIGHT

Saturday night is big in the newsstand business even when there isn't much news. People eager for the color comics, the sports scores, the want ads, throng the newsstand just after the bulldog is delivered. On this night, cars formed a line down Fort Road as Blind Benny bumped along the curb, collecting nickels and handing newspapers into windows. The Alt kidnapping had caused such a run on the newsstand that, even at this dark hour, passersby were crowded off the sidewalk and into the street. I snatched a *Daily News*, pitched a nickel toward the ashtray, and ducked into the Mrs. Sippy Tavern.

In the red glow of a neon beer sign, I set the newspaper on a pinball machine, paged in trembling hands to the Personals. There it was.

Come Home. All is Forgiven. Richard.

I folded up the want-ads and beat it fast down Third Street, a vicious freezing wind whipping up from the river. I dodged across the street nearly getting smashed by a city bus. Across Rice Park I ran, and made myself slow to a walk as I approached the Hotel

Saint Paul. I didn't want some bellboy to remember me as an out-of-breath madman.

Up at room 914 I gave the coded knock three times to no response. I leaped the stairs until I reached the ground floor, finessed the coat check girl, and circulated around the edges of the Grill Room. No George.

Finally, reluctantly, I approached the front desk.

A slender young man was bent over its marble top, scribbling in an account book.

"Right with you sir."

I couldn't help it, I beat my palms on that desk top.

"Right away," muttered the desk clerk.

His red thinning hair was combed over the bald spot, which, with his head down, seemed aimed right at me.

He crossed a T, and stepped back, as if he was Picasso finishing a masterpiece.

"Now," he said. "How may I assist you?"

"Messages for Mister Taylor."

He turned, revealing the stretched back of an ill-fitting blue blazer, a size too small for him.

"Mister Taylor, Mister Taylor," he muttered.

"Check 914," I said.

"So familiar," he said. "Taylor, Taylor, Taylor. Haven't I seen you around, Mister Taylor?"

"No," I suggested.

"Taylor, Taylor ..." he snatched a note from the pigeon hole. "Yes. Mister Junker, is that it? Junker in 914. Mister Junker is at the opera and is expected to return at 11."

He gave me a triumphant smile.

"May we be of further assistance?"

I had a vision of my hands around George's patrician throat, strangling him, those Aryan blue eyes bulging, finally, with understanding. He was not supposed to leave the hotel. He was not supposed to create any memorable scenes. The whole Taylor-Junker messaging bit was supposed to be for emergencies only. Opera!

Again in the dark I hustled through Rice Park. The city's opera house was called, with complete lack of imagination, the Opera House. Its lit marquee was like a dull rectangular moon just across from the federal building. I stood outside its brass doors alongside an emaciated old gentleman in top hat, tux and tails. He had a cheap, dirty cloth coat thrown over the tux, to keep him warm whenever the opera swells were not in sight. He ignored me, paced the curb, sipped from a silver flask held in a white-gloved hand.

"When does it let out, do you know, chief?" I asked.

He ignored me and walked the curb line. A white-and gold horse-drawn cab slipped around the corner, the driver calling for his silver steed to halt, the horse's breath creating clouds around its magnificent head.

A taxi crept over from the Hotel Saint Paul. I turned to see a poster for the opera, a big Italian woman, her forearm covering her head like she was in despair. The woman held a bloody knife. The word TOSCA was written over her head along with GIACOMO PUCCINI. The were smaller words in Italian I had no hope of deciphering. The playbill gave no time for the performance.

Another taxi pulled up and idled. The doorman removed his top hat, let himself in and sat in the relative warmth of a Yellow Cab. He passed that silvery flask to the driver. I stomped my cold feet, paced in front of the gilded doors. Hoping for the warmth of the lobby, I tried the doors, they were locked.

Despite everything, I was lit up with hopeful feelings. This whole thing could be over by Monday, the gang on the road,

Richard Alt freed, the dogs safe, my home restored, and as a bonus, Lap Weaver would abandon Myrtle.

A whole fleet of Yellow Cabs pulled up, as if ordered by the Gods of Opera. The horse stomped his hooves and the white carriage lurched as the driver called whoa. A fur-wrapped socialite and her mink-coated husband appeared in the lobby, the first of a burst of swells as the doorman leaped out of the taxi and unlocked the doors.

I stood aside as a buzzing wave of beautifully-dressed humanity flowed out those doors. George brushed passed me unseeing. He escorted a fur-wrapped blonde beauty whose red dress fell to her black leather boots. George approached the hansom cab driver and began negotiations while his date waited, demure. A young opera buff shivering in front of the Tosca poster lit a cigarette, and I bummed one from him.

George gave his date a hand up into the cab, then stepped in too. I hustled over, put my foot on the carriage's steel step, and said to George:

"Hey buddy, you got a light?"

George glared at me with killer eyes.

"The impertinent riff-raff in this town," he said to his date.

He, wearing kid gloves, patted the arm of her fur coat.

"Let me deal with this man directly," he told her, and stepped out of the cab. We walked off a pace.

"What?" he demanded. With an ivory-and-gold lighter, he lit the cigarette in my lips.

"We're ready," I whispered. "We're go."

"You know what to do, then." He removed a glove, opened his overcoat, dug into a suit pocket, handed me a hotel key.

I retreated into the opera crowd. He climbed into the cab and the horse drew it off into stalled traffic. When I reached the hotel, I

took the crowded elevator. I got off on the wrong floor, slipped up
to 914 and let myself in.

I flicked on the light. I was in the sitting room, bedroom off to
the left. Two green plush chairs beckoned, and I threw my
overcoat over one and slumped in the other, grateful for an
overheated room. Across from me was that roll-top desk and
typewriter. Above it was a huge framed photo of the Saint Paul
river docks and railroad yards, featuring busy steamships and
locomotives.

A sleek modern telephone on the desk rang.

I hesitated to pick it up, hovered over it, fear not blood coursing
in my veins.

It kept ringing.

I snatched the business end and merely listened.

"Hello old sport."

I sighed.

"I'm rather busy at the moment" George said, "so are you ready
for dictation?"

"Over the phone?"

"We are talking on the phone aren't we?"

"Wait."

I put down the phone, removed my suit coat, loosened my tie,
rolled up my sleeves, cracked my knuckles, approached the
typewriter, picked up the phone again.

"Okay," I said. "If this is how you want to do it."

"You see I've caught a fish and I'm rather afraid she might
wriggle off the hook."

"I'm ready," I said. I put my gloves on, rolled a fresh sheet of
Blackstone letterhead into the platen. I removed my gloves.

George cleared his throat. "You are to bundle the money into
two suitcases," he dictated.

Phone pinched between ear and shoulder, I typed.

"Make that two strong suitcases. The money will weigh 60 pounds altogether."

I typed *strong* above the word *suitcases*.

I heard laughter and piano music faint. Was this madman phoning me from a nightclub? I listened, typed and after about five minutes of that, read him back the ransom note.

> There is an 8 a.m. bus departing Union Station for Rochester on Monday. The priest and the money should be on that bus. He is to sit on the right side of the bus and watch out the windows at all times. At some point he will see a man standing next to a burning trash can. At that point he is to insist that the driver let him off at the next intersection. There he is to abandon the suitcases and walk south, never looking back.
>
> You are warned to make sure there are no coppers on the bus. We will have men on the bus to make sure of this. You are doubly warned that the money should not be marked.
>
> If the money is not marked, we will release the boy unharmed. There will be no further communication until we get the money.

On read back, George seemed satisfied.

"Leave the key at the desk for me and Powers, don't fail to deliver."

"I'll get it to them as fast as I can," I said.

"No, no," said George. "Anything but fast. Around midnight tomorrow would be ideal. Don't give them time to think up tricks."

"Anything else?" I said, but he had already hung up.

I could have worried about how to deliver the ransom note, but my bigger concern was my midnight appointment with Big Ryan. If the man could shoot dead his friend and partner in the shakedown business, what chance did I have? There were just over 90 minutes left until the rendezvous.

What the hell, I called room service.

It was a sumptuous last meal: roast beef, mashed potatoes, string beans, apple pie, and a double-strong old fashioned. It tasted even better because it was charged to George's bill. After I downed the old fashioned, I began to gulp George's expensive brandy, right from the bottle. By quarter to midnight I was half smashed and well fed, and ran out the door in panic when I realized I had just enough time to drive to the Eagle.

There, in the winter midnight, in the street-lamp shadows, I idled my Terraplane sedan to keep the heater going. The brandy was catching up with me and I began to relax, feeling silly, almost giggly. I had the ransom note in an envelope in my inside suit-coat pocket. It would make a fine play in the newspapers: BODY OF EX-BOOTLEGGER, 42, FOUND WITH ALT RANSOM NOTE.

And that's when I realized Big Ryan wasn't going to kill me.

Not until I had delivered my last note.

I filled my pipe and lit it with Sadie's lighter. I won't be joining you, unlucky girl, not tonight, I said, out loud and to no one. I puffed up a cloud of smoke just as Big Ryan's Plymouth turned the corner. That dark armored squad car crept down Summit Avenue, circled around, parked in front of me, and opened the passenger door.

I popped out of my car and into his. For a long moment Big Ryan just looked over me. I could sense anger, I could almost feel Serious Bobby's ghost in there.

Big Ryan had been drinking, and even half drunk myself, I could smell it.

"Tomorrow you're going to drive and see the boys," he said, never looking at me, but staring through the windshield at the streetlights.

"If everything goes right," I said.

"Everything *will* go right," he said.

He lifted his schoolteacher's eyeglasses and rubbed his face with a big meaty hand.

"Tell the boys I'm shut out," he said. "No more meetings with G-men, or Dahill, they've shut me out."

I cleared my throat.

The Plymouth engine rattled and died.

"Not that it matters," he said. "We're almost home."

He pushed the starter button.

"I still get my cut," he said. "Remind those boys, I get my cut if they know what's good for them. Now get out of my car."

I shouldered out, slammed the door, and backed away. Ryan's Plymouth, lights out, made a U turn and rolled down the steep Ramsey Hill.

I hustled back to my Terraplane, relit my pipe, sat back for a think. Ryan had been shut out. He'd been Dahill's top man in the kidnap unit, he'd been in conference with the G-men, and now? Somehow they had come to suspect him. Somebody had leaked. Had Papa Alt finally seen through his so-called protector?

CHAPTER ELEVEN

SUNDAY MORNING

On Sunday morning, throbbing with gout and a headache, I
tried to read *Tender is the Night*. Fitzgerald was, after all, the most
famous person to ever come out of Saint Paul. I couldn't quite
figure out what he was writing about, since it seemed to take place
in the south of France, and nobody had been murdered in the first
few pages. *Scribner's Magazine*, however, made a perfect wrapper for
the ransom note. I encased magazine and envelope in my suitcase,
and shut the closet door on it. I had fifteen minutes to eat a
breakfast of aspirin and coffee, and to hobble down to the
Cathedral.

The Alt family "owned" the ten o'clock Mass. It was invariably
celebrated by their special friend at the Cathedral, Father McCarthy
O'Sullivan. I entered at the Summit Avenue doors, which meant
the entire congregation had its back turned to me. Fedora in hand,
I walked up the side aisle, and at the twelfth Station of the Cross,
genuflected and sat in an otherwise empty pew.

Mass, apparently, was going be late. The congregation was
restless, coughing, murmuring, banging the kneelers in and out of
position, shuffling up and down the flagstone aisle. The Cathedral
is truly a mammoth thing, and on an ordinary Sunday Mass, wasn't
much more than half full. But today it was jammed, and I was lucky

to find an empty pew, way off to the side. A good number of Saint Paul's citizenry had turned out for the show, crammed forward for a better gawk.

They soon got it. The side altar doors opened and in walked two men. They stopped and surveyed the crowd. Their overcoats were floor length to hide their tommyguns. I didn't know either of these G-men, which meant they were probably from Washington or Chicago. As they stood grim and serious, the door behind them creaked open and Papa Alt shuffled in, eyes cast down. He genuflected and slid into the front pew.

He was followed by two policemen in Saint Paul's green uniform. The shorter, darker one was Lieutenant Charles Tierney. The cop who looked like a banking executive, his graying hair greased back, was Chief Thomas Dahill. The uniformed cops, good Catholics, knew to remove their caps, and stood holding them, surveying the congregation.

The rest of the Alt family entered behind them. The young bride Emily, accompanied by gawky husband in red earmuffs. Between them Richard Alt's five year old daughter and his wife Marie. The older Alt daughter Belinda with her tax attorney husband and three children. Doctor Mark Koenig, tall and dignified and in his late 60s. And finally family retainer, and Myrtle's former boyfriend, Andrew Stockwell. All blessed themselves with holy water upon entrance, and genuflected before entering the pew.

When all were seated, Big Joe Ryan, in brown pinstriped suit, stood as doorman, hat on his head, smirk on his face. He looked to me like a wolf, studying the sheep, trying to figure which one would be the tastiest. Chief Dahill and the G-men had thrown him off the case, still he had the brass balls to show up as self-appointed doorman.

It was a well-managed show, because only when the Alts settled in their front pew did the bell ring and Father Mack exit the sacristy in company of two altar boys.

Every day of the year is a Catholic feast day, and today's Mass commemorated Saint Germanicus of Smyrna, or so it said in the bulletin. He was a martyr who had been thrown to the lions. I read the Introit in Latin, trying to jog some meaning from the altar boy remnant of my brain.

But like all the rest of the thousand-plus souls in that Cathedral, I was waiting for the homily.

As Father Mack mounted the lectern to speak under a painting of the Holy Ghost, the Alt family pew was bookended by one uniform cop and one federal agent at each end. Big Ryan had not moved from that side door, except to slouch against it.

The Cathedral of Saint Paul was modeled after Saint Peter's at the Vatican. The design that worked well in Rome, all that Mediterranean air rising to the dome, made it impossible to heat in the depths of a Minnesota winter. Few in the congregation shed their coats, and some even kept their gloves on. The sun did little more than send gray cold light through the stained-glass windows. Up in the loft, the organist wore a yellow scarf and wrapped in a thick coat.

Father Mack, in red and gold vestments, stood on the lectern and glared the chilled congregation into a silence broken only by muffled coughing and the cries of babies.

"Fellow Catholics," he said into the microphone, and even those two words betrayed his origins. On his tongue those words sounded more like: *Fella Cat Licks.*

"It can always be said that we live in treacherous times."

He paused and I could swear he managed to make eye contact with everyone in the pews.

"But these times are more treacherous than most."

Big Ryan shifted on his feet.

"The judgment of God can be delayed," he said, his voice rising, echoing from the stone walls, " but it cannot," he pounded the lectern with a thud that echoed off the stone walls, "be denied."

He pointed his finger at all of us.

"Somewhere in this city lurks a heart of evil."

He paused and there was rustling in the pews.

"A festering heart that pumps bile, not blood, through its veins."

"A heart capable of the most cold and callous acts."

Somebody threw a kneeler. Some latecomer opened the rear doors, thought better of it, retreated.

Father Mack gripped the lectern as if he needed to keep from falling over.

"We will find that dark heart," he whispered into the microphone. "And we will expose it to the terrible light of the Lord."

I have attended hundreds of Masses, but had never witnessed a homily cheered. It is against all tradition. But when Father Mack stepped down, a spontaneous applause broke from the congregation, and all but the Alt family, it seemed, stood and roared as if the priest had scored a game-winning touchdown. Father Mack ignored this, turned his back on the congregation, and signaled the altar boys to rise.

Big Joe Ryan, arms crossed over his massive belly, glared impassive at the crowd.

It was like after a thunderstorm, the atmosphere had changed. People talked to the people next to them, even as Father Mack muttered the Latin of the Consecration. A murmur of joy ran through the congregation.

Even with an auxiliary priest to help give Communion, it was going to take a while to administer the sacrament to the hundreds lined up for it. Since I was in the state of Unconfessed Mortal Sin and unworthy of receiving the Host, I ducked out back for a smoke.

I lit my pipe with Sadie's lipstick tube lighter. Yes, now that a rich family had been targeted, all the resources of God and Man had been brought to bear. Franklin Roosevelt! J. Edgar Hoover! The Archdiocese of Saint Paul! The two most powerful institutions in human history, the Catholic Church and the United States Government, were determined to avenge a crime against the Alts.

But how about the skinny, homely, Jewish prostitute who had lost this lighter on her last night on earth? The Alt family had poisoned their own well, getting rich on gangster money and illegal beer. Sadie Carmacher, all she had done was get on a train with her new friend Rose. I could only imagine that poor girl's horror when Jack Peifer delivered them to the docks after midnight. And then the two thugs Swede and Rico started beating them, Rico carrying a beaker of acid, Swede with gasoline and matches, the helpless terror of that last moment, when Sadie knew her terrible fate.

True, Swede and Rico were dead, both by my doings. But they were only the mechanics, and whoever had arranged the murders of Sadie and Rose was simply too powerful for a corrupt system to prosecute. In the end Sadie and Rose were dispensable: prostitutes, one of the wrong faith, the other of the wrong color.

Chilled by a nasty wind, I entered the Cathedral just in time to see Shotgun George Ziegler. Having just taken Communion from Father Mack, he arose from the red velvet altar kneelers, eyes closed, and blessed himself. Head down, hands folded at his belt, he did the post-communion shuffle down the flagstone floor and, looking humble as a schoolboy, veered into a dark corner and sank into a pew, head down, in deep prayer.

I backed out of the Cathedral, and walked around to the Sibley Street door. I hid myself in a snow-plowed parking lot amid dark sedans. A couple of uniformed rookie cops eyed me, suspicious, and then dismissed my presence. In a few minutes the G-men poked their heads out the side door, and then they and Dahill and Tierney led the Alt family to two Lincolns, packed them, and gave them a police escort down toward their riverside mansion.

As the cars began to peel out, I stationed myself at a low wall between Cathedral and Chancery.

"Father Mack!"

"I've no time, Mick, I've to be off."

"A word," I said.

"Then come into the kitchen and have Mrs. Bold make you a cup of tea."

I followed him into the back door of the Chancery. The kitchen was vast, and sparkling clean, and could have serviced even the biggest restaurant in town. The round, white-haired Mrs. Bold was almost lost in it. Father Mack hurried down the hall toward the Library.

Mrs. Bold served tea immediately.

A dozen eggs were piled in a white bowl on the counter, a slab of bacon sat raw on a steel broiling pan. The table held a variety of cakes, and a bowl of pineapple and canned cherries.

"He's in a hurry," Mrs. Bold said.

Father Mack overheard me and called in: "Much to do."

"His excellency wants to leave and there's so much preparation," said Mrs. Bold. Seeing the blank look on my face, she added: "The wheelchair."

"What wheelchair?"

"His Excellency is now confined to a wheelchair," said Mrs. Bold. Then she whispered. "We're afraid he'll never come out of it."

She broke eggs into a Pyrex measuring cup, set the shells back into the bowl.

"I see. So where is the Archbishop going, then.?"

"Saint Cloud," she said. "Dinner with the Bishop Busch." She whispered. "God knows what they talk about. Between you and me, I think they just play cards and complain about the laxity of their priests. Even with Father McCarthy and two nurses, it takes an hour just to get the poor man into a car."

"Father Mack's taking him up to Saint Cloud?"

"Oh yes."

"And spending the night?"

"Oh, His Excellency won't ride in a car after dark, not with the nefarious doings in this town." Again she lowered her voice. "He feels so vulnerable, he's so afraid of kidnappers. Thank God for Father McCarthy."

The teacup rattled in my hand. No! No! No! Father Mack cannot leave town! Mrs. Bold read the panic in my face.

"Are you feeling all right, Mister Powers?"

I stumbled out into the cold sunshine, across Summit, turned and stared at the Chancery. The entire plan was about to blow up in the worst possible way. Perhaps we could make a last-minute switch of emissaries, but one of them was dead and Shotgun George had been adamant that he wanted the priest and only the priest.

If I could get the ransom note to the Alts now, maybe they could detour Father Mack. But an early delivery of the note would anger Shotgun George, and I never forgot that he'd been a Capone executioner. George had insisted that the Alts have the minimum time to react. I didn't want George to suspect me of collusion or trickery. I was not one of "them" and had stayed alive for years on the fringes of gangland by never fatally pissing off a murderous stone eyed killer.

I ran down the long stairway to the bottom where the streetcar came out of the tunnel and caught the next one for downtown. I headed for the Lowry Hotel intending to find Janie and there she was, at a window seat in the Terrace Café, having breakfast with reporters, all of them men. I pantomimed, hoping to God the other reporters wouldn't see me. She left the table and met me on the lobby balcony.

"What, Powers? I'm in the middle of breakfast."

"Upstairs in your room," I said. "Now. This is big. Scoop of a lifetime."

She sighed. She had a linen napkin in her hand and stuffed it into the pocket of her blue shoulder-strap dress. We waited for the elevator. With a white turtleneck blouse and thick white cotton stockings, she exposed little flesh to winter's bite.

"Well?" she asked.

"Wait," I said.

Her room was on the fourth floor and when she let me in she said: "Kind of a mess."

"Look, I need you to call the Chancery."

"Okay."

"Like within the next five minutes."

"Powers, you're sweating. Why are you limping? Are you sober?"

"Call Father McCarthy O'Sullivan. Tell him he has been designated as go-between by the kidnappers. The ransom drop is imminent. He will be handling the ransom."

"He doesn't know that yet?"

"He might suspect it but he doesn't know the timing. The transaction has to take place tomorrow morning. He must be in town. Must. Must Must."

"How do you know this?"

"You tell him who you are and that you have a very reliable source who told you off the record, and on deep, deepest background."

"How do I know ..."

"If Father Mack is not in town, it could be the end for Ricky Alt. These kidnappers are not fooling around, and they are getting very nervous and they are drinking hard. Go ahead, Janie, lives are at stake, don't you dare stall."

"Powers, I'm afraid that you ... oh heck, I think you're nuts. You know, this kidnapping has brought every nut out of the woodwork. The phones never stop ringing with hoaxers and nut cases, even the G-men are swamped with bad tips."

I walked to the window and looked down at the Sunday traffic.

"We're all dead then. If Father Mack leaves town, it's the end of the world, Janie."

I turned around to stare at her. "I tried stop him, I wanted to ask him to have a beer this evening. But now he's going to Saint Cloud with the Archbishop and won't be back until it's too late. He's got to carry the ransom. The kidnappers will only deal if he carries the bags."

She stared at me, lips moving, impatient, eyes searching me.

"Call and stop him," I pleaded.

"How do you know all this?"

"You know I can't tell you, kid."

"I'm not a kid, Powers, I'm a reporter for United Press. The words I write go out to all the world and they must be true."

I dropped to my knees. I grabbed her warm hands in my cold ones. I looked up at her.

"They're blackmailing me. I'm the messenger boy. If you leak that, I'm dead and maybe you're dead too."

She gave me a hard, searching look. "You're serious, I guess I do believe that Powers."

"These people have left many bodies behind. They'll kill us without flinching. Janie, make the call. For the rest of your life, you'll be glad you made this call..." I held up my hand, "I swear before God."

"All right," she said. "You're making me nervous."

She went to the phone and flashed it.

"Operator," she said. "Chancery of Saint Paul, Father McCarthy O'Sullivan, person to person."

She turned around to eye me, as if still not quite convinced. I, feeling utterly used up, limp, sweaty and hung over, sat on the edge of her crisply made bed.

"Father O'Sullivan?"

Janie turned her back on me.

"Janie Vetter, I'm a correspondent for the United Press. Father, we met one time at the Chancery, you might remember, it was Kentucky Derby day, we listened on the radio."

She paused.

"Fine, Father, and how are you? Father, I don't want to shock you but a gangland source whom I know to be reliable has just informed me ..." she took a deep breath ... "that you are the designated courier between the Alt family and the kidnappers."

She paused, I could hear her breathing hard.

"Yes, Father, I can give you a number in Chicago where an editor can confirm who I am. I have been told that the ransom drop will take place sometime between tonight and tomorrow, and that it is most urgent that you remain in town."

She listened again.

"No, Father, the authorities know nothing of it."

She glanced at me, I nodded encouragement.

"Yes," she said into the phone, "they want you and only you to deliver the ransom. They refuse to deal with anyone else, I've been told."

She listened for a moment.

"Yes, I'll be here, at the Lowry, that's V-E-T-T-E-R, ring 431."

And then she hung up.

"Powers," she said in a shaky voice, "what have you gotten me into?"

"You wanted a story, I gave you a story."

"What did you mean, blackmailed?"

"I mean blackmailed, threatened with death. Well, not in so many words but these guys don't use words. They give you the wolf glare, and you know."

"You do realize, don't you, that the U.S. Justice Department has made solving this crime its number one priority."

"I can't think about that right now, Janie. I need to grease the wheels and make this thing work."

"Where are they holding Ricky Alt?"

"Can't tell you."

"Who are they?"

"No dice, Janie. Maybe someday I'll call you from Cuba, maybe Mexico, I don't know, I'll give you the story exclusive and you'll be a big star in the detective mags. But right now anything I told you would only endanger your life. And Alt's life too. You cannot even write what I just told you. You cannot be so foolish as to write that Father Mack is the man, because that would jeopardize the whole operation."

She sat in the desk chair, huffing, frustrated.

"Right now, we're in the phase of freeing Ricky Alt. When he's back home, then we get to the phase of finding the kidnappers. Okay? That's the way it's got to work."

"I don't know how you get mixed up in all this, Powers."

"You know there was a time, before the Crash, I had a chance with the Great Northern. It was only a brakeman's job. Should have taken it, I guess. You're young, you don't have any regrets, do you?"

Her face flushed, she stared at the floor.

"Oh," I said, embarrassed as a fool.

CHAPTER TWELVE

SUNDAY NIGHT

On Sunday evening around suppertime, I parked at Union
Station and rented a coin-operated locker. I put the ransom
instructions in there, wiped clean with Windex. The station seemed
hollow and almost empty: the occasional straggler sitting on a
bench with a stack of luggage, the two bums trying to keep from
freezing to death, the lone porter pushing a broom over the
gleaming marble floors. The ticket windows were shuttered. On the
balcony café above them, a lone busboy rolled up white tablecloths.

If anybody remembered me at all, they might only describe a
limping man, coming in from the cold, only his eyes exposed
behind ski mask. They might mistake me for a war-wounded vet,
but it was only a gout limp. Even if a professional photographer
took my picture, no jury could have identified that bundled up
man.

I drove uphill to the Cathedral and sneaked in the side door. In
the Alt's pew, I reached into the rack, opened a hymnal, and taped
the locker key to the back cover. A young priest in thick overcoat
arrived to lock the doors, and I escaped just as he entered, at a
quarter to midnight.

I drove to the Barking Dog, on the way passing the lights-on, shades-drawn windows of Myrtle's apartment. Lap Weaver, I said to myself, I hope you're enjoying your last night in Saint Paul.

Now at midnight, it seemed the whole city, exhausted by the kidnap drama, the big headlines, the radio broadcasts, the police cars rushing through the night, had fallen into the deepest slumber.

In the Barking Dog, the piano player had given up on music, and was drinking at the bar with the female owner and the hardcore drunks, all men. I used the third phone booth, the one in the darkest part of the hallway nearest the door.

My call was answered on the first ring.

"Hello."

I couldn't tell whether I was talking to Andrew Stockwell or Doctor Koenig, and I didn't care, I only wanted to get off the phone quickly.

"This is Blackstone," I said. "Listen carefully. Go to the Cathedral. In the first pew, nearest the Sibley Street door, you will find a hymnal. Taped to its back cover will be a numbered key. Take that key to Union Depot and open the matching locker. Follow the instructions you find in there and things will work out."

I hung up. I sneaked out. Snow flurries were whirling in the streetlamp halos, a capricious wind blowing out of the North Pole.

MONDAY MORNING

The next morning, I rewarded myself for a job well done with a platter of scrambled eggs and potatoes, and a mug of Commodore coffee. This was served in a small cafe, a barroom converted for morning duty. Two stray businessmen looking over order books were the only other diners.

The morning's *Pioneer Press* led with the headlines:

HUNT SANKEY IN ALT KIDNAPPING

FAMILY AWAIT GANG'S PROMISED SIGNAL

The story said that J. Edgar Hoover had issued an urgent call for the arrest of Vern Sankey, who was wanted in previous kidnappings and was now the prime suspect in the Alt snatch. The Feds had gone off the trail once again.

The news story said police had ordered a chemical examination of the blood stains in the snatch cab, and found that they'd come from a human. This knocked down the theory that it had been animal blood used as a "stage effect" to frighten the Alt family.

As of press time, the story added, the family was anxiously awaiting ransom delivery instructions from the kidnappers. It was a strange feeling, to be able to predict tomorrows' headlines.

I followed that story off the front page and came to another on the jump page:

U.S. INCOME FALLS SHARPLY, 40% SINCE 1929

Rather than rely on the distracted and bored waitress, I got up to refill my coffee at the vat at the end of the bar. The barroom's Christmas decorations had been up almost a month now, and it seemed suddenly depressing, like we were all stuck in time and couldn't get moving. All of us, not just the gangsters and the cops, but the whole country.

The coffee was stale, too.

I stood there looking out the red-curtained windows into a courtyard, where a fountain had been rendered pointless by winter. I mulled over how things would go from here. In less than two hours, Lapland Willie Weaver would light a trash fire that would cause a Rochester-bound bus to stop. A linebacker-sized priest would get off with two suitcases, which he would deposit in a frozen cornfield before walking off. Weaver would put a fortune packed in two suitcases in the back seat of his jalopy. He would check into a hotel room and examine the money. Once he saw it was not marked, he would call George, who would send me the go signal. I would set out for Eagle River. At 5 p.m., Weaver would phone the Lone Buck tavern in Eagle River. He would ask for Mister Green. The bartender would hang up after getting no takers. A small red-headed stranger would finish his beer, walk out the door, and never return.

A half hour after that phone call, Ricky Alt would be on the way home. Some time tonight, it would all be over.

But that might be when my real troubles began. The Barker Gang, I suspected, wanted me back in Eagle River so they could dump their hostage on me. They would take off for their rendezvous with a fortune, leaving Ricky Alt's deliverance to me.

And Ricky Alt could identify us all. Obviously, the Barker brothers and Karpis did not care. They were relying on terror tactics to keep the Alts from identifying them. They could count, too, on the bumbling of police and prosecutors. The Barker-Karpis intimidation method had worked in the Hamm kidnapping, which looked like it would never be solved. William Hamm was still a nervous wreck, and on learning of the Alt kidnapping, had taken his family for an extended stay on Waikiki Beach.

I poured my coffee dregs into the sink, walked into the lobby and sat near the crackling fireplace. There I read through the newspaper while awaiting George's signal.

A flashy red Studebaker coupe pulled up into the driveway, followed by a beat-up black Ford sedan. Both cars had frosty windows. Out of that red Studebaker leaped a young man who was dressed for a day on the tennis courts. He bounded through the brass revolving doors and into the lobby, and paced in front of the elevator. He was in his late twenties, with a trim athletic build and startling mop of platinum curly hair.

He approached the desk clerk, whispered something, and the clerk picked up the phone and spoke into it. This conversation seemed to satisfy the curly-headed man. He glanced at the driveway where his two-car caravan was idling, sending smoke into the winter haze. He sat in a lobby chair, leaning forward as if desperate to leap out of it.

Ding went the elevator bell and out of it struggled a uniformed bellboy yanking a shiny brass cart piled with luggage. Following the bellboy was Ma Barker and a teenage girl. Ma saw me right away, grinned and waved. She had lost a tooth. Her hair had gone from fake blond to scraggly gray. She was wrapped in a mink stole over spangled white dress.

She was almost assaulted by the man with curly hair. He made excited gestures toward the cars.

The bellboy pushed the cart toward the door, looked back over his shoulder.

"Just wait," called the curly-haired man, who then held an angry whisper session with Ma Barker. The teenage girl, a dark-haired skinny thing in a sailor dress, kneeled to re-tie the laces of her ankle-high black boots.

I set down the newspaper, wandered over to stick my nose in.

"I'm not going to leave my clothing behind," Ma told the curly-haired fellow. "And neither is Dolores. You just go out there and make room."

He flinched and for a moment I thought he was going to punch her. Cursing at the perplexed bellboy, then pushed through the revolving doors.

"Mister Powell," Ma said. "You must live here, for I swear we meet every time I check in."

"Well, it looks like you're checking out," I said.

"Oh, my boys sent Curly to fetch me," Mother said. "Curly and my boys go way back, Oh Lord, just too far back to remember. We're going to Chicago. Dolores is all excited, it's her first time. Dolores, say hello to our friend Mister Patrick Powell."

"I've been to Chicago, Mother," said Dolores. I had seen her before, but couldn't immediately remember where. She was a pretty girl. Her blue eyes sparkled, as did her diamond earrings. I guessed her age at fifteen. I shook her petite hand.

She curtsied.

"How do you do, Mister Powell."

"They can't expect us to go to Chicago with no clothes," said Ma.

Dolores worked into a dark cape, fished in its pockets, brought out a pack of Chesterfields, offered me a cigarette, and then slipped one into her lipstick-heavy lips. I noticed then how much makeup she wore: powder, mascara, eyebrow pencil. I lit her cigarette with Sadie's lighter.

"Oh that's cute," she said. "Mother do you see this lighter? It's a lipstick tube." She shot me a strange look. "It's not a man's lighter at all," she said.

She blew smoke away from my face, stepped over to the desk to swipe an ashtray off it. She held that ashtray in one hand, tapped it with the cigarette in her other hand, as if determined to capture every speck of ash.

"Mrs. Smith?" ventured the desk clerk. "Your bill."

Ma approached the desk, opened her pearl-studded purse and pulled out a rubber-banded wad of bills.

"I'm afraid I can't cash that," said the clerk.

Ma squabbled and fussed and began sorting bills on the desk. As far as I could tell they were of the hundred-dollar denomination. Finally she found a fifty and pushed it at the clerk.

"Obscene amount of money they give her," Dolores whispered, and tapped her cigarette. "And she does nothing but complain about them."

"About … ?"

"Her boys. How they run around with bad women. How they never come home. How they booze and gamble. How they forget they were raised Christian."

"Right," I said.

At the desk, Ma began disputing charges with the clerk. She had not made a call to Saint Louis, she insisted, and had not ordered champagne. Dolores led me deeper into the lobby, cigarette smoke trailing over her frizzy dark hair.

"How well do you know these people?" she asked, and from her face I sensed she realized it was a dangerous question.

"A little bit," I said.

"Something's going on," Dolores whispered.

"What do you mean?"

"Suddenly we have to pack up for Chicago. Do you know her boys?"

"Yes," I said.

"Little Shorty and Big Shorty?"

"I have met them."

"Then you know Ray."

"Ray?" I said.

"Ray Slim," she said.

"Does his real last name begin with a K?"

She nodded, blew smoke.

"I know him." Now I realized I had seen Dolores, with Karpis at the Green Lantern.

"Get a message to Ray," said Dolores. "Tell him I'm being kidnapped. Tell him I'm being kidnapped by Curly Davis. Tell him that…" she tugged at the sleeve of my suit coat. "Please. Tell him I don't want to be with this man. He gives me the creeps."

I looked out the lobby windows at the two-car caravan and saw that the autos were now surrounded by well-dressed women, who with Curly Davis were rearranging luggage in the trunks. I recognized two of those women: Paula, girlfriend of Fred Barker, and Gladys, wife of Harry Sawyer. A third woman, with narrow shoulders and a very wide butt, I had never seen before. There was also a little girl, bundled in pink, the adopted daughter of Harry and Gladys Sawyer.

"You're not really being kidnapped, are you?" I asked Dolores.

"Well, I don't want to go."

"How old are you?"

"Sixteen." She smashed that cigarette butt out in the ashtray.

"Don't fuss, I'll be okay," she said. "I'm just annoyed, that's all. Tell Ray to come get me in Chicago. As soon as he can. Tomorrow if he can."

She set the ashtray down on a leather hassock just as Ma approached, waving a hotel bill.

"Did you order champagne when my back was turned?"

"No!" said Dolores. "I ordered it when you were in the shower."

"Lord, a little thing like you drank all that champagne."

"I didn't drink any of it, it's in my luggage."

"Ah," said Ma, as if she'd solved a puzzle. "For the honeymoon."

Underneath all that makeup, Dolores blushed.

Curly Davis bulled into the lobby. "Let's go now," he snapped.

"I'm not riding with that Paula," said Ma.

Curly snorted.

"I don't care," said Dolores. "I don't mind Paula."

"Well it's a coupe," explained Curly, a current of anger in his voice. "Edna and I are in the coupe. Mother, you have to ride in the sedan."

"I will not ride with that hussy," said Ma.

"Paula's the only one who can drive it," said Curly.

"That girl has smashed up more cars than a wrecking yard," Ma said.

"I'll be in the lead. She'll follow. I'll make her drive slow."

"Is she sober?" Ma said.

"For God's sake," said Curly.

"I've never seen her sober," said Ma.

"Little missy," said Curly, "can you drive?"

"I can try," said Dolores. "I'll bet I can."

Curly turned his back and walked off as if he was going to abandon the whole enterprise, then whirled with a new idea. He snapped his fingers.

"How about this guy," he said. "Can you drive, pal?"

"I've got appointments here all day," I said.

"Freddy is going to fucking kill me," said Curly.

"Language!" said Ma. "You're in the company of Christian women."

"Do you want to see me dead?" said Curly. "Is that what it is? Because you are killing me, Mother. Now get in the goddamn car with Paula." He whirled. "They stuffed all your luggage in. I'll tell you what, Mother. You ride in the Studebaker with me. Edna can ride in the Ford."

"I will not allow Dolores to be driven anywhere by that drunken trollop."

Curly huffed. "I'll talk to Gladys. She can drive. She doesn't want to drive but I'll talk her into it. You won't have to ride with Paula, you won't even have to see Paula. Okay? Can we get out of here?"

Ma shuffled behind him.

Dolores winked and made kissy lips.

"You promised now," she whispered.

And then they all were off, packed into two cars and motoring for Chicago.

I waited in a much quieter lobby. But my insides were churning. Big Ryan had been a midnight no-show, and I didn't know what that meant. And now this guy Curly was packing up the Barker Gang's women and rushing them out of town. Since Gladys and the child were along, that meant Harry Sawyer was in full panic mode.

Something had gone terribly wrong but I had no idea what.

I paced along the big lobby windows, awaiting George's go signal. George had arranged it so a drugstore delivery kid would approach the front desk with a bottle of cough syrup that had been ordered by a Mister Wagner. The clerk would check the register and either find there was no Mister Wagner registered, or would call the room of a perplexed guy named Wagner. Either way, the arrival of the cough syrup was my signal. George did not want to risk contact at this delicate stage. On the signal, I was to drive straight to Eagle River.

But until George's signal was delivered, I could not leave the lobby and the clerk was getting suspicious, asking me twice if he could be of some assistance. As it passed ten o'clock I calculated that the bus had surely reached Rochester by now. Perhaps at 9:30 or so, Father Mack would have alighted with the ransom suitcases. Give Weaver an hour to check the money. I expected the drugstore boy any time now. I worked the crossword puzzle in the *Pioneer Press*. Twenty-eight across. What's a six letter word for "trying time" and ends in an S?

By 11 o'clock I was cycling dreadful scenarios through my mind and expected any moment that a car full of G-men might show up and shoot me through the plate glass windows. But no cars rolled up, except the ones driven by valets and left to warm for departing guests. By 11:30 I was pacing the street in front of the hotel, watching for that drugstore boy. George had failed to arrange for a disaster signal, and I was stuck in Limbo now.

At just after noon, I ordered a whiskey at the bar and ducked into the lobby phone booth to call United Press and ask for Janie.

"It's Powers. What the hell is going on?" I demanded.

"Madhouse," she said. "Can't talk."

She hung up on me.

"Mister Powell, you called for a cab?"

That was the desk clerk, approaching the phone booth.

"I did?"

I peered out of the booth to see a Yellow Cab in the drive and a tall, thin gray cabbie waiting cap in hand at the front desk.

"You're Mister Powell?" the cabbie asked.

"I am."

"Okay, one for the Paramount."

I worked into my overcoat and followed him out the door. The cab was warm and stank of cigars and sweaty feet. The less said the better, so I sat back. The cabbie, looking into the mirror, engaged me as we turned down Summit Hill.

"Everybody's got it better than me, you know," he said.

"What do you mean?"

"All day long. Everybody I pick up. They got it better than me. Like you, for instance. Matinee movie in the middle of the day. You know what I call that?"

"No."

"The good life. You see, I got a sick wife, two kids in school, what are you gonna do."

He shrugged.

"Right?"

"Right." I figured he was working me for a sympathy tip.

"What's your racket, pal?"

"Unemployed," I said.

"I'd trade places with you buddy, I'll tell you that. You don't want to drive a hack twelve hours a day. And don't get me started on these streets. Does the city own a snow plow? If they do, where are they hiding it? In the mayor's garage?"

I lit my pipe, which added my own layer to the cab's aromas. I cranked the window down an inch to let the smoke out.

As he nosed us through the Seven Corners traffic jam, the driver said: "I should have been a cop."

"You think so?"

"Oh yeah, what do those bums have to do all day?"

I didn't answer.

"Kidnappings," he said. "Now if I was working that case, you know what I'd do?"

"No," I said.

"You know he was a friend of mine, Arnie, that kidnapped cabbie."

"Oh yeah?"

"Yeah, the guy they stuffed in the trunk. He ain't saying a word about it now. G-men got him hidden away, see?"

A cop standing on a concrete stanchion blew the whistle, held a white gloved hand to halt us at the nexus of the intersection, between Blind Benny's newsstand and the Mrs. Sippy Tavern.

"Chicago newspapers offered Arnie twenty bucks to talk, and the G-men took him away. A hack finally gets a chance, and the cops pull it our from under him. How do you like that?"

We finally cleared the intersection and motored down Seventh, the driver weaving around delivery trucks, streetcars, ice patches and dashing pedestrians.

"Could Arnie end up in the movies?" the driver asked. "Maybe. Imagine that, a cabbie in the movies. Now why couldn't that happen to me? Two hours in a trunk, and you're famous the rest of your life. The *Chicago American* gives you twenty bucks a word."

We pulled up at the Paramount's marquee. I dug for change, not wanting the guy to remember a big tipper. Thirty cents for the ride, a nickel for the cabbie.

"Jimmy Cagney," he said. "Now that guy's got it better than all of us."

"Show's started," scolded the ticket lady. I paid her a quarter and pushed into the lobby, where a high-school boy in sloppy uniform ripped my ticket. The movie was "Mayor of Hell," starring Cagney. I whispered "back row" to the usher and he escorted me with his flashlight. There were maybe twenty people in an ornate theater that could hold two thousand. The management had not bothered to provide an organist, and that grand instrument stood unattended off to the side of the screen. I sat, fiddling with my pipe, too worried to pay the least attention to the movie. What was I doing at the Paramount, mid-day on a cold Monday?

I found out shortly as Shotgun George sat beside me. He was dressed in vanilla suit that nearly glowed in the dark. He set his coat and fedora in the chair beside him.

"Disaster," he whispered in my ear. "Complete shipwreck."

I'd never felt so sick. Hangover, attack of nerves, flare-up of gout, throbbing eyeballs, headache like a steel band around my skull, stomach in full revolt, balls retracted into my body for quick flight.

"Our bus kept going," whispered George. "The hillbilly lit the trash fire as planned and ..."

He huffed. "Zoom."

"What went wrong?"

"That's where you come in," said George and patted me on the shoulder. "Find out and meet me here for the six o'clock show."

The Lowry Hotel stood across the street from its bigger, fancier sister the Hotel Saint Paul, and it too was in sight of both the Alt bank and the Federal Building. I was overcome by the feeling that I was very small, a dark figure on the winter streets, a sneak, a shadow. I ducked into the lobby and mounted the stairs and stood outside the United Press office with my dripping fedora in hand.

I stood paralyzed by either hopelessness or fear until Janie opened the door, rushing out, stopped by the surprise of seeing me.

"I've got to know something," I said.

I grabbed the sleeve of her dark green blouse.

"Let go," she said and pulled away.

She crossed the hall toward the door that said LADIES ROOM.

I pushed in behind her, held the door open.

"What went wrong?" I whispered.

She stood, eyes blazing with anger, before a wall of green-painted pipes.

"Michael Powers, I will call the police on you."

"The police? You're in Saint Paul, remember?"

From somewhere in the dark depths of that bathroom, a woman screamed as if she had seen a monster.

I let go of that door, ran down the steps, out onto busy Wabasha Street and, hustling toward the police station, passed shoppers and clerks and homeless bums and one street preacher squawking about the end of the world. At the police station I ran breathless up the wide stairway and turned in at the Bertillion room.

McAmbly was huddled at the counter with Lieutenant Tierney, Chief Dahill, Federal agent Roland Heater, and two other fellows whom I took to be G-men.

"Wrong door," I said and retreated.

But McAmbly was my only hope, so I retreated to the Town Talk determined to wait until the big shots cleared his office. It was just past 1:30 now and Opal was slumped at the counter, enjoying the post-rush cigarette and coffee.

"Don't get up," I said.

"Wasn't going to," she said.

I glanced over my shoulder at the cop table, and saw only Bulldog McMullen, without his majesty the Inspector. McMullen was absorbed reading *Modern Detective* and smoking a cigar. A paperboy burst in with the *Dispatch* and I bought a copy, as did just about every one else in the place. Kidnapping had been good for the newsboys. When I unfolded the *Dispatch* the headlines screamed:

ALT FAMILY SCRAMBLES
TO MEET RANSOM DEMAND

The story was no help to me, since their latest news was that sometime after midnight, a man had called with final instructions for the ransom drop.

Opal, beside me, yawned and popped a stick of bubblegum into her mouth.

"Whole thing went sour," she whispered. "Did you hear?"

"What went sour?"

"The ransom drop. They don't know nothing in the news."

"How exactly did it go sour?"

"Dummies," she said. "The bankers. They had the money under a time lock. You know, one of those safes you can't open until morning. It was too late." Her lipsticked mouth formed an expression of delight, as if the big shot bankers were proven to be rubes after all.

"The bus had left and the money," she elbowed and lowered her voice a bit, "all that money, was stuck in the vault."

"How do you know this?"

"Are you kidding?" she said. "The cop table. I wish the tips were as good as the gossip."

She pushed her coffee cup across the counter.

"That's why they call this place the Town Talk."

I felt like I had sunk into a low, dark place from which there was no escape. I left the Town Talk and wandered downtown, enveloped in my own haze of anger and fear, bumping into people, slipping on the icy sidewalks, turning over in my boiling brain the implications of that missed ransom drop. I needed relief, and there were only two that had ever worked for me: booze and horse racing. Needing a clear head for the coming days, I turned in at the Royal Cigar Store.

It was quiet. Mondays were dark days for most American racetracks, and the big chalk board listed only Agua Caliente, the Tijuana track, first race in twenty minutes. The place was clean and practically deserted, even the tellers windows unmanned. I approached Reilly's window and reached into it to filch a copy of the Racing Form. It was mostly feature articles, charts from Sunday's races, and in the back, the dope on Caliente. The first race was a lousy maiden claimer. This was a race for horses that had been brought to the races at great expense, and had exhibited no desire to please their owners or the betting public. The owners of these animals, just by entering them into such a race, were signaling that they had surrendered their dreams and were hoping only to snag a few bucks to pay the stall rent.

"Scared money never wins" said a voice. I looked up to see Pat Reilly, he of the greasy blond hair and bad teeth. He wore a bowling shirt with his name sewed over the pocket, just underneath the emblazoned name of his team: HAMM'S.

"Now exactly what does that saying mean?"

"Come on," he said, and lit a Lucky. "It's the oldest saying in the books."

"Speaking of books," I said, "give me a deuce to win on Tippecanoe in the first at Agua."

I pushed two dollars at him, looked over my shoulder. The only other soul in the joint was asleep on a bench near the silent teletype.

"Scared money," I said in a quiet voice. "Are you trying to tell me something?"

"What?" he said, lips drawn back in a snarl, cigarette bobbing in his teeth.

"Oh, I don't know, are you going to tell me a tale about a bus?"

"You planning on leaving town by bus?"

"Come on."

"Everybody else is leaving town."

"Meaning?"

"Harry split," Pat whispered. There was a wounded look in his eyes. "Just like that."

"What about Gladys and the kid?" I said, just to test him.

"Gone," he said. "Nobody knows where. Heap big mystery, chief."

"Federal heat?"

"McMullen drove out this morning. At dawn. I don't think the Bulldog has ever been up at dawn once in his life. But there he was knocking at Harry' farmhouse door."

"With bad news for Harry."

"With awful news for Harry," Pat said. "They nailed the Lantern shut."

"Who?"

"Dahill and them guys."

"I didn't know they could do that."

"They could do anything they want," said Pat. "This is Saint Paul."

"Why the heat on Harry?"

"Don't bullshit me," said Pat. "Two bucks on Tippecanoe? Save it. You'll need it to pay the lawyers."

"Give me the ticket," I said.

Staring at me intense, he pulled the lever of his ticket machine.

"No radio from the Mexican tracks," he said. "You'll have to wait for the wire."

"I'll be back," I said.

"I doubt it," he said. He pushed the ticket across the counter. "Good luck, mister longshot."

CHAPTER THIRTEEN

TUESDAY AFTERNOON
ON THE ROAD TO EAGLE RIVER

I dreaded bringing bad news to the Barker Gang. The drive was five hours with nothing to do but worry, about the gang's reaction, about sliding off the icy road and tumbling into a ditch, which I sometimes thought might be the better option. The tires, gone hard in the cold, were wobbling and thrumming as I drove through Ladysmith, the halfway point. A right turn on Route 27 offered an escape to Iowa and points south. Were it not for Snowflake and Hula Girl, I might have turned south and sped away.

I had met Shotgun George last evening at the Paramount, filled him in on the missed bus and the time-locked safe. He wanted to try another scheme immediately, but I insisted that Fred, Karpis and Doc expected me back no later than Tuesday afternoon, and I had to make the drive no matter what. I promised to return to Saint Paul as soon as possible. During our whispered conversation, George smelled of liquor. Even as he'd sat beside me, he was drinking from a flask.

A flat tire just outside Ladysmith added to my misery. I had a good spare fixed to the back, and changed the flat roadside. It was after 2 p.m. when I turned off Sunset Road and down Cindy's snowy driveway. As I approached the cottage, I saw a dead dear hanging from a tree, bloody snow underneath.

The house seemed dark. No dogs barked. All sorts of boot-prints led to the front and back doors and I wondered for a moment whether there'd been a raid. I expected to see shell casings in the snow. I mounted the porch steps, knocked timid like a stranger.

Karpis opened the door with a cigarette in his mouth.

I walked in after knocking the snow off my boots.

"Where's the dogs?" I asked.

"Out with Doc, what's the word?"

I peered into the parlor. At the dining table was the leavings of a sloppy drunken poker game.

"The word is," I whispered, "no go."

Karpis blew smoke toward the ceiling.

"What do you mean no go?"

"They missed the bus."

"What bus?"

Only then did I realize that the gang knew nothing of the ransom plan, and that George had made it up on his own.

"Where is everybody?"

"They went for a walk in the woods," said Karpis. "Everybody."

"Including the dogs?"

"What's this about a bus?"

"The ransom was supposed to be taken aboard a bus. But the money was under a time lock in Papa Alt's bank. The bus left before the vault could be opened."

Karpis sat in a chair, thinking over this setback. He tapped his cigarette into an ashtray stand. Sunlight filtered through the big window onto his shoulders. He wore a salmon-striped shirt, held up by blue suspenders over dark trousers. He had the hunched worried look of a man who'd just been told: Cancer. Weeks to live.

"More bad news," I said. "Our copper's shut out."

Karpis looked up at me. I had never seen him anything but tough and cold and now he looked almost pleading.

"They're on to Big Ryan," I said. "Under suspicion. G-men are watching him now."

Karpis, feet up on an ottoman, snuffed the cigarette. He stared up at the ceiling, as if the answer to his problems were printed there in bold face.

"You know what this is?" he said.

"No."

"Catastrophe." He heaved a deep sigh. "Which is what I told Harry when he hatched this hare-brained scheme."

Eyes closed, he said, "Maybe Fred and I made a mistake. We should have gone to Hot Springs. We'd never have returned to Saint Paul if it weren't for Peifer."

He opened his eyes and stared at me. "How well do you know Peifer?"

"Pretty well."

"He got us started in the snatch racket. The son-of-a-bitch played me. Flattery, see, and I fell for it. Easy, lucrative jobs here and there. He was softening me up. What Peifer wanted all along was the Hamm snatch. He was scheming on me, long range. And then Harry talks us into this disaster."

He sat up and pointed a finger at me. "You. You should have known better. You know the ins and outs of that goddamn city. You should have talked us out of it."

"I didn't know nothing about it until you showed up with the Alt boy."

"Bullshit," said Karpis. "It was planned at your girlfriend's apartment."

"She didn't say nothing to me. She's not my girlfriend."

"I never knew a woman could keep her mouth shut," said Karpis.

He picked another Chesterfield out of the pocket of that beautiful shirt.

"We've lost our copper," he muttered, as if trying to make himself believe it. "Now what?"

"We try again," I said. "The Alts have the money. They're willing to pay. It's just a bump in the road."

He lit that cigarette with a gold flip-top lighter.

"You know," he said, "I'm sick of this racket already. When we get done I'm heading for foreign lands and I'd advise you to do the same."

"I'm thinking Cuba," I said.

He glared through his own cigarette smoke. "You stay out of Cuba."

"Why say that?"

"Let's just quit talking about it."

An ugly silence filled the room. The fireplace had gone cold, the radiators were silent and only now, when I took off my heavy coat, did I realize the room had a chill.

"Anybody stoking the furnace?" I asked.

I walked into the basement, and indeed, found weakly glowing ash in the coal furnace. I shoveled in coals, very few so as not to smother what little heat was there. You had to crouch under the low ceiling of this basement and I yanked the light cord and looked around. The coal bin would be the place to shelter should the law come for us, behind concrete foundation and a pile of coal. This tiny window, just big enough for a coal chute, made the smallest possible target for federal bullets or tear gas. I poked around just in case Cindy's father had hidden a shotgun down here, but the search was interrupted by the high-pitch yipping of my dogs.

I ran up to the kitchen door, and down the trail they rushed from the frosty golden-lit woods, romping happy up front as they were bred to do, looking behind them at the hopelessly slow humans trudging through knee-high snow. Snowflake and Hula Girl bounded into the deer-fenced yard, Snowflake rolling in the snow, and Hula Girl using her muzzle as a snowplow. I opened the door, let them in, they shook off the snow and I embraced them like they were my children.

Doc Barker, carrying a tommygun in red-gloved hands, pushed through the door.

"Well," he said. "What's the good word?"

"Let's talk in the parlor," I said, "when we're all here."

Ricky Alt was next, snatching a watch cap off his head and shrugging snow off his shoulders. He looked as if the walk had put him in good spirits.

Fred Barker, almost lost in a trench coat, shut the door behind him.

"Trouble," said Doc.

"Ricky," said Fred, and jerked his thumb. Alt, hunched over, slipped into the side bedroom and closed the door, obedient.

Doc opened the refrigerator, which seemed to contain only wrapped meat, eggs, and bottled beer. He pulled a butcher-wrapped package and from it chose bits of raw meat.

"Raw meat?" I said. "That ain't good for the dogs, is it?"

"Hell, they love it," Doc said. He held these meat chunks high in the air and made the dogs jump for them. They leaped high, snapping their jaws in greed.

"What trouble?" asked Fred.

"Big trouble," said Karpis, blocking the doorway to the parlor.

Fred shed his trench coat, reached into the pocket of his hunting shirt for a cigarette.

"Papa shitbird won't pay," Doc guessed, teasing the dogs with a bloody strip of meat.

"He'll pay," I said. As they all glared at me, I explained the basics: choosing the priest as an emissary, the want ad, the bus plan, and the time-locked safe.

Doc finished feeding the dogs, put the bloody plate on the floor for them to lick. They never fought, my dogs, but each tried to crowd the other out.

"Parlor," said Fred and all the humans moved in there while the dogs licked and sniffed at the kitchen floor.

In the parlor we had two walls and two rooms between us and the captive's bedroom.

Doc, wearing a home-knit sweater that featured Santa and his reindeer, heaved wood into the fireplace. Fred stood hands on hips staring out the picture window at the frozen lake and the piney woods.

"Kidnapping," Fred said. "This ain't right. How did we get into this, brother?"

Doc lit the fire with twisted up newspaper.

"All I know is I ain't had no pussy in a week."

"Ray, what do you say?" asked Fred over his shoulder.

"I say we drown him in the lake," Doc said. "Cut a hole in the ice and shove that son of a bitch into it."

"I was asking Ray," Fred snapped.

Karpis, hands in his pockets, joined Fred at the windows and he too stared out at the lake as if the answer would rise up out of the ice.

"What would Jesse James have done?" asked Fred.

"Shoot 'em and run," said Doc.

"That's my vote," said Fred.

"And leave all that cash?" said Karpis. "They've got it ready for us."

"Hell, they'll figure some way to mark it," said Fred.

"We cleaned it up good last time," said Doc, and hovered around the fireplace as the fire began to consume the wood.

"You forget how long it took," said Fred, "you and gramps on the train to Reno, and those casino boys, we got lucky."

"I vote we shoot and run," said Doc. "He's a per-nis-shit son of a bitch."

"A what?"

"Pernishit," said Doc. "You know, mean, rotten."

"Where'd you learn a ten dollar word like that?" asked Fred.

"I read the dictionary every day in prison," said Doc. "Learnt three words a day. It's like having a high school degree."

He dusted off his hands and my dogs trotted out and circled him like he was their hero.

"These are some mutts you got," said Doc. "These are intelligent, these here."

He squatted, cuffed them playfully and they play-fought with him. As he stood up, he fished a flask out of his hip pocket.

"Let's give the fat cats another chance," said Karpis, leaning back against the frosty windows.

"But we've got no copper," warned Fred.

"The day I need a copper … " said Karpis. "I never liked that bastard."

"One thing I want to do before I die," said Fred, "is stick up a train. We could do it Ray. Just like the James gang, only nastier."

Doc sat at the dining table, pushed aside chips and coins, reached for an ashtray, his rolling papers, his tobacco pouch.

"Son of a bitch, the more I think about it," said Doc. "Stuck here another week in this shithole."

He rolled a cigarette, licked paper.

"Ray's right." Fred tossed chips and coins across the dining table. "There's money on the table. What's three more days. Can you drive at night, Powers?"

"Sure," I said.

"Two hundred fifty," said Karpis. "The price just went up."

I said: "But now they got two hundred in suitcases, Ray, let's not get greedy."

"You're telling me not to get greedy?"

"Fight nice boys," said Doc, blowing smoke. "I say shoot the banker son of a bitch and we'll be in Chicago before midnight."

"And what good will that do?" said Karpis.

Doc swigged. "They won't fuck with us next time."

"There ain't going to be a next time," said Karpis. "I'm done with the snatch racket. I'm with Fred. We take down a train."

"Payroll," Fred said, "remember how that went."

"Machine Gun Kelly," said Karpis. "That poor bastard."

"Hell, Kelly was always kinda stupid," said Doc.

"I remind you," said Karpis, "that the money-changing bastard in that bedroom has seen all our faces."

"Which improves my point," said Doc. "Dead bankers tell no tales."

"And pay no ransom," said Karpis. "Take the dough. It's waiting for us, all bundled up. George got it last time and he'll get it this time."

"Fuck that son of a bitch George," said Doc, and looked at his cigarette as if he had just discovered a nasty burning thing in his nicotine stained fingers.

Doc ducked into the kitchen and returned with the tommygun. He stood in the doorway with the machinegun held at cross arms. The dogs retreated underneath the dining table. I became aware of odd things: Doc's boots dripping on the polished wood floor. The crackling fire. Wind blowing off the frosty lake and rattling the windows.

"I'll do it if you boys ain't got the stomach," said Doc.

Fred shook his head.

It hit me like an electric shock when I realized that if they did shoot Ricky Alt, they would soon figure that I, too, was a dangerous witness.

"I can get the money," I said. "I give you my word. Life and death, I can get it."

"Well, Lap's gonna pick it up," said Doc.

"I will get it to Lap. I can play Saint Paul like a piano. Listen boys," I stood up, like this was the speech of my life, valedictorian of Gangster High School. "I will drive back to the city and George and I will hatch a plan and I will wrest that money from Papa Alt if it's the last thing I do. Give me three days. Come on, guys, it's worth three more days to get your hands on a fortune."

"Three more days," said Karpis, and shot Fred a serious look.

"And a fourth to get back here with the good word."

"Shit, now he's stretching it," said Doc.

"Why don't you shut the fuck up while we're thinking?" suggested Fred.

"Kiss my ass," said Doc, and aimed the tommygun out the window. "Pow you're dead G-man."

He turned to us. "Nobody's taking Doc Barker alive."

"Powers," said Fred, "you are right persuasive."

Karpis, looking relaxed now, said: "Give a man his chance. And this is the last chance, Powers. You understand that."

"He understands it," said Fred.

"Piss on it," said Doc. "Bunch of son of a bitching cowards."

"Watch your tongue, brother," warned Fred.

"Enough of you, little man," said Doc. "Ray's the brains of the outfit."

"And Ray says hold on."

"Shit," said Doc.

He walked to the front door with his tommygun and with only that Santa-reindeer sweater for a coat, stepped out onto the porch. He heaved a frosty breath, and walked down ten paces to the lakeshore. There he raised his tommygun and sent a long burst of bullets over the lake.

Karpis moaned.

"Gotta let a dog bark," said Fred.

CHAPTER FOURTEEN

WEDNESDAY MORNING
EAGLE RIVER

That night I slept restless, alone and cold in the porch-bedroom.
Snowflake and Hula Girl chose to spend the night with Doc.
Maybe he smelled of venison, or maybe it was my tossing and
turning that drove them away or maybe, I thought in the middle of
the night, they recognized Doc as a fellow predator.

But I had other worries. Sound carries a long way in winter, and
even far-off neighbors could tell the distinctive sound of a machine
gun. I wouldn't have been surprised by a morning visit from the
sheriff. I began to picture it, how I would greet him at the front
door, and say, yes, sheriff, I did hear that and I was mighty worried,
and then I heard a car speed off down Highway G and I guess it
was a bunch of Chicago hoodlums up here taking target practice in
the woods and yes sir, I'll let you know if I hear it again.

But the sun rose behind the pines and no sheriff. I had
persuaded the gang that I should not leave in the dark, because if I
went into a ditch, ended up in the hospital or worse, they might
never get their money. So I arose with the sun , stoked the stove,
and fried thin tubes of venison sausage on the grill, warmed the

cast iron pan to receive scrambled eggs, and made coffee from a diminishing supply of grounds.

The dogs begged for breakfast and I had nothing to feed them but venison. Doc followed them into the kitchen, stretching, dressed as if it were summer, in a sleeveless t-shirt, the tattoo of a big blue cross on his shoulder. Scratching at his red hair, he poured himself a cup of coffee, sat at the table, and stared at the sunrise.

"Ma made a hell of a breakfast," he said. "Biscuits and gravy. That woman. Cantankerous, but she can cook."

He sipped coffee.

"You met her Powers?"

I hemmed, I hawed. Dangerous question.

"I don't remember."

"Oh, you'd remember," he said. "Fiery old bat."

Fred ambled in, barefoot, in boxer shorts, a leather vest over skinny bare chest.

"You let the prisoner out of his cell?" asked Doc.

"He's in the bathroom," said Fred, and headed for the coffee pot.

"Reminiscin on Ma's breakfast," said Doc.

"I am sick of eating deer," said Fred. "Never liked it."

"Are you a country boy or not?" said Doc, scratching his head. "Took it downtown, got it all wrapped up and civilized, hell, you can't tell it from a cut of beef now." Doc looked at me. "I'd a cut it up myself, but Fred won't have no part of butchering."

"I ain't no butcher," said Fred, sipping coffee.

"Survival skills, Jesse," Doc said, and then filled me in. "He thinks he's Jesse James."

"And who the hell do you think you are?" said Fred.

"Why I was named for Doc Holiday."

"A goddamn dentist," said Fred.

"Yep, he did like to drill people," said Doc.

First a shadow, then the man who cast it appeared at the kitchen door.

"Morning, fellows," said Ricky Alt. "Smells like coffee out here."

He was dressed in a red and black flannel shirt, pajama bottoms, and paint-spattered slippers that had belonged to Cindy's father. He shuffled toward the coffee pot, picked it up, banged it back on the stove.

"Ricky's got a plan," said Doc. "He was telling me yesterday."

Ricky took the beat-up coffee pot to the stove, rinsed it and began spooning grounds into it. It was cowboy coffee, simple as water and grounds and egg shells. When he set that pot on the hottest part of the stove he said: "Doc, I was telling your brother …"

Snowflake barked at the back door and I let him in.

" … how it works," finished Ricky.

Fred leaned casual, skeptical against the counter.

"Tell him how much," said Doc.

"Two hundred," said Ricky. "Thousand."

Fred pursed his lips as if to say: What a coincidence.

"How'd you get that much on a horse race?" asked Doc.

"You lay it off," said Ricky. "Track in Chicago, bookies in New York, Mexico, Des Moines, twenty thousand here and there."

"On one horse race?"

"Are you kidding?" said Ricky. "It's done all the time."

"Tell him how the son of a bitch works," said Doc.

"Simple," said Ricky. "You tell the rube you've got a sure thing, fixed race."

"You know somebody who fixes horse races?" said Fred, suddenly interested.

"They don't need to. They don't want to pay off a jockey, a trainer, a fixer. This way it's simpler. The mark thinks it's a sure thing, he puts two hundred thousand down, thinking he's sure to make three-to-one. Minus a commission of course. All the operator does is keep the money, it's that simple. The horse loses, and at 3-1 he probably will. The operator fumes and says he can't understand what went wrong, sorry pal, we've been double crossed. If the horse wins, you say you couldn't get the bet down."

"Shit," said Doc.

"Worst case," said Ricky, "he's got powerful friends, you give him his money back minus commission and find another mark. So it's twenty grand at worst."

"So you pulled this yourself?"

"No. Dutch did. You know One-armed Dutch, downtown, the pawn shop guy, it was his scheme. All I did was act as cashier. I held the money. See the mark, he was in hock. An embezzler. You can't cheat an honest man. He was a stocks and bonds man trying to cover up for missing funds. Which just happened to be parked in our bank."

"What happens when the mark realizes he's been cheated?"

"Why, he goes to the county attorney. Who's our friend."

"Who called you to the Grand Jury?" I asked.

Ricky shrugged. "No harm there. No indictment, that's for sure. Thunder and lightning, that's all."

"What if the cheated man picks up a weapon?"

"He won't because he knows better. See, he's gambling with his boss's money, so now it's him who could end up in jail, so the best thing for him to do is leave for the coast."

"Hmm," said Fred.

I poured scrambled eggs into a hot buttered pan.

Doc said: "Where you a find a son of a bitch stupid enough to fall for that?"

"Well, like I told you boys, he was an embezzler to begin with. And he was deep in it, and the only way out was three to one, so he was desperate. That's the easy way to get two hundred thousand. No firearms involved."

"Well I'll be a son of a bitch," said Doc. "We been outsmarted."

"You boys could be the enforcers in that kind of scheme," said Ricky.

Doc said: "We ain't going to be anywhere near that shit hole Saint Paul once we deliver you."

"Never again," said Fred, "I don't know how you people stand these winters."

I dropped egg shells into the coffee pot.

"Hmm," said Fred. "So Rick, you're friends with Harry Sawyer."

"We go way back," said Ricky. "Harry was in charge of Pop's beer runs. We handled money for him. For all of them. Cops came in checking Harry's accounts, we played dumb. You ask Harry, he'll tell you about some of the deals we made."

Doc and Fred exchanged glances.

"Then Harry's another guy," said Fred, "who'll be glad to see you home."

CHAPTER FIFTEEN

WEDNESDAY AFTERNOON
HOTEL SAINT PAUL

My seven-note knock on George's hotel room door was answered by a round-faced boy with a crew-cut.

Surprised, I stepped back and checked the number on the door: Right, 914.

"Donny, I told you," said George's voice, "do not answer the door."

George appeared behind the boy. Half of George's face was covered in shaving cream, and he held a straight razor at his side.

The boy was maybe ten years old, a sparkle in his dark eyes, a mischievous grin on his lips. He wore a crisp white dress shirt, a blue vest over it, decorated with the golden monogram of a Catholic school.

"Go play," commanded George. He gently hauled the boy away from the door, then opened it for me, gave a suspicious look up and down the hall, closed the door, double locked it and threw the chain.

"This is Donny," said George. "Donny, this is Mister X."

"Hi Mister X," said Donny.

"I'll be out momentarily," said George and waved the straight razor at me.

He retreated to the bathroom and stood there in a halo of light, humming an opera tune, finishing his shave.

Donny, on hands and knees, ran a red-steel toy fire truck over the shiny hardwood at the edge of the Persian rug.

"Emergency!" he said, and then answered, "I'm on it, Joe. Vroom Vroom Vroom."

He pushed that truck through the doorway and into the bedroom.

"Inventive little boy," said George from the bathroom doorway. He toweled his face, threw the blood-specked towel to the white tiled floor.

"It will be a brief custody I assure you," George said. "Business first!"

"Daddy," said Donny from the bedroom. "Can I get a grilled cheese sandwich?"

"Not now," said George. "Children," he said, "What happened to seen and not heard? An entire generation going to rot."

"Please!" begged Donny.

George shut the bedroom door on him.

"Oh crap," said Donny from behind it.

"The boy has discovered room service," said George. "He called this morning and asked if they could deliver a cat. He misses his pet kitty, you see."

I removed my coat and threw it on the desk chair. My eyes went to that typewriter. How were we going to write a ransom note with a little boy in the next room?

"We've got a deadline of four days and today counts," I said.

I expected George to be grateful, or even relieved that I had succeeded in wresting patience out of the Barker Gang.

He walked to the window, stared down at the Federal Building.

"Strategic thought," he said, "is not their strong suit."

I had no idea what he meant.

"They should trust us. Open ended, that's what we need."

He slammed his hands on the window sill, walked to the phone and barked into it.

"Send the bellman to 914."

"Daddy," whined Donny from behind the door, "can I come out now?"

"In a few minutes," growled George.

"I have to go to the bathroom."

George raised his eyes to the heavens, opened the door, and gave the boy a playful swat as he ran for the bathroom.

"I didn't know you had a son," I said.

"Neither did I," said George, and lowered his voice. "The 'daddy' is an affectation. He is adopted. Irene adopted him. The milk of motherhood proved to be thin indeed. She is out of patience, and doesn't see how he'll fit in when we get to Florida."

"Irene?" I said.

"The wife," George said.

He lit a Camel.

"Irene has social ambitions, you see." He looked at me as if he had never seen me before. "In Florida. Palm Beach society. You are unmarried, I take it?"

A knock came at the door. George peeked first, then opened it and asked the bellboy to stay at the threshold. When Donny emerged from the bathroom, George called him to the door, put his arm around the boy's shoulder and said, "This gentleman will take you to the café, and sit with you while you enjoy a sandwich and an ice cream sundae. There is no hurry, linger for a half hour or so."

He palmed the bellboy two rolled up bills.

The bellboy winked at Donny. The child, full of trust, eager for adventure, walked down the hall with the bellhop.

George closed the door, locked it and stood in front of it as if preventing my escape.

"Powers, we are in a desperate situation. If they kill Ricky Alt, it will be the electric chair for all of us. I trust Fred and Karpis, but Doc Barker I fear. The man's brain is literally pickled in alcohol, and it wasn't much of a brain to begin with. There's very little his brother can do to stop him, when he gets into his drunken rages."

"We'll get the money," I said. "That's all they want."

"How?" asked George. "Because my plan is useless now."

"The roadside drop," I said. "It worked in the Hamm."

"In the Hamm we still had our copper. And we had Serious Bobby. It was crucial to have the pickup man in on the scheme. Now we've lost our copper and instead of a crooked insider we must work with an honest priest. We're in a predicament, Powers. How do we get our hands on that money?"

"Airdrop," I said.

"Hmm," said George, and sat in the red velvet plush chair.

"The suitcases will burst," he said. "Any container will burst. Believe me, I am trained as an engineer. We would have Lapland Willie chasing bills all over the landscape."

He leaned forward. "Can the priest be corrupted?"

I shook my head. "No way. I've known him for years."

"The priest," said George, "loads the money in his car and drives out of town. We choose a certain highway. You drive behind to assure he isn't followed."

"Not me," I said.

"Nonsense," he said. "This plan will work. You see, the priest only knows to drive until we deliver him another message. That message diverts him on a path that could not have been known heretofore. He will make our specified turn on a deserted rural road where we once again ascertain he is not followed. We once again get him a message for one final turn. When we are sure he cannot possibly be followed, he drops the suitcases for Lap to pick up."

"How do we get him the messages?"

"There is a note in the car. It is our car, we steal it and we prepare it. When he gets into the car he is never to get out until instructed. Once he drives straight out of town he is instructed to open the note at a certain milepost. The note gives him the next turn and tells him where to find the final directives. He does so, abandons the car, alone on foot in the wilderness, and Lap drives that car a short distance, transfers the ransom to his own car, and is on his way.

"The priest cannot leave the car, and so cannot tell the coppers where the first diversion will be. If he makes that point without being followed, we monitor him until the second diversion. That's where you need to be. It will be way out in the country, and the police cannot follow without being noticed. If he makes the turn at that second diversion…"

"I like it," I said, "and here's why. I don't need to tail him. We put Lap at the second diversion. Why risk two men? Lap sees he is not followed. The priest sets out the ransom and walks off. If there's nobody in sight, Lap scoops up the money and drives off. There's no way for the coppers to know or guess where this would be unless they follow him. Even an airplane would be obvious out there in the snowy prairie. You don't need me and that's why I like it. I'm just the messenger, remember?"

"So we need a car and it must be in good working order."

"No problem," I said. "I know the right guys."

"You're a good man in the trenches, Powers. By the way, where did you serve in the War?"

"The trenches of Brooklyn," I said.

CHAPTER SIXTEEN

WEDNESDAY NIGHT

That evening I drove past the Green Lantern, just to see for myself that the famous old gangster tavern had gone dark. It was like they were already ghosts, all of those gangsters who had made a pilgrimage here: Bonnie Parker and Clyde Barrow, Harvey Bailey, John Dillinger, Jelly Nash, Verne Miller, Machine Gun Kelly, Pretty Boy Floyd, and add to that a thousand gangsters nobody ever heard of. End of an era, marked with two-by-fours nailed in a cross over the doors of a shabby tavern.

When I arrived at the Commodore, the clerk retrieved a message for me. It was from my sister Kelly. Call me, urgent, it said. When I phoned it turned out she had some papers for me to sign, so I drove over to her house on the East Side.

I parked a block away, just out of general suspicion. On my walk to her bungalow I passed the home that once belonged to Ralph Tallerico. The lights were on. I told myself as I crept past that Tallerico had forced my hand, and he himself was a killer so …
Still, it was an eerie feeling to pass the house of man you have shot, and I walked gut sick, hunched into myself up to my sister's back door.

"Are you hiding from someone?" she said.

I stepped into her bright, messy kitchen. She was a tall, strawberry blonde with a hint of those childhood freckles, an apron thrown over her fine dark blue dress.

"You look sick. You don't have the flu do you?"

"Where's Gary?"

"Drinking," she said.

"The girls?"

"Out," she said. "Their whole vocabulary is two words now. Out and Fine."

She transferred dirty dishes from table to sink.

"Pie and coffee?"

"Of course. So what's this about a sale?"

"We found somebody."

"A farmer?"

"Developer."

"Who's building houses nowadays?"

"Smart people are buying land now." She laughed. "That's why we're selling it, because we're not smart."

"So he's a speculator. How much?"

"Three thousand, three hundred. He wants to see Cindy's place too."

That alarmed me. Would this speculator be nosing around the property?

"Cindy won't sell, he can forget that," I said. "Tell him that. Tell him don't bother looking at Cindy's place. You think $3300 is fair?"

"Doesn't matter," said Kelly. "We need the money."

She delivered cherry pie, coffee and a short stack of papers to the kitchen table.

"Eleven apiece," I said, signing the papers.

"Not quite," she said. "Realtor's commission. County fees. We're lucky to clear a thousand each."

I signed, hard to believe that a few signatures would deliver a grand into my hands.

"Thank you Aunt Doris," I muttered.

This good fortune would double down on my determination to take none of the ransom money. If I was ever hauled into court this would be my ultimate defense. But then again, if they got me into a courtroom, they'd have to drag me up from Havana.

"What are you going to do with the money?" I asked Kelly.

"Are you kidding?" she said. "In debt to the eyeballs. I know what Mona's going to do. She'll hold a $1000 party. How about you?"

"Get me started in Cuba," I said.

I peered out the window at the Tallerico house, Rico's 1932 Chevy sitting in the icy driveway.

"His nephew still partying day and night?"

"It keeps getting worse," Kelly said. "I'd call the cops, but …

"Yeah, right."

"More pie?"

"This nephew's driving Rico's car and everything?"

"Bullet holes and all," Kelly said. "He shows them off. This is where my uncle took a bullet, you know. Oh, he wants to be a gangster, just like Uncle Ralph."

"Bullet holes?"

"Yeah, Ralph was shot out at that nightclub. The Plantation."

"That wasn't the car," I said.

"What do you mean?"

"I know somebody who was out there that night. Your neighbor was shot, all right, but that car…"

"Maybe the nephew put bullet holes in that car to impress his friends. Punk. I wouldn't put it past him."

CHAPTER SEVENTEEN

THURSDAY MORNING

That night I called Filben and requested the theft of a specific auto, and by morning Rico's 1932 black Chevy sedan was in the rear garage at Herb's, getting a paint job, new plates, a fake registration, new tires, battery, plugs and belts. Meanwhile at the Saint Paul Hotel, room 914, George and I wrote several drafts of instructions for Father Mack, burned the drafts, and produced two finished notes on Blackstone stationery.

Our instructions were: Father Mack was to drive down State 13, directly south, about 40 minutes through the cornfields toward the town of New Prague. When the highway made a right turn toward the town, he was supposed to retrieve the first note from the glove compartment.

That note instructed him to turn left and make sure he wasn't followed. At the lonely intersection of highways 19 and 23 he was to open the final instructions, which were in an envelope underneath the back seat. This note instructed him to turn back to the north and drive for five minutes over the prairie until he saw a frozen creek on his right. At that creek, he was to turn off onto a dirt road, where a mailbox was painted with the name: Schmitz. He was to exit the car, leave the ransom money in the back seat, and walk east.

I stored those notes in a box of kitchen matches so I could burn them if the federals came knocking at my room.

All I needed now was to wait for the blue paint to dry on Rico's car.

CHAPTER EIGHTEEN

THURSDAY EVENING

That evening I was dining on the Commodore Commercial: Salisbury steak, mashed potatoes and green beans, when the bellhop tapped me on the shoulder. I had a call at the front desk, a voice I hadn't heard in many months: Sam Tanaka.

"Powers," he said, "I thought you should know."

I turned my back to the desk clerk.

"Myrtle is here with an ugly man," Sam said. "Mick, it looks like she went ten rounds with Max Schmelling."

"What do you mean?" I asked but I knew what he meant.

"Saph is watching them," said Sam. "There'll be no monkey business here."

"Thanks," I said. "I'll slide over."

I called Myrtle's friend Loretta from the Commodore bar.

"Glad you're home," I said.

"You're back in town?"

"How about dinner at the Hollyhocks?"

She belched. "I've eaten."

"Cocktails then. It's important. It's about our mutual friend."

"You truly, truly are a pain in the ass."

"I need to see you," I said. "I'm coming over."

"I'll meet you at the bar," she said. "I don't accept rides from strange men."

I drove to the Hollyhocks, slipped the parking valet a dime and sneaked in the kitchen door. The help, Japanese and Colored most of them, worked amid clattering dishes and shouted orders. The waiters and cooks and dishwashers kept bumping into each other, for Jack in his reckless generosity hired too many people. I slipped into the barroom and there at a stool in the darkest corner, Loretta sat hunched over a drink.

She was a short, frizzy haired, stocky woman in her late 30s and tonight she wore a heavy white dress that could have done double duty as a lace curtain. Acne scars were like punctuation marks on her pale face. What had turned her to a life of bitter prostitution, I didn't know.

"Did you see our friend?" I asked.

"No," she said into her drink.

I peered around a white column into the dining room.

"She's out there," I said.

"You know the story?" she asked as I sat on the stool next to her. To the barman, an ancient Japanese fellow, I said: "Ginger on ice."

"The story is," Loretta said, "this creep shows up out of nowhere and moves in on her. Like you're mine, you know. Possession is nine tenths of the law."

"I saw her with bruises."

"Yeah, well that's not all." Loretta still hadn't looked at me. "See that's why I don't like your kind. Keep your brute hands to yourself, is that too much to ask?"

She sipped from her lowball glass. "I don't tolerate that. I don't know why she does."

She fumbled for a cigarette and I lit it with Sadie's lighter.

"Check that," Loretta said. "I know why she does."

"You going to tell me?"

She blew smoke.

"He put a gun in her mouth. The barrel. Right in her mouth."

The bartender slid my drink in front of me. I turned to look for Lapland Willie and Myrtle, but couldn't see them from my stool. I did see Saph McKenna working the front door. He was the rare white guy among Jack's employees, a punch drunk heavy weight enforcer, dressed in a tuxedo that did not hide his menacing physique.

"She's got mixed up with a crazy thug," Loretta said. "She can't phone anyone. She can't have friends. She can't leave the apartment without him."

I stood, pushed the barstool away, and said into Loretta's ear: "A few words to the man upstairs, a few bucks to the bouncer, and this Weaver clown is a bloody heap in the snow."

"That's your crappy solution?"

Loretta sucked down a lungful of smoke. "Brutal meets brutal, huh? Great. What happens after the beating, when the brute gets home? He blames Myrtle. And then what? Use your imagination on that one. You just make it worse."

I couldn't tell Loretta that Lapland Willie had jumped bail a couple of years back and the sheriff was looking for him. Lap had to be a free man, at least for the next few days. I was stuck with that.

"When he drinks it's the worst," said Loretta. "In the mornings its tears and apologies, then its flowers and candy and maybe a nice blouse and then the next time he's drunk..." she punched her open palm.

"If we could keep him sober," she said, "the kid's got a chance but I don't imagine he's sipping ice water right now."

"Champagne, I think."

"What's he celebrating?"

"Loretta, I know a secret," I said. "I can't tell you how I know, but Lap's going to skip town soon, maybe tomorrow, maybe the next day, but real soon."

She looked me over with big brown skeptical eyes. "He'll drag her along."

"No," I said. "Not on this adventure, believe me."

"You know this for sure?"

"I do."

"Well that ain't going to … shit," she said. "There they go, look."

Lapland Willie followed Myrtle up the carpeted stairs toward the casino.

"That ain't going to help tonight," Loretta said. "They'll ply him with free drinks up at the roulette wheel. I can pretty much guarantee another black eye when he goes home a loser."

I watched Myrtle swish into the casino in her elegant spangled blue gown.

"Idea," I said.

I patted Loretta on the back.

"You made me spill my drink," she said.

I barged through the busy kitchen looking for Sam Tanaka and found him on the back porch, taking a frosty smoke break. Occasionally he waited tables, but mostly he was house manager, man behind the scenes, watching for sneaky moves by casino dealers, bartenders and wait staff. He wore a red silk shirt and a dark vest and smoked with hands cuffed around his cigarette.

"Thanks for the call," I said.

"You're so very welcome," he said, his voice as frosty as the night.

"I owe you now."

"No you don't."

"I couldn't do you that big favor, Sam. I just couldn't."

"It is already forgotten," he lied.

"Now I need a favor from you, though."

"So ask."

"The comp rooms. Occupied?"

"Not yet."

He still hadn't looked directly at me. The last conversation of our long friendship occurred this summer, when Sam had asked me to suggest to Federal agents that Harry Sawyer was the man behind the Hamm kidnapping. The purpose was to divert suspicion from his boss, Jack Peifer, who really was the finger-man.

"What will it take to put Myrtle and her friend in the big one for the night?"

Sam shrugged.

"And me and Loretta in the little one."

Sam tossed the cigarette, an orange point, into the night.

"How about twenty bucks apiece?" I said.

"They are for high rollers," Sam said.

"Look, this Weaver guy is trouble, and if I can keep him busy a night, two nights, it'll go good for our friend the fur thief."

"She should not try to work her magic here."

"Never, Sam. Absolutely off limits. She only works the high class stores."

"Not what I heard."

"She doesn't do the coatrooms. Stealing from people, that's low."

"People like her are the reason we have a coat-check girl."

"Sam, we've all been friends for years. You know I'm sweet on that kid."

"Okay, Mick, you've worn me down. Twenty five the night."

"I appreciate it."

"Jack will have a fit."

"You know how to work the man, Sam."

"I am a high wire walker, yes," he said. "That's why I never look down."

The plan was simple. Loretta and I bunked in the smaller comp room, dozing, reading, listening to the radio until just after 2:30, when Myrtle and Weaver stumbled into the room next door. If Weaver got rough with her, we would hear it, and with Saph on duty until the last sucker went home, we could be sure to stop it.

But there was no need. Maybe Weaver had done all right at the roulette wheel, or maybe he just drank himself into a stupor, for there was no sound whatever coming from next door.

Loretta left sometime in the night, while I was dozing in bed. I awoke at dawn and took a shower in the tiny closet of a bathroom. Soap and hot water felt exceptionally good. Today, if the ransom car was ready, if the Alts still had the money, I had the prospect of getting Lapland Willie out of town and the Barker-Karpis gang out of my cabin.

CHAPTER NINETEEN

FRIDAY MORNING
THE HOLLYHOCKS CASINO

I had to dress in the stinky clothes I wore last night, which smelled of cigarettes, sweat and booze. In my stocking feet I slipped out into the hall, listened at the door where Myrtle and Lapland Willie slept, and then tiptoed downstairs. Through the empty casino I walked and into the dining room with all its upended chairs.

Violet Peifer was sorting pictures at one of the tables. It was Jack's habit to take photos of his patrons, which flattered their egos and, I sometimes suspected, set them up for potential blackmail. Jack was accumulating evidence, it seemed, of how many Twin Cities big shots played the gangster game at the Hollyhocks.

Out of the kitchen burst a boy pushing a huge red steel fire-truck.

"Donny," said Violet, without looking up. "Not on the carpet."

"Okay Missus Jack," he said.

He backed the fire truck down the tile hallway, making vroom vroom sounds. He wore a sky blue shirt way too big for him, and pants that had been cut off at the knees.

"I thought," I said to Violet, "that was ah, isn't that uhm…"

"George's boy. Do you know George?"

"I might have met him."

"Chicago friend of Jack's," she said. "Amazes me. Jack has more friends than any man I've ever known."

"Generous man," I said.

"Too generous," she said. "We're the only casino in town that's run like a charity."

"What's that mean?"

"We're an orphanage now."

"But he's George's..."

"Do you know Irene? George's wife? I'll bet you don't, because if you did..." she circled her ear with her forefinger. "Certified lunatic."

"Oh."

"She wants the boy, she doesn't want the boy."

Donny abandoned the fire-truck and stood in front of the cigarette machine. He looked over his shoulder and reached in, mischievous, to work free a book of matches.

"Donny," said Violet.

"Huh?"

"Firemen don't play with matches."

Chastised, he sat on the floor and pouted. I saw then that he was barefoot. I realized then that someone had refashioned a man's shirt and trousers for this boy.

"Poor boy," whispered Violet. "Nobody knows who his father is, and his mother was a prostitute."

"Ah," I said.

Donny pushed the fire-truck onto the hardwood floor of the bar room.

"Where's the fire, chief?" he said to his imaginary fellow firemen.

"Now it's up to Jack," Violet said, "to find him a new home."

"Why is it up to Jack?"

Violet shrugged and sorted pictures.

I looked at that boy, and my hair stood on end as I realized whose son was playing with that fire truck.

I talked Janie into an early lunch at Martinucci's. She met me at 11:30 at a table that was set in front of a huge window and covered with a checkered cloth.

"It's cold here," she said. "Can we move back?"

"I asked for this table for a reason," I said. "The view."

"Of the frozen river?" she said.

"How's that baby?" I asked.

"I call to check on him twice a day. Mom's great about it, but…" her eyes went somewhere else "I can't sleep, worrying about him. It's odd. I miss him like he's part of me. It's like my arm's been amputated, but I can still feel it."

The Martinucci's chubby, beautiful, almost blonde teenage daughter served us salads consisting only of iceberg lettuce and sliced radishes.

"The small lasagna," said Janie. "With white sauce."

"Two meatballs," I said. "Just the meatballs and sauce."

When the waitress turned away I said: "Remember a snowy Sunday in March, a kid reporter covering the weekend cops beat, a burned Buick, two corpses inside?"

"Of course I remember."

"Well we know now, don't we?"

"What do we know?"

"Rose was the wife of Denver Bobby, one of the stickup men who robbed the Denver Mint. That money was laundered right here," I pounded the table. "At Papa Alt's bank. That money was the founding fortune of Papa Alt's bank, and enabled him to buy a brewery that Prohibition had put out of business."

"Okay."

"So ten years later, Papa, with the help of Saint Paul's underworld, has turned the brewery and the bank into money machines. Now Rose shows up in Saint Paul, drinking and running her mouth in taverns. Papa Alt wants to know what she's saying. Is she spouting off about the Denver Mint and the Alt bank? So Papa Alt asks his confessor Father Mack to recommend a man who can conduct an quiet inquiry. That man being me."

"So in your mind, Powers, Papa Alt had those girls torched."

I shook my head.

"Rose and Sadie were both busted for prostitution in Duluth. They became friends by pure chance, because they were both let out of the workhouse on the same day. Rose said she knew people in Saint Paul who could loan them money for a fresh start. They couldn't get Tom Filben on the phone so they called Jack Peifer, who wired them fifty bucks. Motive?"

"Well, Jack could add a couple of prostitutes to his stable."

"Correct," I said. "But when Rose and Sadie got here, they drank with gangsters, slept with gangsters and soon learned two facts. One, the town of Hudson was offering a $500 reward for the arrest of the gang that had raided them back in January of '32. And two, they learned via pillow talk the identities of the Hudson raiders: we know them now as the Barker-Karpis gang."

"So Rose and Sadie, their fatal mistake," said Janie, "was going to the Saint Paul cops to try to collect that reward."

"Correct. Now. Who do the cops call when they have a problem with a prostitute?"

Janie, her cold red hands wrapped around a mug of tea, said, "Jack Peifer, master of prostitutes."

"Correct. Now stay with me. Those prostitutes are a threat to Fred Barker and Alvin Karpis. Why does Jack Peifer care?"

"That's the missing link," said Janie. "He has no reason to care."

"Yes he does. Jack is the master of long range planning. Even back then, Jack was scheming up the Hamm kidnapping. Karpis was the key. Karpis had just hit town and Jack used him for small jobs, and found Karpis impressive. Karpis is smart, for a gangster, and shrewd. Jack wanted Karpis to lead the kidnap gang. Jack foresaw that William Hamm would try to shake free of the underworld once beer was legal. So Jack planned the kidnapping to serve a warning on Hamm. Jack and his friends had been making protection money off the Hamm brewery for years."

Our salads sat cold and untouched. The waitress brought over our lunches on stylish black plates.

"You were right years ago, Janie. It was Jack who called for them at the Hotel Saint Paul on the night they were burned up. His motive was to protect the Barker-Karpis gang. He didn't want to risk using Fred and Karpis for the simple job of eliminating two prostitutes. So he hired Swede and Rico, two dummies he always considered disposable. For all I know, Jack brought Swede up from Chicago for this purpose."

"Peifer delivered those girls to Swede and Rico," Janie said. "I always knew that."

She glanced out the window.

"You know," she said, "I'm not hungry."

"Not the end of the story," I said. "Sadie had a son. He's ten now. Name is Donny. He's currently residing with the man who delivered his mother to her executioners."

"Wait," she said, and pointed a shiny fork at me. "Let me get this straight…"

"I found out from Violet. Jack of course soft soaped it. He told Violet what a shame it was: this desperate Duluth prostitute had been murdered in Saint Paul, and she'd left an orphan back in Duluth. So right after Sadie's murder, Jack had the boy brought down from Duluth and he lived with Jack and Violet for a couple of weeks. Then Shotgun George and his wife Irene arrived for a stay at the Hollyhocks. Probably that visit marked the beginning of the serious planning for the Hamm snatch. Irene was smitten with the boy and she and George took him back to Chicago. Now they're tired of him and they're dumping him back on Jack."

"That's just plain wrong."

She cut into that oozing, steaming lasagna with her fork. Then she pushed her plate away. "I can still smell that awful fire."

"Stays with you, doesn't it?"

"I'm calling Child Welfare."

"The kid will be gone by the time they fill out the paperwork," I said. "Violet doesn't want him around. They'll pawn him off on another gangster. See, the boy is valuable as camouflage. He can make a bunch of gangsters look like a family."

"Then we've got to take him, Powers. You've done dicey things, Powers. Have you ever kidnapped anybody?"

Two blocks from the Hollyhocks is a monster sledding hill. It's a switchback road built to make the steep cliffs of the Mississippi negotiable for cars. But in winter the road is not plowed, and it's a child's delight. Janie and I bought a Flexible Flyer down at Freidrich's Hardware and tied a red bow on it, with a card attached. The card said "For Donny. A Late Gift from Santa." I waited near the windy river bluff while Janie, unknown to the Hollyhocks staff, dropped that sled off on the front porch.

It only took an hour for the boy to cross the boulevard, dragging that wood-and-steel sled on a rope. He was dressed in a shabby adult's coat that dragged on the ground, and, I guessed, had been abandoned in the nightclub's cloakroom. As Janie and I watched from my idling Terraplane, Donny shed that coat and lay on the sled, and kicked off for the long, switch-backed ride to the river.

Janie got out to stand guard. I drove ten blocks down Cleveland Avenue to a tavern, from which I phoned Billy McAmbly.

By the time I returned to the river road, Donny was out of breath, red faced and talking to Janie. I sat in my car and watched until Billy drove the squad car up and parked. Billy got out of the car in uniform, squatted to talk kindly with the boy. The boy reacted in fear, then reverted to shyness, and then allowed Billy to put the sled in his squad car's trunk. Janie put her arm around the boy, who, warmed by sledding, had shed even his red sweater and was now in t-shirt and rolled-up trousers. I joined them, Donny recognized me and I promised hot chocolate. Billy sounded the siren to the delight of the boy, and off we went, all of us, toward the McAmbly home.

"Maureen!" Billy shouted as he bulled through the back door.

You'd have thought the McAmblys had a maid, that's how neat the kitchen looked. Only a box of Kellogg's Corn Flakes disturbed the perfection of the red-and-white checked table cloth. Dishes stood in the sink drainer like soldiers at attention.

"Maureen," Billy bellowed, "Kevin, Kathleen, Brian, James, Coleen, get down here and meet your cousin."

Donny, overwhelmed by overcoat, steam heat and shyness, leaned into Janie, who put her arms around the boy's shoulders.

Maureen, in housecoat, tipped barefoot down the stairs.

"This is Donny," Billy said, and guided the boy forward with a big, meaty hand. "He's going to be a McAmbly for a while."

Maureen looked at us as if we were all insane.

"Well, look after him," said Billy. "Take his coat. Are you Irish or heathen, Maureen? Get the boy a warm drink and something to eat."

"I got a new sled," said Donny. "Want to see it?"

Janie helped him out of his overcoat. Underneath he wore those absurd, cut-down shirt and trousers.

"Hot chocolate?" asked Maureen.

"That's the spirit," said Billie. "Hospitality. Now you're an Irishwoman." He looked around. "Did everybody else abandon ship?"

Maureen began the sibling litany of who was playing hockey, who was at the movies, who was visiting a friend. Billie half-listened and led us adults into the living room. He shed his coat, draped it on the couch. It had been quite a while since I had seen him home, dressed like this, in full forest-green uniform, with cap, Sam Browne belt, pistol, handcuffs, as he might have looked on his first day of patrol.

"He'll end up in an orphanage," Billy said in a quiet voice, "there's no away around it."

"Better than being dragged around by gangsters," I said, "and dumped whenever he becomes inconvenient."

"How did this boy fall through the cracks in the system?" Janie asked.

"What system?" I said.

"Child welfare," she said.

"Do you know anybody over there?"

"Aye," said Billy. "A good woman. German but a good woman. Gertrude."

"He'll never know, will he?" whispered Janie. "About what happened to his mother."

"Maybe that's good," I said.

"Gone to Heaven," Billy said. "That's all he needs to know. Just like the children of this house, think of your mother in Heaven, I tell them." He picked up his overcoat. "In the meantime, we've no extra bed but there's this couch. This an Irish house, I tell you, and we may be poor and crowded but we turn away nobody in need."

CHAPTER TWENTY

FRIDAY MORNING

Snelling and University is a busy intersection, but it's miles from downtown Saint Paul and the joints on its corners belong to other gangs. The Boulevards of Paris nightclub operated under the protection of a Jewish mob from Minneapolis. The Green Dragon Café has for years been run by Italian gangsters that were connected to New York City. Parking Rico's repainted Chevy out there would, I hoped, throw suspicion on those gangs, and put the cops off our trail.

I checked to make sure Herb's boys had ground down the car's serial numbers. But even if the cops managed to identify this car, they would find it belonged to a man who's been dead a while, and whose gangster connections are the stuff of vague rumors.

I drove that car up the hill from Herb's, parked it in the lot behind the Boulevards of Paris. I put an envelope marked 1 in the glove compartment, and slipped an envelope marked 2 under the back seat. Even though I'd worn leather gloves most of the time in this car, I wiped everything I'd touched with a rag soaked in Windex.

I rode the streetcar back to downtown, walked a block to the Library. On the second floor I walked deep into the stacks of engineering books. In gloved hands I pulled out a book nobody would borrow in the next hour. I stuck the note in there and memorized the call number. Then I loped across the icy Rice Park and down Saint Peter Street to Ace Billiards. From a phone booth in the dark quiet recess near the men's room, I dialed the Alt mansion and demanded to speak to the old man.

"Mister Alt is not available," said the male voice. "You can speak to me."

"Blackstone," I said. "Put Papa Alt on this phone."

"He can't come to the phone, he is too ill right now."

"Who am I speaking to?"

"Stockwell. I speak for Otto Alt."

"All right Stockwell, listen up. There's a book in the library with your instructions. It is the Engineer's Manual of English by W.O. Shepherd. Dewey number six two one point eight. Follow the instructions exactly and the kid will be free by this evening."

I hung up.

I immediately dialed back.

"The downtown Saint Paul library," I said.

I hung up and walked, head down, out onto the street of bawdy houses and taverns, quiet at this respectable hour.

My next move was across the street and up the stairway to room 914 in the Hotel Saint Paul.

"Powers," said George, blocking my entrance. "Is something wrong? I was hoping to never see you again."

I barged in.

"Front row seat," I said.

He was wearing a deep blue cardigan sweater over a white shirt, khaki trousers and black leather slippers. He could have passed for a professor of philosophy or literature. I pushed past him to the window and looked down.

Rice Park was below me. The Alt's River State Bank was across the street and on the west, or far side, of the Federal Building. The Library was on the south side of the park, to my left. I brought my racetrack binoculars out of my overcoat, slipped off the black leather case. I could smell the cigarettes on George as he came up behind me.

"We'll see the whole thing," I said.

"This is your scheme, Powers, and I hope for your sake it works."

He lay a patrician hand on my shoulder, middle finger occupied by a gold-and-ruby ring from the University of Illinois.

"There simply won't be another chance," he said.

"Couple of minutes," I said, and fetched the desk chair, shoved it in front of the window, and sat to watch. I kept my back turned to George, and more or less shut him out of my existence.

I worked my Dublin bent pipe in my hand, as if it were a giant key to all the vaults containing all the mysteries. My breathing was shallow, my throat tight, mouth dry, and I became aware of a pulsing headache. The Alt mansion was, at most, a five minute drive from the Library. I pulled out my pocket watch and set it on the window sill and watched the second hand move. It was Dad's watch, time and numbers had been his life. A railroad man's prize possession was a good watch, and for my old man it had kept time to a decent life. He had lived and died in honor and obscurity. What would he think of his only son now, a rum runner turned killer and kidnapper? I hoped there was no afterlife, so I would never have to explain to him in shame how I had got caught up in something so twisted and so wrong.

Five minutes went by, then a sixth, then a seventh. I saw my own reflection in the window, a worried soul, a dark soul, a man with only two fates now, Alcatraz or Cuba.

A black Lincoln pulled up in front of the Library and two men in overcoats got out. I watched through binoculars but their backs were turned to me. The one in the white hat might have been Andrew Stockwell. The hatless man in the dark coat was definitely Father Mack.

Up the broad steps they walked and through the heavy doors.

"There they go, into the library," I said over my shoulder.

George, lying on the gold-brocaded divan, was wearing spectacles and reading a book.

"Splendid," he muttered.

"The priest and Papa Alt's man Friday."

"Splendid prose," George said. "You simply must read it."

I turned back to look across the bare trees of the park to the Library's door.

"Are you a literary man at all, Powers?"

"No."

"Shame," said George. "You're missing out on an entire ..."

"Shut up," I said. "Please shut up, I can't stand it."

George slapped the book closed. The cover said: *Lost Horizon*. He sat up, shook out a Camel, slipped it into an ivory holder, put that in his lips, fired it with a golden lighter. I simply stared at him.

"My good man, you're under a great deal of stress," he said, and blew smoke. He rose, disappeared into the bathroom, and returned with a glass of water. He handed me a tiny blue pill.

"Calms the nerves," he said. "My doctor prescribes it."

"No thanks," I said.

"Powers, you're the very vision of a nervous wreck. There are a great many situations, believe me, where even a steady man can use an assist from modern pharmacology."

I put the blue pill on the window sill, drank the water, turned from George and watched the library, intent.

"If there are any coppers tailing them, we'll see it from here," I
said.

"There's no shame in taking prescribed medicine, Powers, we're
in a nerve-wracking profession."

"Yes, I know, the communications business."

"I believe I'm being mocked," George said, "and I will write
that off to your anxiety attack. Which you could alleviate, but
stubbornly choose not to."

Andrew and Father Mack hustled down the library steps and
around the far end of Rice Park. They crossed in front of the
Opera House and the Wilder Charity Building and slipped behind
the Federal Building and into the double glass doors of the River
State Bank.

I watched through binoculars, swinging the view from bank to
Federal Building.

"They are good men," I said. "They are not followed."

I put down the binoculars.

"It's going to work like a charm," I said.

I felt proud of myself, even though this was a dark and shameful
operation. I was going to pull it off smooth. I was going to get rid
of the Barkers, save Myrtle from the brutish Lapland Willie, free
Ricky Alt, save my dogs, deliver Sadie's son from gangland, all in
one clever afternoon. As a bonus, all of this was happening within
sight of the baffled G-men. I was feeling pretty proud of myself for
maybe a full minute, but then noticed a couple of fellows gathered
at the doors of Papa Alt's bank.

I looked back at George, who was gently snoring, *The Lost
Horizon* on his chest.

Across the park, I watched in horror as that gathering of a few
men at the bank's doors began to swell. A couple of curious
secretaries drifted over from the Wilder Charity Building. A group
of schoolboys leaped off a streetcar and stood peering into the big

windows. A newspaper photographer showed up, huge camera slung around his neck by a leather strap. I put down the binoculars, turned my head and said:

"George? Trouble."

I realized then he was in a doped-up, half drunk sleep. I turned my attention back to the street, via binoculars.

A cop on a horse trotted over to the crowd, and people were streaming out of their offices now, most not even bothering to put on a coat. I saw Post Office workers in shirt-sleeves, vagrants, shop clerks, prostitutes, daytime drinkers, housewives, and now a taxi pulled up and disgorged a gaggle of newshounds, including a man who began setting up a newsreel camera. The crowd spilled into the street, blocking a streetcar, whose passengers streamed out to see what was going on. People parked their cars at odd angles and leaped out to join the crowd. Janie, strawberry locks under a red beret, rushed past the Federal Building, notebook in hand. A police car pulled up and out of it got Chief Dahill and Lieutenant Tierney, both in plainclothes. Down the steps of the Federal Building ran Agent Roland Heater and four of his Washington G-men, and they pushed their way through the crowd.

The ransom was being moved and everybody in town wanted to see it, maybe to have a story to tell their grandchildren.

"Complete and utter disaster," I muttered, and with a slug of cognac, swallowed George's blue pill.

What could I do now that this had turned into a circus?

I shook George awake, led him groggy to the window.

"Look at this madhouse," I said.

George yawned.

Down on the street, a Saint Paul cop maneuvered Father Mack's Plymouth as close as he could to the bank's front doors. The cop on horseback tried to drive people away from that car, but the crowd was like an oil slick, reforming as the horse moved around.

A paddy wagon, lights flashing, arrived at the edge of the crowd and spilled out green-uniformed cops. They bulled through the crowd and into the bank. Even nine stories up and a block away, I could hear through closed windows the angry honks of blocked truck and car drivers.

Out of the bank burst Andrew Stockwell and Father Mack, each carrying a straw suitcase to the priest's Plymouth. The crowd was swirling crazy now, cops clearing the way for that Plymouth, and it crept through the crowd with Saint Paul police and the G-men following in a whole procession of cars.

"Quite the spectacle," said George, yawning.

"Maybe," I said. "Maybe the cops will let them go once they get to Snelling and University to switch cars. There's no way to be sure now. We've got to play it, George. We've got to give the money carriers a chance to shake the cops. Call your man. Give him the go."

"I suppose you're right, Powers," George said. He picked up at the telephone, dialed, let it ring three times. Then consulting his gold wrist watch, he waited exactly a minute, rang another three times, and hung up.

"You are correct, we have no choice but to send the man," George said. "We can't have the suitcases arriving in the cornfields without our liaison there."

He stared out the window as if he were just waking up.

"Don't worry," he said, "our man will be able to see if the priest is followed."

He clapped me on the shoulder. "Thanks to your clever scheme, Powers."

He settled down and picked up the book. "Absolutely splendid work of literature."

His cigarette had gone out, and burned a dark spot into the mahogany coffee table. He picked up the holder, examined it as if the cigarette might be a small, wounded animal, and then lit it again with his gold lighter.

He lay back and covered himself with the hotel's purple bathrobe.

"In a few hours," he said, "we'll all be home free."

But it wasn't just the cops tailing the ransom. It seemed that half the citizens of Saint Paul leaped into their cars and made something of a rolling parade that turned down Saint Peter Street, passing all the gin joints, bawdy houses and billiard parlors on the way to University Avenue. A guy driving an ice truck joined the parade, as did a plumber's van and two ladies in a taxi. As far as I was concerned, this parade of fools was marching toward Alcatraz.

George's lips fluttered in a gentle snore as I paced the plush red rug, thinking, scheming, envisioning every form of disaster: plane crashes, train wrecks, buses falling off steep cliffs, cars rolling into ditches. I wandered dazed into the gleaming bathroom and faced myself in the mirror and said aloud: "My God, what am I going to do?"

I threw my overcoat on, ran out of the room and down the stairs, pounded down the slippery Fifth Street four blocks to the ornate Saint Francis Hotel. Its ground floor was rented by storefront businesses and agencies, and I stood at a travel agent's window, mesmerized by a huge color poster that said HAVANA. It depicted a relaxed pipe-smoking gentleman, a passenger in an airplane that was circling Morro Castle, looking down on a lovely tropical city.

I walked in.

"How much?" I said to the woman at the sales desk. I leaned in, a maniac, so close she pushed her chair back.

"To Havana," I said.

"For one person?"

Without waiting for her answer, I pushed out the door and into the nasty cold of a Saint Paul January. Making a fool of myself now, in my panic. I rushed through the revolving doors of the Saint Francis, across the brass and mahogany lobby, and toward the sign that said: PUBLIC PHONES.

I dialed the Alt Mansion.

"It's Blackstone," I said. "I'll wait for the cop to hang up."

"You are speaking with Doctor Koenig."

"Okay, doctor, I want whatever cops are listening to hang up. And then I want you to put Papa Alt on this phone, I don't care how sick he is. If he isn't on this phone in thirty seconds, you'll never see Ricky again."

"But..."

"Now, doctor! You've wasted ten seconds."

There was a fumbling noise and many many awful seconds later Papa Alt said into the phone a weak: "Hello."

I realized with a jolt of panic that he might recognize my voice, but it was too late to back out now.

"Mister Alt," I said, "I apologize." Even to myself, I sounded like a bumbler. "I don't want to cause you any more pain sir, but we must get this thing delivered now. The priest and the money are now being tailed by a whole procession of onlookers. He will not be able to make the transfer and leave as planned. I assume he will bring the money back to the bank. When he does, here's what I propose. Mr. Alt?"

"Yes?"

"Are you listening?"

"Of course I am listening."

"When Father Mack and Mister Stockwell return with the money, have them stay in the bank a few minutes, and then have them get into a Yellow Cab. They should make a show of putting those suitcases into the cab. The suitcases should be empty. Let

Stockwell and the priest form a decoy procession, and let them head east, with all onlookers following. Once the decoy leaves town, have your head teller drive the money out to the blue Chevy, license plate 62113, parked behind the Boulevards of Paris."

"Yes."

"Have him put the money in the car, which will be unlocked. We will be watching. If there are no police, we will take it from there."

"Mister Blackstone," said Papa Alt. "If my son is returned unharmed, I will consider this a fair exchange. The police will pursue you, but they will get no cooperation from the Alt family. But if Richard is not returned in health, I will use every resource at my command to hound you and your friends until you are dead or in prison. Is that clear?"

"Your son is fine. He's playing cards with us. He's eating well, enjoying the occasional glass of Altwasser. All will be well if the ransom is delivered and the cops are held back."

"I hope for all our sakes you are telling me the truth."

"Get the cash out there, as soon as you can, and we'll free Ricky."

I hung up. Using my ski mask, I wiped the phone clear of fingerprints, I hoped. I knew the cops had tapped the phones of everyone connected to the Alts, and in my swollen imagination I imagined a phalanx of G-men waiting for me in the lobby.

But out there was only the usual collection of sharply-dressed salesmen, loose women, bellhops, layabouts and touts. I pushed through the revolving doors and out into winter.

I bought a newspaper and hopped a streetcar and as it rounded the Loop I caught one piece of luck: the ransom procession led by Father Mack's Plymouth had already given up and returned to the bank, followed by its motorized entourage of gawkers. They could not have possibly gotten as far as University and Snelling. Father

Mack, or maybe Chief Dahill, had realized the hopelessness of their enterprise and turned back.

I needed that luck of timing, since I would have nowhere to hide out at Snelling and University. It was warm enough on that streetcar that I couldn't use my ski mask without arousing suspicion, so I put the newspaper up to my face, tipped my fedora low and read the sports pages with zero comprehension.

Just as we entered the Selby Tunnel, and went from bright sunshine to flickering lamps, I was stunned to see a familiar woman approach me. It was my former landlady, Mrs. Holy Reardon. She was a skinny, wiry, tough old bird with curly gray hair wrapped up in a kerchief depicting the Vatican. Her unfocused eyes always seemed to look in two directions at once. But one of them beamed at me.

"Mister Powers," she said. "What brings you back to town?"

I choked out some gibberish that only sounded half-human.

"May I sit down?"

I squeezed next to the frosty window as the streetcar lurched back into daylight.

Mrs. Reardon, dressed in a light jacket and dark skirt, sat next to me. She carried a blue empty shopping bag made of twisted strands of some hairy fiber. Outside her jacket flapped a scapula, dangling a holy picture too tiny for me to make out. She saw me staring at it.

"Saint Benedict," she said, and fingered the scapula. "Protection from hoodlums."

I folded the newspaper, resigned to conversation.

"Well, you've come back to a town that is all agog," she said, and blessed herself as the streetcar lurched past the Cathedral.

"Weren't you raised Catholic?" she said. "With a name like Powers?"

I blessed myself, Father, Son, Holy Ghost.

"Oh, when Mister J. Edgar Hoover gets hold of those kidnappers," she twisted her lipsticked lips into a pucker. "I feel sorry for them."

"How is Mister Reardon doing?" I asked.

"He is making his Novenas, preparing for the end," she said.

"Oh," I said, "I didn't realize he was sick. Sorry."

"He's quite well. Mister Powers, every one of us is a creature of Heaven, on loan to the Devil during our time on Earth. We should welcome our approaching death, because that's when we return to our true home."

She looked around as if hoping the other passengers would acclaim her philosophy.

"Let me pray for you, Mister Powers," she said. "I sense that you need prayer."

I did. We held hands glove to glove as Mrs. Reardon muttered, chapped lips working, closed eyelids fluttering.

We passed along Selby-Western, and all its busy storefronts, where the Colored and White neighborhoods intersected like a jigsaw puzzle. Mrs. Reardon let go of my hand. The conductor, in slovenly dark blue uniform, stuck his hand out for our nickels and issued tickets. An elderly Colored lady in a lovely flowered hat alighted. She was bent over with flowing gray hair and I seized the moment. I, Saint Paul's most gallant gentleman, excused my way past Mrs. Reardon and offered the lady my seat. The old woman looked at me with wet, rheumy eyes, the pain of life in them, thanked me and sat with Mrs. Reardon.

I strap-hung on that lurching streetcar all the way down University, past the car dealers and chicken shacks, the pawn shops and taverns. When Mrs. Reardon got off at Snelling, I tipped my hat to her. A block later, I got off through the back door.

Perhaps Mrs. Reardon was right, and we are all tools of the Devil. I certainly felt that way slinking past the Bloomenfeld

Butcher, hams hanging in strings at the windows. I dared not stop in any of the taverns or cafes, so I walked, slouched and miserable, around and around the block, as if I were window shopping. I could see the Chevy from almost any vantage pint, looking lonesome in a parking lot that was only jammed at night. Two squad cars roared by, their sirens jangling my nerves. My feet and hands grew so cold they no longer felt part of me. No good outcome seemed even remotely possible. Half the time I was convinced the cops would pounce on me once I got into the blue Chevy, and would beat me until I revealed all I knew. The other half the time, I reassured myself the police pressure wouldn't start until after Ricky was freed.

I prowled the aisles at Essenmeyers, looking at the wilted winter vegetables, and wondered where the hell they grew Iceberg lettuce. On an iceberg? I filled a shopping basket just to look normal, took my time doing so, a view of that blue Chevy out the grocers' big picture windows. After I could stall no longer, I abandoned that basket in an alcove leading to the manager's office, and, a bit warmer, slipped back out to the street.

Hands in my pockets, breath condensing in the crisp air, I stood as if waiting for the streetcar. After maybe five minutes a Yellow Cab pulled into the Boulevards of Paris lot. I leaned against a streetlamp pole and watched as it stopped at the blue Chevy. Papa Alt had added his own wrinkle, for out of the cab popped not a cabbie, but Andrew Stockwell in white hat and Lieutenant Tierney in brassy uniform. They opened the trunk of the blue Chevy and deposited, I could see it plainly, two large straw suitcases. It made sense the moment I saw it: Papa Alt wasn't going to trust $200,000 to a Saint Paul cabbie. Father Mack, I concluded, was miles from here, leading the decoy parade.

Detective and brewery manager slammed the trunk shut, hopped back into the taxi and it roared off.

I watched it go down Snelling until it disappeared just past Rondo Street.

I could hear Myrtle's voice in my head: *You're not yellow, are you Mick? You never was a coward.*

If I wasn't a coward, I sure felt like one. I willed myself to cross the street, looking away from the traffic cop who worked the intersection with white glove and whistle. Did he know or didn't he? Was he a G-man in Saint Paul cop's clothing?

I sauntered down an alley of dirty snow and sagging garages. I kept that blue Chevy in sight. I turned the corner and came up behind it. The lot was frozen mud, the snow plowed into hills, and I passed behind casual, sure I would see G-men lurking. No. A middle-aged Chinese cook dressed in white stood, smoking a cigar, at the back door of the Green Dragon across the alley. As far as I knew the G-men had no Chinese agents.

Head down I walked up University, feeling a surge of, well, I had once been shocked by an electric toaster and that's what it felt like, raw and unpleasant, but that feeling propelled me toward the blue Chevy. I ripped open the door, sat behind the wheel, and my hand went into the door pocket.

No key.

I looked around in panic. The bastards had trapped me, Tierney must have palmed the key, and here I was sitting, dead duck, I opened the door, ran in blind panic down University and stopped only when I was out of breath, looked back and saw that Chevy, nobody near it, driver's door hanging open.

I looked around, expecting to see people at their living room windows, pointing and laughing at me, a fool on his way to prison. I caught my breath and my courage and marched back to that blue Chevy, sat in its cold seat, removed my gloves and searched thoroughly in the pocket and this time found a tiny frozen slip of metal, the key.

The car's windows were already frosted over. I let out the choke and started the engine. With red-bare hands I attacked the frost on the windows as the engine sputtered, making cold, ugly sounds.

Greed began to sing its enticing song. *Two hundred thousand dollars, Mick.*

The engine stalled and I started it again.

Fear answered.

But the dogs. Doc Barker will kill Snowflake and Hula Girl.

I began to hatch an elaborate and stupid scheme to lure the Barker gang out of the cottage and then rescue the dogs, free Ricky Alt, and abscond with all the money. That fantasy lasted only as long as it took for me to move the gearshift into first gear.

I eased the Chevy out of the lot. No panic driving, I told myself, no getting pulled over by the police. At University and Snelling, the traffic cop held up a white-gloved hand that seemed the size of a catcher's mitt. I stopped the car. I fed the engine just a little gas, eased the choke in a nudge. *Don't stall, don't stall, don't stall.* The traffic cop waved that mitt, and I was off, down University, reminding the Holy Ghost that I had recently paid him tribute and that this would be the worst possible time for a flat tire.

I drove a route that kept me well north of Downtown and hooked up with Route 12 on the east side of the city, just past the Hamm's Brewery. I looked in the mirror as much as I looked forward, but if anyone was following me, it wasn't obvious. Two miles short of the river that divides Wisconsin from Minnesota, I pulled into the parking lot of hamburger stand, watched the traffic go by, and the aroma of grilling meat got to me. I said to myself: *Why not? You're a dead man anyway.*

I ate a hamburger and fries and drank a root-beer at a red-painted counter facing the frosty window. The hamburger stand was surrounded by frozen prairie, and no tail car could have been hiding anywhere close by. My back was turned to the dining room, where farmers and truck drivers grumbled about the weather. A red van pulled in that said ARROW DELIVERY in gold letters on its side. Here it is, I told myself, a truck full of G-men. But out of it popped a uniformed man and maybe his son, hustling toward warmth and food, and they brushed behind me shouting to the burger cook.

"They let the ransom go," said the driver.

"We was just downtown," said the helper. "It's a madhouse. Cops going crazy."

"You don't say," said the cook.

"Bunch of lunatics," said the driver.

"It's like a riot," said the helper.

"People all over the street," said the driver. "You know who's got the ransom now? You wouldn't believe it. Catholic priest!"

"He's in on it," said the helper. "I'll give you two to one."

"Aw go on," said the driver.

"Make mine well done," said the helper. "If there's one thing I hate it's bloody meat."

They ordered and moved around the corner to the pickup window, their exclamations reduced to muttering.

As I balled up my greasy wax paper wrapper, the driver walked to the end of the counter to grab an ashtray.

"They wouldn't try this stuff in Illinois," he said. "They got the electric chair down there. They know how to deal with these scum."

That statement was a revelation. Now I knew in full why the Barker-Karpis gang had chosen my place for a hideout. If the job went wrong and they ended killing people, Wisconsin had long ago abolished the death penalty.

I walked out of that burger stand with renewed confidence. No Sherlock could possibly follow me for four hours down a lonesome highway without me noticing. No police agency had any interest in preventing the ransom delivery. By the time I stopped for gas, I was whistling along with a movie tune playing on the radio.

Who's Afraid of the Big Bad Wolf, the Big Bad Wolf ...

Fueled and fed, I opened the trunk just for a reassuring peek at the suitcases. I drove across the Saint Croix and cruised up the hill into Wisconsin. I checked the rearview, but not so often. Thanks to Herb's Garage, I had a new spare tire, a toolbox, and gallon of antifreeze. I veered north through the town of Amery, where I pulled over to watch traffic go by, nothing suspicious behind me. I did the same in the parking lot of a café in the resort town of Turtle Lake.

An hour or so into Wisconsin, I began to imagine the perfect ending: Ricky Alt back in his bank, pulling his deals and swindles. Papa Alt brewing up a fortune, this $200,000 barely a hiccup. Lapland Willie Weaver would flee Saint Paul, probably tonight, leaving Myrtle safe. Shotgun George would take the train for Chicago, where the Barker Gang and their women would reunite. Doc would gamble his share away. Fred would spend his dough trying to impress women with extravagant gifts. Karpis would bury his money, for he talked about having a son someday, who would go to college and live straight.

That left me and the dogs. I would shut down Cindy's cabin, drive to Key West, and wait for my sister to wire the money from the sale of Aunt Doris' burned-over farm. I would phone Myrtle and invite her to the warm life. I expected rejection. So then it would be me and the dogs, a new life in Havana. Would the G-men ever round up the Barker Gang? I didn't know, but they hadn't been very good at it so far.

I drove through Barron, a town where they slaughtered a thousand turkeys a day. The radio, which had lost the Saint Paul station, picked up some scratchy Wisconsin broadcast, Mae West singing: *I Like a Man What Takes His Time.*

It was an hour to Ladysmith and another gas up, and an hour more to Minoqua, a lakeside town mobbed with Chicago tourists in summer but deserted in January. The sun was dropping big and bold behind the pine trees when I stopped in Minoqua for coffee and donuts. It was only then that I began to worry about Lapland Willie.

With everything else going on, and maybe because I had taken George's dopey blue pill, I hadn't realized that Weaver would be out in the prairies waiting for a ransom that would never arrive. Weaver had no way of knowing I was delivering the ransom. He would be calling the Eagle River tavern tonight at five, and would give the code red. Doc Barker would finish his beer, return to the cabin, and Ricky Alt would be a dead man.

It was quarter to five. My cabin was 45 minutes away. I leaped into the car and drove like a madman down Route 70, raced down Sunset Road.

By the time I turned into Cindy's driveway, it was full dark, a startled doe staring back at my headlights.

I slipped and slid that car through the ruts and down the hill, my headlights illuminating the cabin.

No lights were on.

No smoke wafted from the chimney.

The Pontiac was gone

No dogs barked.

When I killed my engine it was utter, dark silence.

I opened the front door, weak kneed. I flicked on the light, expecting to see the corpse of Ricky Alt on the floor. But all I saw was a hellacious mess left by four sloppy men. I pushed into the kitchen, the three bedrooms, I was about the check the basement when first Hula Girl, then Snowflake bounded in through the front door, panting like they had run for miles.

I squatted and petted them and talked softly to them and rubbed their cold bodies. How long they had been in the woods, I didn't know. Can a dog's eyes be desperate? It seemed so to me. I shut the front door, the house was losing what little heat it had. I opened the icebox, ripped off some venison sausage links, threw them into a cast iron pan. The stove was warm. The gang had left not long ago.

I checked my Dad's watch. It was thirteen minutes to six. If Doc had got the code red at five, he would have been back here a half hour ago. Ricky could be already dead and lying in the woods.

I led the dogs down into the basement, half expecting to find a body there. I stoked the furnace, climbed the stairs and fed the dogs venison.

Now what? With the heat rattling the radiators, I sat down at the kitchen table, opened a bottle of Altwasser as the dogs wrapped themselves up at my feet. I had $200,000 in the trunk. I did a quick calculation and came up with the figure 300 years. This was 300 years pay for a working guy like my brother-in-law Gary. Six working lifetimes worth of cash.

Unmarked.

Small denominations.

I would never have to work again, I would never be anyone's messenger boy, I would be free of these murderous, manipulating monsters. I began to envision that beach house in Cuba. Modest, but right next to the ocean. If Myrtle refused to come down, Cuba was known for its charming women.

I drank that beer. Altwasser. Founding brew of a dark and criminal fortune. They were all criminals, weren't they, the rich? And now I was about to join them. A rich criminal living in luxurious, tropical exile.

The code red had been sent and Ricky, I was pretty sure, was already dead. The Barker gang might come hunting for me, but they'd never betray me to the cops. I would live in Cuba under another name, in a small home far from Havana.

I could feel the warmth of Cuba, or was that the coal heat piped up from the basement?

"Dogs," I said, "we are about to go on a scary adventure."

I was in the basement rummaging through boxes of summer clothes when I heard a car's engine rumble in the quiet dark woods. I ran upstairs and gawked out the parlor windows, lightning bolts of fear lighting up my brain. The dogs went into a howling barking frenzy. Headlights flashed through the woods.

A long dark sedan stopped just behind the Chevy. I imagined the sheriff but the fellow who got out looked like a banker, tall, dressed in a tweed overcoat, a dark fedora, and calf length boots. He left the engine running and headlights blazing as he, alone, approached the porch.

I stepped out to greet him and locked the barking dogs in.

At the bottom of the stairs he said: "Would you be Michael Powers?"

He was a guy in his fifties with the saggy face of a kindly insurance salesman.

"You are?" I said.

"Oglethorpe. Jim Oglethorpe, your new neighbor."

I shook his leather gloved hand.

"Just closed the deal," he said. "Thought I'd say hello."

"Hello," I said. I had not even begun to recover from my attack of nerves and could barely squeak that word out.

"My wife Daisy, in the car."

Someone waved a white glove at me from inside that sedan.

"I'd be interested in purchasing this place too, if your cousin wants to sell someday."

"Sure," I said.

"Now's the time to buy property," he said. "Say, did I hear gunshots a while ago? That wasn't you at target practice, was it?"

"No," I said.

"Well, it sounded like machine gun fire."

I gulped.

"Probably came from across the lake," he said. "You know how sound travels. Well, Mister Powers. Just thought to say hello. We'll be out in spring, we're going to put up a cabin in that meadow near the road. You know."

"Right," I said.

"I did see a few roughnecks around here yesterday. Do you worry much about vandals and break ins?"

"No never," I said.

"Well, nice meeting you," he said, and got back in the car, reversed it, and drove it up the snowy hill.

The dogs leaped all over me when I opened the door. I pushed them away and gave them a serious talking to.

"The banker is dead," I said.

I walked into the kitchen and stood staring at I don't know what.

"Ricky Alt is dead," I said, with only my dogs as audience. "The bastards have done it."

I washed my hands at the big white porcelain sink, using a harsh bar of Fels Naptha laundry soap, scrubbing under hot water.

"Machine gun fire," I said. "They should have just let him go."

I dried my hands with a rough towel.

"Dogs, we have to skedaddle."

I opened the front door and they ran out.

"I can buy all the clothes I need in Florida," I said.

I locked the door behind me, let the dogs into the car and pushed the starter button. The car, engine still warm, purred as I drove up the hill and approached the intersection of Sunset Road and Highway G. Where would they have dragged the body?

That question began to worry me as I drove toward town. They might have left his body on my property as a form of revenge. That would focus the investigation on me. Cindy and Aunt Doris had between them 160 acres, far too much land for me to search, even in daylight.

I had to know. I was going to pass the Lone Buck tavern anyway.

I drove straight down Railroad Street past the train station and the lights of downtown and pulled into a dark, pine-tree studded lot. The Lone Buck was a log cabin, surrounded by icy, rusty cars and trucks.

Inside it was one long bar and two billiards tables. Deer heads and fish were mounted on the wall, the windows were painted over in red. A few men, dressed in plaid, idled at the bar. Two barrels of beer stood out in the open near the restrooms, steel taps on top.

The bartender was long and lean and had a halo of black hair above a sharp face.

"I'm Mister Redd," I said. "Anybody call for me?"

"Who?"

"Mister Redd."

"Hey Barney, you get a call for Mister Redd?"

"Who?"

"Somebody was supposed to call me here at five o'clock. I'm a little late."

"Sorry pal. You want a beer?"

I backed out of there, and sat in my Chevy, let it idle while I lit up a pipe. Did Lapland Willie somehow know that I'd gotten the money? It didn't seem possible. Was Lapland dead? Had some cop pulled him over, found out he was a bail jumper, and put him in the hoosegow? Had he simply lost his nerve? Gotten drunk? Because he should have sent the red code.

I burst back into the bar.

"Give me a beer," I said to the barman.

He set a small glass in front of me and I slid him a dollar.

"Little guy, comes in here, five o'clock every day for the past week," I said.

The barman shrugged.

"He's a stranger in town."

"I don't start until six. Barney, little guy…

"Yeah, I heard," said Barney. He was a hefty man, blonde hair greased and combed straight back, plaid shirt and suspenders.

"Only about five-three," I said. "Red hair, parted in the middle. Maybe you noticed a tattoo or two. Kind of surly."

Barney and Gene looked at one another.

"Southern accent."

"Oh that guy," said Barney. "One beer and out. Drank tomato juice in his beer. Strangest thing I ever saw."

"He in here today?"

"Nope," said Barney.

"Thanks." I drank up, left 95 cents in tip, and went back to the car.

I was maybe two days from Cuba. Every hour I drove toward it, the weather would get kinder. But if I fled with the ransom it would be sure death for Ricky Alt, if by some chance he was alive. And that would be a black mark on my soul for all eternity.

I lit my pipe and prayed to the Holy Ghost for His guidance. I felt that He would only sentence me to Purgatory for Swede and Rico, men who were trying to harm me. But was it was Hell Eternal if I was responsible for the death of Ricky Alt. And the man had a wife, a daughter, sisters and a father. Ricky was a banker, sure, and people hated bankers these days, but he wasn't the worst of them. The Alts weren't the most splendid people in the world, but then again, neither was I. Who was I, Mick Powers, to condemn a man to be murdered by these soulless Barker thugs?

Damn it, if only I knew. Was Ricky dead or alive?

Doc had missed his five o'clock beer. What did that mean? Lapland Willie had not called, what did that mean? Machine gun fire in the woods, what was that? Maybe the gang had given up, shot Ricky, called Lapland Willie and told him to blow town. That was the best I could figure. Maybe this rube Jim Oglethorpe, poking into the property, had spooked the Barker Gang, who mistook him for the sheriff.

But it was nineteen degrees and dropping, and dark, and the Barker Gang had to be somewhere. They could have driven down dark, forested, icy roads in the night, but it wasn't likely. If they hit an icy patch unseen and skidded off the road, that would deliver them into the hands of the sheriff. Most likely they were waiting for dawn. They either broke into a summer cabin or rented at a motor court. Summer cabins had no heat, though. So I decided to check the motor courts for a blue Pontiac.

It didn't take long. There were few motor courts open in winter, and only skiers and ice fishermen to rent them. I drove along Route 70, and the fourth court I passed had exactly one car parked in the lot.

Swede's blue Pontiac.

The bright red sign said VACANCY.

The dark billboard said FRITZ FAMILY MOTOR HOTEL

I drove over a little bridge and parked in the lot of a tavern just across a stream from that cluster of tourist cabins. I sat and smoked and watched.

It was an awful thought, dark, selfish and cruel, a Mortal Sin of a thought. But something wicked in me hoped that Ricky was dead. That would be the simplest, safest and by far most lucrative for me.

If Ricky was still with them, I would turn over the ransom, and if the Barkers didn't kill me on the spot, I'd be a broke criminal on the run.

But if Ricky was dead, I would soon be a wealthy man living in tropical splendor.

I briefly thought of driving back to Saint Paul, turning over the ransom, and telling the whole story to the cops and the press. But given what the cops were like, and what the criminals were like, I figured that would give me a life expectancy of three days. I did not care to meet the fate of Sadie and Rose. How many witnesses had disappeared under Big Ryan's watch? And since he was one of the planners of this fiasco, I could be sure that I would never live to testify in court.

I could think of only one thing to do.

I locked the dogs in the car. I walked over the bridge, hands in my pocket, headed for the one cabin with lights on. I passed Swede's Pontiac and gave it, for some reason, a friendly thump. In gloved hands, I stood under the spotlight and tapped on the door.

It cracked open, then flew open.

"Well I'll be a son of a bitch," said Doc. "Lookity here."

Fred and Karpis were playing cards at a tiny table.

Doc pulled me in rough, and locked the door behind me.

"It's a bum from Saint Paul," said Karpis.

"What do you know?" said Fred.

"Where's our friend?" I asked.

"We got him," said Doc. "Don't you worry."

"I've got some news for you," I said.

"Let us have it then," said Karpis, and twirled a black .45 on the card table.

I hedged my bets. "The Alts are going to come through," I said.

"Too late," said Doc.

"Way too late," said Fred.

"We took care of him," said Doc. "Son of a bitching German beer master."

Karpis pushed his straw hat back on his greasy head.

"We sold him off," said Karpis.

"Highest bidder," said Fred.

"Like a race horse," said Doc.

"He's alive or not?" I asked.

"Oh," said Doc, "the son-of-a-bitch is breathing."

He jerked his thumb.

"Over there next door."

"We gave him something to kill the pain," said Karpis.

"The pain of life," said Fred. "He's sleeping."

I asked: "What do you mean you sold him off?"

Karpis folded his cards, stood up and stretched. No more hunting outfits for him, he was dressed in a suit that would have looked swell on Michigan Avenue. He said: "You don't want to know, Powers, you'll get your cut. Won't be as much. But you'll get it. Fred's a man of his word."

"Unlike Papa Alt," said Fred. He lit a cigarette and blinked away the smoke.

I sat down in a cheap chair someone had knocked together from raw pine limbs. A picture on the wall, of a deer in a forest, hung crooked over Fred's head. I wanted to straighten it. It bothered me somehow.

Fred took a slug of whiskey out of a silver flask.

"We get $50,000," said Fred. "Gang in Chicago's driving up to get him. Let them deal with Papa Alt."

I said: "What does this mean, you sold him off?"

"We sold the rights," said Karpis. "Think of it that way. These Chicago boys will take the risk, they'll scare the $200,000 out of the Alts. The $50,000 is our commission. We might do it this way from now on, snatch and sell to the highest bidder. Makes sense."

He tapped out a Chesterfield.

"The son of a bitch is going to shit a brick when we hand him over," said Doc.

"It's the fault of that cheapskate old man," said Fred.

"See these Chicago boys, they got no scruples," said Doc.

"They ain't like us," said Fred. "We was raised to Christian hymns."

"They'll cut this boy's finger off and send it in the mail," said Doc. "That'll light a fire under Papa Alt's skinny ass."

"No maiming," said Karpis. "Not us. We kill a man or leave him whole."

Fred laughed, his gold teeth leaking smoke.

"Ray's squeamish."

"So the Chicago boys…" I started.

"They'll mail body parts until they get the money," Doc said.

Everything I'd ever dreamed of evaporated in that moment. My ten happy years with Peggy, my Saint Paul penthouse, my love life with Myrtle, my beautiful friend Janie and her happy baby, my career as a rum runner and gangland messenger, and finally my dream of Cuba, of opulence, of warmth and freedom. All of it rose like smoke from a trash fire and disappeared in a whirlwind leaving an ominous dark sky.

My eyes leaked tears. In front of the baddest gangsters alive, I began first to cry and then to sob into my hands.

Doc laughed.

Fred kicked back in his chair, a look of sheer amusement on his face.

Karpis said, "Somebody get this guy a towel."

"I'll be a son of a bitch," said Doc. "Crybaby gangster. What's the matter kid, did somebody take away your tommygun?"

I stood up, grabbed my overcoat, walked out the door and slammed it behind me. Doc Barker in sleeveless t-shirt came running up behind.

"You shut my dogs out," I said. "Asshole. They could have frozen to death."

He held a pistol at waist level, ran around in front of me.

"Some tall son a bitch came nosing around the cabin," Doc said. "We was seen. It was time to leave."

I expected to be shot. I no longer cared. The money would sit in my car until the sheriff discovered it. Ricky Alt would join me in Hell. This gang of thugs would be staring through iron bars for the next thirty years.

"Out of my way," I said, and Doc Barker, oddly enough, stepped aside. I suppose he didn't want to shoot me and attract attention before the $50,000 deal went down. He watched me go. I crossed the bridge and with him glaring at me across the river, I made a decoy move and entered the tavern.

I drank a beer. Doc walked back to the lit cabin. As soon as he was inside, I sprinted for the Chevy. My dogs seemed squirrely, as if they had picked up all this tension. I petted them calm. We'll soon be out of it, I told them.

I opened the trunk and grabbed the suitcase handles, one in each hand.

I crossed the bridge lugging those suitcases.

Underneath the spotlight again, I kicked the cabin door.

Fred opened it. He didn't see the suitcases at first.

"Let the crybaby in," shouted Doc.

I burst in and threw the suitcases on the narrow iron bed.

"What the damn hell is that?" said Fred.

"Open it."

But Karpis was on it first. Doc behind him used a bowie knife to cut the ropes. Karpis snapped open one suitcase. Fred the other. They opened to deep piles of banded green cash.

"I'll be a son of a bitch," said Doc. "We done it."

Karpis turned and looked at me, the first emotion I'd ever seen in those lizard eyes.

"All of it?" Karpis asked.

"Every dollar," I said.

Fred ran his hands through the money.

Doc picked up a band of bills and riffed through it.

Fred began counting the bundles out of the suitcase.

Doc poured whiskey all around, into water-glasses and coffee cups. "Ma's right," he said as a toast, "there is a Jesus watching over us all."

There was a lot of business after that, but I left it all to them. They had to somehow find Lapland Willie and George and tell them to scatter. I declined to be their messenger. They told me I'd get my split after they laundered the money in Chicago, and I should look them up by asking at Louis Cernocky's tavern. I said I would. But I had no intention of spending another moment with these murderous creeps.

I assumed they would free Ricky, but I had done my part, had given up a fortune that had been in my grasp, and all I wanted to do was run out of that cabin. After one drink with the gang, a lot of backslapping and insincere promises, I slipped out and hustled for the Chevy. I drove it deep into the woods off Sunset Road. I burned the ransom notes. Tried to wipe the car's surfaces clean of fingerprints. Maybe ten months from how, some deer hunter would come across this car.

My dogs and I walked to Cindy's cabin through the woods, and it took us nearly an exhausting hour. When I got home I lit a huge fire in the fireplace, fed the dogs the last of the venison, and fell into a deep, satisfying sleep.

In the morning I took a taxi to the train station, where I had to rent a couple of dog kennels from the agent, as the dogs could travel only as freight in the mail car. It took all day and three transfers, but I finally did get us back to Saint Paul.

I phoned Myrtle, knocked at her door, no answer either way, and Loretta wasn't home either. The purchase of Doris' farm had not cleared yet, so I begged a $100 advance from my sister Kelly, which she'd deduct when she wired me the money after Aunt Doris' will cleared probate.

Saint Paul's afternoon papers ran page-high headlines.

ALT FREE!
RANSOM PAID

At a drugstore across from Myrtle's apartment, I bought copies of the *Dispatch* and the *Daily News*. Neither newspaper named any suspects. I drove home, packed a suitcase full of clothes, put my dogs in the back seat and headed down Highway 61, intending to drive until my tires touched salt water.

CHAPTER TWENTY ONE

HAVANA

Three days after we left Saint Paul, the dogs and I arrived in
Havana on the S.S. Cuba, a six-hour float from Key West. I rented
a hotel room near the harbor. Expecting to find a revolution in
progress, I found a Depression instead.

I should have been tipped off by the ferry ride, because the S.S.
Cuba was not even half loaded when it left Key West. Havana
hotels were mostly empty. A *Norteamericano* and *dos perros* looking
for an apartment had plenty to choose from, at bargain prices.

I rented a three-room second floor apartment on a street named
O'Reilly. The apartment came equipped with stodgy Conquistador
furniture, a bed big enough for a king, queen and retainers, huge
windows and a balcony with views of the harbor. My landlords,
Senor and Senora Oliva, spoke good English and offered to
acquaint me with the city. They too were dog people and doted on
their tribe of Dachshunds.

They may have been sister cities in corruption, but otherwise,
Havana and Saint Paul could hardly have been more different.
Outside the bawdy districts, Saint Paul, especially in the cold
months, was quiet. Havana was hot, humid and noisy everywhere.
During a Saint Paul winter, you might not see your neighbor for

three months. In Havana, your neighbors swarmed the streets, visiting each other, drinking, smoking, walking arm-in-arm, selling vegetables, cigars and sodas, stopping for gossip. Musicians played on street-corners, and radios and record players blared from every apartment. For the first night I was annoyed by my neighbors, but that was just Saint Paul wearing off me. On the second night I began to accept street music as a fact of Havana life, and fell asleep to its rhythms.

The next morning I walked Obispo, the crowded narrow shopping street, and at Western Union, wired my sister Kelly so she'd know where to send my $900 inheritance. I wrote Myrtle a post card in plus-5 code.

ANXNY UTBJWX 050 TWJNQQD MFAFSF

VISIT POWERS 505 O'REILLY HAVANA

At a panaderia I made a breakfast of potato empenadas and the darkest, most delicious coffee, which Cubans insist on serving with cream and sugar. I paid twenty cents American for a Montecristo cigar from a wizened old toothless man, and lit it up while walking back home. It was a heady smoke, almost dopey, and I told myself I might become a cigar man.

I leashed Snowflake and Hula Girl, and walked them toward the sea. An urban square called Plaza De Armas was crowded with vendors and patrolled by menacing soldiers. The dogs and I kept going toward the Malecon. I talked to an old man who was dressed in splendid but threadbare white jacket. He wanted to practice his English. He had dreams of visiting New York City, where his younger brother lived.

The dogs and I walked the Malecon, where crashing waves sent up spray and created puddles of sea water. Cars roared by, leaving a

stinky exhaust that settled in among many smells: Sewage, tropical
flowers, cigars, grilled meat.

I turned off to a palm-shaded boulevard that was studded with
benches, picnic tables, chess tables, monuments, vendor stalls,
coconut trees, and children's swing sets. An artist offered to paint
the dogs for five American dollars each. A man in an alley hinted
that his sister was available for a price. I bought a tropical fruit
drink from an old lady with arthritic hands whose stand was sun-
yellow and adorned with painted flowers. I purchased spicy chicken
cutlets on a stick and shared them with Snowflake and Hula Girl. I
wrapped their leashes around a wooden bench. The dogs panted in
the cool dirt. I watched Havana swirl by. The men were partial to
white suits, while the women mostly wore billowing dresses in
floral patterns.

Sitting on that bench in the rising heat, I began to calculate that
I'd soon have enough money to last a year, maybe longer. Surely, I
could find some way to make a living given a year's grace.

At an open-air barber shop I tied the dogs in the shade of a
palm tree and went for a quick haircut. The barber taught me how
to ask in Spanish whether dogs were allowed. So after my haircut I
stopped at the rum joint next door and ordered a Cuba Libre.

"*Permitido perros?*" I asked the bartender.

"*Si,*" he said.

I was going to like this town.

As the days began to stretch out, I became tropically lazy. My
morning walk was always the same. Through the Plaza De Armas,
to the Malecon, curve around to the Passeo, down to Parque
Central, and back home along O'Reilly. Under the tropical canopy
of the Paseo, I bought a painting of the ocean, coconut-scented
candles and cigars. The Cuban staple of pork with rice and black
beans agreed with me, and my apartment had only a one-burner

hot-plate, so I never cooked at home. It was a mystery to me, anyway, how Cubans could make ordinary black beans taste so fabulous.

It was easy to make a feast from the fruit markets, with all their bananas, grapefruit, papayas, oranges and pineapples, along with fruits I'd never tasted before. Delicious, simple meals such as fried chicken and potatoes were available at stalls all over the city, and it was hard to pass a panaderia without stopping in. The dogs were thriving on chicken and rice, and a home-based veterinarian gave them each a rabies shot and pronounced them healthy.

In the afternoons I left the dogs at home and explored Havana by streetcar. Near the end of the line was the racetrack, Oriente Park. It was a seedy disappointment. Like the tourists, the horse trainers were abandoning Cuba and the track was rundown, dirty and maybe dangerous. Muggers, one tout told me, sometimes were tipped off by mutuel clerks, and winners were relieved of their cash on the way home, sometimes with a beating for good measure.

So maybe my new life, I'd decided, didn't need to include the Sport of Kings.

As the weeks went by, I became convinced that I had made a successful escape. I learned bits of Spanish. Fortunately for me, but unfortunately for Cuba, prices were crashing.

I found it easy to squash thoughts about my former life. J. Edgar Hoover, Alvin Karpis, Shotgun George, Harry Sawyer, Big Ryan, Doc Barker, to hell with them all. At Pan American News on Obispo I sometimes stopped to read the headlines of the New York and Miami papers, or took an *El Mundo* home to try to dope out the Spanish.

I delighted in the discovery of the Hotel Ingleterra, where the staff spoke good English and the rooftop bar offered splendid views of the city. Downstairs in the dining room, the roast chicken dinner became a Sunday night treat. I met a fellow expat named

Doreen, a honey-haired heavy smoker in her mid-40s and took her
to dinner at the Ingleterra. She was on the run from a bad husband
in Atlanta. We got along okay, but after our third date, she
disappeared, leaving her landlord shrugging and short a week's rent.

I speculated about Myrtle, and assumed that Lapland Willie
Weaver had abandoned her to go into hiding, and that she had
found another sugar daddy.

Naturally the Cubans I met were curious about me and wanting
to practice their English. But I noted a recurring theme in these
street conversations. Cubans wanted out of Cuba. It might not
matter to tourists much, but Havana was a city ruled by one tin-
horn dictator after another. Friends and relatives with political
opinions were snatched off the streets. Batista, the new strong man,
had spies everywhere. There were no jobs, and little prospect for
work, and so Havana had become a city of sharps and hustlers.
One Cuban after another told me Cuba was hopeless, beautiful but
hopeless, and when they spoke of America I could see the light in
their eyes.

Just after St. Patrick's Day, I got jolted back to gangster reality.
According to the Chicago Tribune, a man named Fred Goetz was
shot gangster style as he emerged from a tavern in Cicero, Illinois.
His gangland name was Shotgun George Ziegler, the Tribune
reported. He was suspected of being a former operative for the
Capone Outfit and participant in the Saint Valentine's Day
Massacre.

There was no mention of either of the two kidnappings George
had helped to engineer.

George was dead on arrival at the local hospital and police had
suspects but, of course, made no arrests.

I began to monitor the Chicago papers more closely and three
days later, hysterical headlines proclaimed that the Alt kidnappers

were spending ransom money in Chicago. The money, apparently, had been secretly marked. It was showing up in banks all over town and the G-men were now focusing: They had narrowed the suspects down to the Barker-Karpis gang, and were knocking on doors all over Chicago.

That night I squirmed and sweated, alone in my Emperor-sized bed. I wondered whether it had been Doc and Fred who had killed Shotgun George. If so, the eliminations had begun and Curly Davis and Lapland Willie Weaver might be next. I fretted about Myrtle and one day visited the telephone company, where you could call long distance to America from a special booth.

But Myrtle's phone was disconnected.

That winter, John Dillinger had escaped from an Indiana prison using a fake gun. It was an event I hardly noticed until Easter Weekend when the newspapers erupted with the story of a Dillinger shootout with G-men in Saint Paul. Three weeks later, Dillinger and the G-men went at it again, at a Wisconsin resort named Little Bohemia. Luckily for me, Dillinger was replacing the Barker Gang as the top target of the obsessive Mister Hoover.

That spring I caught a bad flu and met a nurse who spoke Spanish and English, Joy Figueroa, who was not Cuban-born but a Spaniard. We went on a couple of chaste, cautious dates. Her hair was black and silver, her face chubby and pleasant, she was in her forties somewhere and had never been married. She wanted to know what I did for a living and from my answer figured out I was a gangster on the lam. She said it would be better for us to remain just friends.

The summer went by and I advanced a little in Spanish and made a few friends among the loafers and chess players at Plaza De Armas, a block from my apartment. I studied up on chess, and it began to replace horse racing as an amusement, particularly when I learned that Cubans gambled on the outcome of chess matches. I avoided Americans, and anybody who might be a gangster. I learned that Chinatown was the dark heart of Cuban prostitution and corruption, and after one curious visit I stayed away.

No news of the Alt kidnapping or the ransom money or the Barker gang made any front page, but in late June I learned from screaming headlines that G-men had shot Dillinger dead outside a Chicago movie house.

Maybe that, I thought would satisfy the bloodlust of J. Edgar.

Early in fall Havana cooled a bit, and so did I. It had been six months since the Barker Gang had made headlines. Like the Hamm snatch, and the Barker-Karpis bank robberies, the Alt kidnapping seemed destined to rest in a Washington file drawer for eternity.

I'd spent more money than I ought to have, including a splurge on a white suit and Panama hat. What few jobs were available in Havana shrunk to almost nothing. The casinos kept laying off. Even the Tropicana was closed a few nights a week. Desperate prostitutes were shouting low prices on the street corners, former casino dealers were robbing shopkeepers, and the streets were more and more filled with people who had no honest way to make a living.

One night in September, Joy Figueroa asked me to the opera. It was held in a theater just opposite Parque Centrale and a few doors down from the Hotel Ingleterra. I didn't understand the opera very well, and only sort-of enjoyed the singing, but I hoped to make a romantic advance on this relationship, so I bought Joy a drink at the Hotel Ingleterra bar.

The bar was built in a square. As I pulled out a barstool for Joy, I saw, staring across it at me, the spooky eyes of Alvin Karpis.

He was sitting with a girl I'd seen in Saint Paul, one of the Delaney sisters, a dark-haired, blue-eyed teenager. Dolores, that was her name. Last I'd seen her, at the Commodore, she had begged me to get a message to Karpis in Chicago.

Karpis glared at me through a haze of cigarette smoke. He tossed a drink down, patted Dolores on the back, whispered in her ear, and headed for me.

"Take a walk," he said into my ear.

I got off the stool and told Joy I'd be right back.

We stood in the dull light reflected from a long, tall buzzing neon sign that spelled out INGLETERRE. Traffic roared by, and we fended off a pimp who wanted to introduce us to a couple of *jineteras*.

"How long you been here?" barked Karpis.

"Couple of days," I lied.

"Beat it," he said. "This town is about to get hot."

"Then what are you doing here?" I asked.

"The fools changed the money here," Karpis said. "The G-men won't be far behind. We're on the boat tomorrow. If you're smart, you'll be a day behind me."

"Who changed the money here?"

"Never mind," he said. "They changed it."

"The money from Saint Paul?"

"It was supposed to end up in Venezuela, but the fools spent it here. It's spread all over town now. I've seen some of the bills myself. So like I said, Powers, beat it."

I stared into the misty night. Rumba music filtered from the hotel dining room as drunken men and women spilled out the big doors. I figured there was half a chance Karpis was lying, that he wanted to scare me off because he didn't want me, or anyone who knew him, in Havana.

And there was half a chance that a planeload of G-men were taking off from Washington right now.

"Thanks, Ray," I said, "see you around."

"Not if I can help it," he said.

The Karpis sighting sent me back to Havana Telephone's special long distance booth. The phone company kept the most elaborate quarters I had ever seen, in a castle complete with turrets. On the ground floor was the special long distance office, fed by an undersea cable to Florida. It was a twenty-minute wait just for the privilege of making a call.

The one person I could trust who might be in the know was Myrtle, but since her phone line had been disconnected, my best call was to her friend Loretta.

"Powers calling long distance," I said. "Long, long distance."

"You're out of town?" Loretta said. "Stay out of town."

"I need Myrtle's number," I said.

"She's not in town either," Loretta said.

"Where'd she go?"

"With that Weaver chump. Didn't you know? Can you hear me? There's an awful lot of static."

"Where?" I said. "Where with that Weaver chump?"

"Allen something. Allen-something Florida. I got a post card somewhere. He bought a chicken ranch. Wait."

"This is costing a dollar a minute," I said.

"I'll be right back."

There were four special long distance kiosks, and in the other three, men were shouting in Spanish, as if the volume was necessary to bridge the miles. Despite the big red sign that read NO FUMAR the room was a miasma of cigar smoke. I was coughing into the phone when Loretta came back.

"Allendale, Florida."

"Chicken ranch," I said. "What does Myrtle know about chickens?"

"She's not coming back here, that's all I know. You neither, Mick. This town is boiling over. I'm layin low myself."

CHAPTER TWENTY TWO

FLORIDA

I packed up what little I had. Shed of winter clothes, I was a man with one suitcase and two dogs waiting on the Havana dock for the S.S. Cuba. It was a long journey to Allendale: the ferry, the bus from Key West, the train from Miami to Daytona Beach. My timing was rotten. On the train I bought a day-old *Orlando Sentinel* and there, atop page three, was the headline:

G-MEN NAB KIDNAP SUSPECT

William Weaver, a known associate of the Barker Gang, was arrested at an Allendale farm by federal authorities yesterday in connection with the kidnapping of Minnesota banker Richard Alt.

Also arrested was his female companion, Myrtle Eaton, who will face federal harboring charges, authorities said.

So I made a detour to the Volusia County Courthouse. It looked like a miniature version of the Cathedral of Saint Paul, complete with green-copper roof. It was approached down a brick pathway lined with palm trees. On benches underneath those palms, lawyers, criminals, deputies and loafers took shelter from a blazing sun.

Behind the courthouse was the jail, and after talking my way past two bully guards and a matron, I was in a stinking hot, green-painted room, with a set of bars like a bank teller's cage, only with no slot. There was a double barrier: those bars and the thick dirty glass over them. On my side was a bar stool. I waited, drumming my hands on the filthy green-painted counter. The walls on either side were notched with initials and curses in Spanish and English, carved into the wall with pen-knives.

The jailers had dressed Myrtle in a rat-grey shift. Her hair was a flat greasy mess, her skin looked like it had never met sunshine, her eyes were dull and empty. She shuffled in slippers, approached the cage head down.

She could not engage my eyes.

"I'm surprised you come to see me," she said through dry, cracked lips.

"I got you a lawyer," I said.

"That's good, I guess."

"I called Tommy Filben. Wouldn't you know, he's got a guy down here."

"Yeah," she muttered, "good old Tommy."

"He's going to plead you out," I said. "He's going to get you months, not years."

Myrtle shrugged.

"You're rid of Lapland Willie," I said. "That's the good thing."

She pursed her lips.

"How they treating you, Myrtle, you okay?"

"I need cigarettes," she said. "Cigarettes is like money here."

"What's the best brand?"

"Camels or Lucky Strikes," she said.

"DiLucca, that's the lawyer's name."

"An Italian?"

"I'd say so."

"Well I guess that's okay down here."

"You'll have to talk the federals."

"I won't do it."

"You will because you want to get out."

"I don't care, Mick."

"Yes you do, and so do I. You're in the dumps, I can tell. DiLucca says they don't want courtroom testimony out of you, because you can only give them hearsay. What they really want is the inside dope so they can catch up with Fred, Doc and Karpis. Anything you can tell them, hell, you'll be out of here by Saint Patrick's Day."

Now she looked at me square.

"And, Myrtle, wherever you're locked up, that's where I'll be. I'll wait it out. When you get sprung, let's go away. Just you and me. No more thieving, no more two-timing. We don't need to get married but we do need to live honest with each other."

She searched me, a wild animal look in her eyes.

"No two timing?"

"No more," I said.

"You neither, right?"

"Me neither. Goose and gander."

"You mean it then?"

"I mean it."

"Mick," she said, and tears welled up, "I been waiting my whole life for ..."

Elbows on that grimy counter, she put her hands to her face and sobbed.

I reached for her, touched only glass.

She gathered herself, sniffled, looked back toward the matron, who was reading a *Film Stars* magazine, utterly disgusted with our little drama.

"What are you going do for money?" Myrtle asked.

"I've got a little cash left, that'll run out, but I'll do something, tend bar if I have to, there's always a need for sober bartenders. And maybe there's a racetrack needs a good numbers man, do the program, figure the morning line. Good times are coming back, Myrtle, things are picking up again. I'll find something straight and legal."

"But there ain't no race tracks in Saint Paul," she said.

"To hell with Saint Paul," I said. "We're going to live somewhere warm."

My time was up. The matron led Myrtle into the darkness. She turned, Myrtle did, and gave me one last chilling look.

I stood outside the courthouse and smoked my last Cuban cigar. Hell, a lot of guys dumber than me had made a living off the races. The trick was to make it a business, not a gamble.

I took the train down to Hialeah and rented a motel room a block from the race track. I bought a typewriter and a stop watch at a pawn shop.

Months and months passed. It never left me, the shadow of my gangster days. I lived in fear, not constant, but always in the background, the dread of the ultimate knock on the door. Gangster or G-man, it wouldn't matter, one was as dangerous as the other.

I found a bright, clean place in Hialeah, a block from the racetrack, where I waited out Myrtle's imprisonment. I applied for a couple of bartending jobs, and for a laundry truck driver, but soon got the message: with a million Florida guys out of work, no Yankees need apply

In January, 1935, the G-men shot Fred and Ma Barker dead at a lake cottage in Central Florida. Doc Barker was arrested on the streets of Chicago, and so was Shotgun George's tubercular friend Monty, whose true name turned out to be Byron Bolton.

The G-men renamed themselves the FBI, and with Dillinger dead, they kept Karpis on the run, naming him Public Enemy Number One, putting his photo in the newspaper every few days.

I'd taken the train up to Daytona every Monday to see Myrtle and finally, in March, 1935, a week after Saint Patrick's, they let her out. Together we rode the train to Miami, celebrated her freedom with a feast, steak and wine in the dining car. She'd lost twenty pounds, hadn't eaten a decent meal in seven months.

We took a cab to Hialeah and I showed off my gleaming second floor apartment. Snowflake and Hula Girl leaped and ran in circles, happy for new company. Myrtle was drunk and so was I and I barely remembered making love before we fell asleep in each other's arms.

Before dawn I roused her. I had already dressed and showered and had walked and fed the dogs.

"You wanted to see," I said.

"Are you crazy?" she mumbled. "It's dark out."

"I'm a businessman now," I said. "Early to bed and early to rise. Etcetera."

She sputtered.

"All right, all right." She arose from the bed and stumbled into the white-tile bathroom.

"You wasn't lying, Mick," her voice echoed from in there. "You got no roaches."

"The landlord sprays."

"That jail, the roaches could have carried you off."

"Come on, come on," I said. "The horses wait for no man."

She dressed in halter top shorts and one of my white shirts, sleeves rolled up. I promised her a clothes-shopping trip after the workouts. As the sun rose over the rooftops, we hustled up the block to Hialeah Race Track, entered at the side door, took the sleek elevator to the press room.

There was nobody else there. All the wise-acres were down at the rail. We were facing out the big windows, overlooking the track, and the pond with its flock of pink flamingoes, as the sun rose out of the ocean.

"So here we are," I said. "World headquarters of Mick's Picks."

I led her past desks topped with racing forms, pencils, calculators, binoculars, ashtrays, booze bottles and torn up mutuel tickets. Mine was the far desk, hardly big enough to hold my typewriter, but it had a locking drawer. From it I retrieved my binoculars and stop watch.

"Well if it's a business," Myrtle said, "you're no threat to John D. Rockefeller."

"It's legal, that's the key. Legit. It's fifteen years since I had job that wasn't against the law."

"So how's it work?" Myrtle asked, but she was staring at the pond and flamingoes.

"This here." I rolled a stencil into the typewriter. "You type it up and you take this stencil over here..." I walked to the Daily Racing Form's mimeograph. "I run off a hundred-twenty copies, pop 'em in the mail to my subscribers. Result? A well-informed betting public."

"How much dough you make on this?" asked Myrtle.

"Well, I'm just getting started."

The look in her eyes was dull, sleepy.

"Where's the coffee?" she asked.

"Downstairs. And free donuts, too."

"Nothing's free, Mick."

"Well, no, you got to be nice to the trainers, it's their treat."

We took the elevator downstairs where Myrtle treated herself to a French cruller and a cup of coffee at a window tended by a cranky old lady. The breakfast was free because there were no rubes at this time of morning. Everyone here was some level of insider: exercise riders, trainers and their assistants, grooms, hot-walkers, Racing Form writers and clockers like me.

I never ate or even drank coffee before I'd done my morning timings. Binoculars around my neck, I led Myrtle across the concrete apron and toward the rail.

The morning air was steaming already, but the earth was cool. The horses, one at a time, were led down the bridle path where Max, an old worn-out guy with a clipboard in his hands and an unlit cigar in his mouth, wrote down their names. Then with a glance over his shoulder, assuring himself all was clear, Max slid open a pole gate and let horse and rider onto the track.

The horse snorted and pranced. The rider laughed, speaking in Spanish to a couple of lounging, seedy-looking, coffee-swilling grooms. Up along the rail was my competition, numbering somewhere between five and ten guys, depending on how many had been kept in bed by hangovers. They too ran clocker mail-order services and they too were only as good as their last tip sheet.

Workouts were wonderfully informal, without the pomp, heat, hype and artificial colors of race day. Sometimes in the low light of the rising sun, it seemed like all one color, the riders in dark jeans and sweat shirts, the horses almost the same hue as the dirt.

I loved this way of life. I could see myself doing this job until Saint Patrick escorted me to the pearly gates. Yes, I would have to worry for years that the feds would dig deep enough to unearth my involvement with Harry and Jack. But they hadn't dug as deep as Tom Filben yet, and I was a layer underneath him. There was nothing to do now but stay straight, keep Saint Paul on my blind side, and say the occasional Hail Mary.

"Numerology," I said, and made a note on my clipboard.

"What?"

"The colt's name," I said. "Numerology. He still needs some gate training. Hasn't had his first start yet. And judging by last week's workout, he needs to wake up."

"What does that mean, wake up?"

"Dig deep. Give it his all. They're all fast. It's the ones with determination, the ones that don't quit in the stretch, they're the ones that win."

"How about you, Mick, do you quit in the stretch?"

"Not by a longshot," I said.

Numerology trotted by, magnificent. He was only a Florida colt but pranced with all the power and dignity of Charlemagne's warhorse.

"Beautiful, aren't they?" I said. "I could watch 'em all day. See this is what was missing in Saint Paul. There you'd go into a smoky room full of ringing telephones, and listen to the races scratchy on the radio. It was only gambling, greed, that's all, stripped of life. Here, this is the real thing."

Numerology and his hooded rider took off at a gentle gallop that soon became a determined run. I set my stopwatch, followed the horse in my binoculars, ticked off his time when he reached the quarter pole. I scribbled notes.

Myrtle finished her cruller and licked her fingertips.

Numerology returned, sweating, tossing his head, snorting. The horse looked pleased with himself, happy to get his run after a week in the stall.

"How'd he go?" Max the gatekeeper asked me.

"Forty nine and heavy change."

Max, disappointed, shook his head and allowed horse and rider into the exit path.

"Gorgeous animal," said Myrtle, paper coffee cup to her lips.

"Yeah, he is," I said. "Gorgeous and slow."

She watched the whole flock of flamingoes rise from the pond and flap toward the rising sun.

"Numerology looks strong to me," she said.

"They're all strong."

"He's a three year old? Maybe he'll run in the Derby."

I glanced at the stopwatch.

"That's five weeks from now," I said.

"So?"

"He hasn't even won his first race yet. Anyway, this horse ain't royalty, he's a couple of ticks slow. Maybe he'll win a cheap handicap someday. But the big time? No. He doesn't stand a chance."

"How about us, Mick, do we stand a chance?"

"We might win a cheap race here and there."

I held a stopwatch in my left hand. Myrtle picked up my right hand and kissed it.

"I learned something in the joint," she said.

I could see it, as the sun rose over the grandstand. I could see the light come back to her eyes, as if she just now realized she was out of jail.

"Okay, I'll bite. What did you learn in there?"

"I found out who my friends are."

April, 1953

CHAPTER TWENTY-THREE

SAINT PAUL AGAIN

I drove up, parked, checked the address and just sat there thinking.

Everything was new.

It was early spring, the trees still bare. You could hear the pounding of hammers. Houses were being built on every block. Saint Paul, clean modern Saint Paul, was reaching out and covering up its last weedy fields with new homes. The home across from me was occupied by Janie Vetter, make that Larson.

I was early so I got out of my Studebaker, stretched and went for a walk one block to the Mississippi. The great river, down in its gorge, was only icy on its banks, free flowing now, muddy with snow melt. I walked past the former Hollyhocks speakeasy-casino. It was only some banker's mansion now, painted white, tennis courts added, no booze trucks, no gangster cars, everything perfectly legal.

I couldn't help but ponder the fate of my old friend Sam Tanaka, who had simply disappeared just after Pearl Harbor. Whether he returned to Japan is a matter of speculation. His family lived in Nagasaki and I could only hope that somehow they had made it out before that city met its unspeakable fate.

Jack Peifer, the criminal mastermind who once ran this casino, killed himself on the day he was sentenced to 30 years for kidnapping. Someone had slipped him cyanide-laced gum in jail. Jack's gorgeous wife Violet, from whom he'd concealed his darkest criminal ventures, married a wealthy attorney and moved to Palm Beach, Florida. The man Jack had kidnapped, William Hamm, had since turned the family brewery into a nationwide beer marketing powerhouse.

The criminal network that once reached from the Hollyhocks to the Green Lantern to Al Capone in Chicago had long since been broken up. J. Edgar Hoover, the nation's cleanup hitter, had made his reputation in the Saint Paul kidnapping trials and had since become a national figure, prosecuting German spies and home-grown Commies.

I kept walking.

I wore an expensive tweed overcoat with leather buttons. At age 63 I had become a prosperous American. Horse Racing was in decline but I had sold Mick's Picks, and its nearly 7,000 subscribers, to my top competitor, Wise Dan. I'd put the money in the bank.

You could trust banks these days.

A lot of other things had changed too.

Eisenhower, the rat who'd turned on his fellow veterans during the 1930s Bonus March, was a war-hero president now. It seemed everybody liked Ike, maybe because so may people had jobs and spending money.

The FBI seemed satisfied that it had cleaned up Saint Paul and so forgot about small fry like me. Alvin Karpis and Harry Sawyer had been locked up in Alcatraz almost 20 years now. Doc Barker had been shot dead while trying to escape from The Rock. Harry's man Pat Reilly was in and out of Minnesota's Stillwater Prison, and might have been better off inside, since he went on crazy benders whenever he was paroled.

My sisters now owned the lakeshore potato farm at Eagle River, Wisconsin. They used Cindy's cabin for summer vacations and otherwise, the land, even the acres Swede had burned, was reverting to forest. I visited every year on my ritual trip north. On a mound overlooking Snipe Lake are the graves of my dogs. Snowflake's is marked with a white rock, Hula Girl's with a dark one. I hoped they were happy there, at the edge of the forest they loved.

I circled the block to a modest, clean white clapboard house on a street corner. I knocked on the door.

A middle aged red head answered.

"Well what do you know," she said with a warm, broad smile. "The prodigal son returns." She stepped aside. "Come in and forgive the mess."

There was no mess.

Janie Vetter had married Jack Olson, who made his money figuring out how long people were going to live, and worked for an insurance company called The Saint Paul. Janie was early 40s and radiant. Her son Dane, fathered by a gangster, intended to be a doctor and was studying at the University of Wisconsin. Her two daughters, Annika and Erica, were at that moment in class at Highland Catholic. Janie had given up the news business for freelancing.

"Your coat," Janie said.

I handed it to her.

"It's light," she said. "No weapons."

"You remember," I said.

"Oh, I do."

We embraced. She had an aroma, pleasant, fresh, like spring itself. She led me into a dining room where on a long dark table she had set up a typewriter, a sheaf of paper, and a cup filled with pencils. In the kitchen she had made coffee in a French press, and she poured me a cup. It was a very familiar cup, white with one blue stripe.

"This cup, you got it from my apartment."

"You left it for me."

"Your gangster inheritance," I said.

"So," she said.

I looked out the bright sunny windows into a yard with two apple trees, just leafing out.

"How's Mrs. Powers?" she said.

"Well, we're not really married," I said. "But we get along. You know how she makes her living now? Garage sales. She's got an eye, let me tell you. She can spot a valuable antique and pay fifty cents for it."

"And you?"

"Thinking of coming back up for good."

"Really?"

"Florida's getting crowded. And Hialeah, well, it's kind of falling apart. Twenty years of humidity and horse racing, I've had it Janie. Plus my sisters and nieces are here, and my old pal Billy McAmbly is retired and looking for a drinking buddy. He never did like his fellow cops much."

She carried her coffee to the dining room.

"So," she said. "We begin?"

"Fifty-fifty deal, right?"

We shook hands like a couple of bankers.

I cleared my throat.

"One time in America," I said, "there was nobody to trust. Not the banks, not your boss, not the cop on the street."

"We can't start like that," Janie said. "Too philosophical. Crime readers don't want philosophy."

"All right," I said and sipped. "Once upon a time..."

"This is not a fairy tale, Mick."

"One evening…"

"Make that a dark winter evening," Janie said, and began typing.

"Should we mention the blizzard in there?"

"Maybe in the second sentence," she said.

"One dark winter evening, not long after my wife left me, I awoke to see a car on fire."

I paused.

I felt for my pipe. I didn't smoke anymore but the reflex was still there. I said: "I myself was a criminal at the time."

Janie sighed through pursed lips and sat back.

"Mick, it was twenty years ago but maybe you should see a lawyer because, you know, technically, you could still be prosecuted."

"No. No lawyers. Put it down," I said. "New paragraph. I, Mick Powers, was a criminal at the time."

AFTERWORD

The Mick Powers series consists of four novels, and is based on actual events of the early 1930s. It re-imagines the lives of many people, some still notorious, some long-forgotten. Among the characters based closely on real people:

Fred and Ma Barker were killed in a shootout with federal agents at Lake Weir, Florida in January of 1935.

Doc Barker was sentenced to life in Alcatraz for kidnapping. He was shot dead by guards while trying to escape.

Alvin Karpis was locked up for more that 25 years in Alcatraz, was deported upon parole, and died in Spain.

Harry Sawyer was sentenced to a life term in Alcatraz for kidnapping. He was released when he was terminally ill.

Jack Peifer committed suicide by chewing poisoned gum on the day he was sentenced to a long prison term for the Hamm kidnapping.

Myrtle Eaton was released from prison after serving a short term for harboring criminals, and disappeared into private life.

Paula Harmon, Fred Barker's girlfriend, returned to her family in Texas and was treated for mental and emotional illnesses.

Shotgun George Ziegler was gunned down in a Chicago suburb. No one was ever arrested for his murder.

Byron Bolton, aka Monty Carter, turned federal witness and testified against his fellow gangsters in the St. Paul kidnapping trials.

Next in the Gangster Era series...

The Resurrection of Saint Johnny

IN THE SPRING of 1934, John Dillinger pulled a Houdini and escaped from jail in Lima, Ohio. How exactly he accomplished that escape is still a matter of debate.

What's not in question is what he did next: Within 24 hours, Dillinger, along with girlfriend Billie Frechette, arrived in Saint Paul, Minnesota.

Dillinger's contact in Saint Paul was the criminal mastermind Harry Sawyer. Sawyer put his errand boy, Pat Reilly, in charge of looking after Dillinger's needs. Bess Green, a tavern hostess, well known in gangland, also became involved in shielding Dillinger.

The Resurrection of Saint Johnny is the story of Pat, Bess, Dillinger, Billie and others during this short, but very eventful, stay in the Saintly City.

Like the Mick Powers series, it is a work of fiction, based closely on historical research.

The Resurrection of Saint Johnny as presented here is a near-final draft of the book. It has not yet been thoroughly edited or proof-read.

THE RESURRECTION OF SAINT JOHNNY

By Tim Mahoney

Easter Saturday, March 31, 1934

BLOOD DROPS
IN THE SNOW

B illie Frechette lay in bed, caressing the rough
stubbly face of the World's Most Famous Bad Guy.
He snored, peaceful. Nothing awoke John early,
nothing.

A rude slam of the front door announced their guests'
departure. Billie had waited them out. Breakfast for five? Billie
was no short order cook, and besides, they were down to two
eggs in the icebox.

Billie rolled out of bed in a white flannel nightgown. She
shivered. They had left the window open a crack, John crazy
for fresh air, and now it had gone freezing. Although it was
Easter Saturday morning, the radiator tooted its winter song.
She lifted an edge of the shade and out on the avenue, saw tire
tracks in fresh snow. She walked out of the bedroom whistling
"Beautiful Dreamer."

What did Johnny dream about? Fast cars and baseball
games, if she knew him. In the too bright kitchen she lit the gas

stove under the tea kettle. She wondered about that Chicago lawyer. He seemed bullshit. Still, she wanted to believe. He had talked to a federal attorney about a deal. Or so he claimed. Amnesty for John. In return, the attorney would be portrayed in a movie: The Trial of Handsome Johnny.

She must have spent awhile in Hollywood fantasy because the tea kettle was whistling. A bag of Salada tea, a white cup, a squeeze of honey, she was morning happy. She raised the window shade to feel direct sunshine, warm and friendly on her face. She sipped tea, watching traffic in the snow. One egg apiece, soft boiled, and toast for breakfast.

Whenever His Gangster Highness deigned to arise.

With that last sip of tea she remembered they were out of cigarettes. Red Hamilton had promised to bring her a carton. But she wanted one now. Hoping to find a stray cigarette, she poked into the living room. Red and his two bedmates had not bothered to raise the Murphy bed, so she lifted it, throwing wrinkled pillows onto the couch. In bed with two sisters, well, Red was quite the adventurer and he could keep them both. All those girls did was complain. Did they ever pick up after themselves? Did Billie look like their maid?

One. Two. Three. Heavy knocks at the door. She tiptoed, looked into the peephole, couldn't see. A rough voice vibrated through the door.

"Carl Hellman?"

It took a moment for a her sleepy brain to process that name. John changed names like other men changed trousers. Hellman, right.

Red, stupid, had left the door unlocked and now Billie hitched the security chain. It made a noise and she could not pretend she wasn't home. She opened the door a cautious inch, rattling that chain.

"My husband is not in," she said. "Try this afternoon."

She closed the door. She still hadn't set eye on the intruder.

"Are you Mrs. Hellman?"

This was another voice from the hallway, smoother, Southern syrup.

"Yes."

"Well, we are officers. We would like to speak to you," said the Southern voice.

John had instructed her for this situation. She was to open the door and drop to the floor. John would take the cops hostage if he could, shoot them only if he had to. But those instructions were worthless when John was dead asleep.

"I'm not dressed."

"We'll wait for you to dress," said the Southern voice.

"No, why don't you come back this afternoon."

She turned the deadbolt and it made a solid clunk.

They murmured out there in the hall, the Rough Voice and Southern Syrup. Billie, tingling all over, going numb in hands and feet, breathing shallow, held that doorknob to keep herself upright. She cast a terrified look over her shoulder, hoping to see John. He was the coolest man she had ever known.

She trembled like a trapped rabbit. Every step she took toward the bedroom felt like it consumed a decade. When she pushed through the door Johnny was facedown, bare-assed, hugging a pillow.

She shook his foot.

"John," she whispered.

"Unh."

"Cops."

He rolled over, naked and twisted in the sheets. He glanced at the windows, as if surprised at the sunlight. Then he leaped out of bed and hopped into trousers, cinched the belt around his narrow waist.

"How many?"

"I don't know," she whispered.

He was on his knees at the closet, pulling out the suitcase, piling into it bank-bundled cash, shirts, belts of machine gun ammo.

He rose to his feet, ripped a starched blue-striped shirt from its hanger and buttoned it over his chest. In three rapid strides he crossed the room and peered through the crack in the shades.

"All right, Billie," he said. "Keep your shirt on. We're going to get out of here."

He glared at her.

"Well get dressed. Why are you standing there?"

He pulled on shoes and socks while she, sweating, wriggled into a dark purple dress. She picked flat shoes for running. After one sorrowful glance at all her beautiful clothing, she plucked a mink jacket from its hangar. She shouldered her purse. From the dresser she scooped her best jewelry. When she turned around John was holding the tommygun, pointed at her, like she was the enemy.

"All right," he said. "Take that suitcase and get moving. Follow me."

Billie grabbed the suitcase, which was heavy like it was full of stones. She stood behind John in the living room and all of a sudden it exploded. Shock waves pierced her ears. Her whole head rang like a bell. The air smelled of vile chemistry and flashes leaped out the barrel of John's tommygun. Bits of plaster stung her face.

John flung open the door. He turned one way and then the other, blasting away with the tommygun. Billie, that suitcase nearly tearing her arm out, followed him down the hallway.

Something down in the darkness flashed three or four times, and a lethal insect buzzed past her ear. John fired toward those flashes, then limped down the stairs. Billie followed, fear gone, exhilaration, intensely alive, the light at the bottom of the stairwell like the glow of Heaven. John pushed out the door, turned to check on her, limped into the snowy driveway.

Blood drops appeared in the snow. John let himself into the passenger side of their Hudson and Billie, with more strength than she believed she had, threw that heavy suitcase into the rear seat. She upside-downed her purse. Jewelry and makeup spilled out. She saw in that split second their doomed future, shot to death in this car because she, stupid ugly Billie, had forgotten to bring the keys.

But miracle, there they gleamed in her lap. She started the Hudson and backed out. Where the hell were the coppers?

She took a hard left turn on Grand Avenue.

"Take it easy," said John. "Drive slow. We don't want to get pulled over now."

"You're bleeding."

"They nicked me that's all."

"John."

"You drive, I'll bleed, okay?"

"Where the fuck are we going?"

"We've got friends in this town," John said. "Patrick will help us. Drive easy, easy, easy."

SIX WEEKS EARLIER…

VALENTINE'S DAY, ASH WEDNESDAY,

FEBRUARY 14, 1934

Patrick Reilly pushed out of the heavy Cathedral doors and into a deep arctic freeze. He lit a Lucky. His gray wool overcoat concealed everything but his pale face and short stature. A driver's cap covered his balding head. Upon his forehead was a black mark, ashes, the thumbprint of a priest.

Memento mori, the priest had murmured when applying the ashes. Pat, having endured seven years in Catholic school, knew this was Latin for *drop dead.* But even on Ash Wednesday, Pat was an optimist. He was young, and up for promotion.

He hustled across the street for his car, an Essex Terraplane, midnight blue, with a new-fangled V6 engine. He had bought it from this guy Mick Powers, who had run off to hide in Cuba.

Despite the cold, that engine fired up with a pull on the choke and the touch of a chrome button.

Pat's wife Dolly veered out the Cathedral's side door, where she waited, sheltered from the vicious wind. Pat pulled the Essex to the curb and pushed open the passenger door. He loved Dolly, deep and true, although she drove him nuts most days. Dolly was a looker: helpless in the kitchen but a genius in the bedroom. She dressed fancy, had a sharp tongue, and didn't take crap from nobody. To top it off, she was a low-handicap bowler.

At Mass and at the nightclubs, Dolly dressed the same: rabbit-fur coat, brazen red lipstick, red pill hat. Her beauty-parlor blond hair, short cut, was almost a helmet. Her pale face was punctuated by thick lips and bright blue eyes.

Your honor, Pat said to his inner judge, *I know Dolly don't have the greatest reputation. But that was before we was married.*

Dolly slammed the door, huffed a cloud of frost and said, "Any heat in this thing?"

"I just started it."

"Eight degrees," muttered Dolly as she dug into her purse. From it she lifted a packet of tin foil. In there was a thin crooked cigarette. She propped the lipstick-stained end of that cigarette between her lips. Pat lit it up, flicking his special lighter. A goofy perfume smell filled the car.

Pat spun the Essex around, eager to get away before Mass let out. Of course, just when you need to zoom, there's a red traffic light in front of you. Pat waited it out, blowing smoke that rebounded off the windshield. Dolly huddled shivering against the door.

"Florida?" Dolly said. "Am I going to see Florida before I die?"

"I got business up here now," Pat said. "Big business."

From Cathedral Hill, Pat had a sweeping view of the city

through the frosty windshield. Pat took a deep drag on his Lucky and his chest swelled with tobacco smoke and pride.

Soon a piece of this city would belong to him. No, it wasn't a great city, like Chicago, where he'd been once, or New York, where he'd only heard tell. But these narrow streets, served by a streetcar loop, had hundreds of places where a fella could have a good time: Taverns and pool halls and horse wires, whorehouses and dice rooms. This wasn't one of those cities run by politicians. Oh there was a mayor all right, but all he did was make speeches on the radio. This city was run under a deal between the cops and Pat's boss, Harry Sawyer.

"Oh, *big* business," Dolly said.

She was what you could call sarcastic sometimes.

"And don't say nothing," warned Pat as the traffic light turned green. "Because it's men's business and you don't know nothing about it."

Dolly was only cranky because of hunger, Pat figured. A loyal Catholic fasted before Mass and Communion, and Dolly didn't do so hot with fasting. She sucked down one last cloud of perfumed smoke, snuffed her stinky marijuana cigarette in its foil packet, and took out her mirror compact. She blotted away the ashes on her forehead.

"It ain't flattering," she said, "going around with black ashes."

"I didn't say you should," Pat said.

"How about pancakes at the Lowry?"

"Jeez," said Pat. "On Valentine's Day, are you kidding? We'll wait two hours in line. Anyway, look. It's Ash Wednesday, right? Ash Wednesday cancels out Valentine's Day."

"Says who?"

"Ask any priest."

Dolly sputtered.

"We'll get breakfast at the Town Talk," Pat suggested.

"Fine," said Dolly. "Dine with the low-lifes."

"You'll feel better with breakfast in you," said Pat. "You're my Valentine, right?"

"For better or for worse," muttered Dolly.

"Oh it's going to get better," said Pat. "Let me tell you."

Pat let Dolly off at McCormack's Town Talk. As she sashayed through the diner's frosty glass door, Pat drove down the icy alley and parked the Essex behind the Green Lantern tavern. From the rear, the tavern looked like a warehouse: chipped brick, rusty gutters, broken downspouts, green paint peeled on the steel door.

But from a dark office in that tavern, Harry played this city like Hampton played the vibraphone.

Chicago had Al Capone, New York had Dutch Shultz, Saint Paul had Harry Sawyer. Capone was in prison, Shultz was dead, but Harry was still going, planning the big snatches and robberies, giving the cops their ten percent, issuing protection orders for gangsters who played fair, laundering cash and bonds with his buddies the bankers, fencing diamonds on jewelers row. Six years Harry had been kingpin and the only time he saw a jail cell was when he was bailing somebody out.

The dirt lot behind the Lantern was frozen hard, so no need for Pat's galoshes. He unbuckled them. A level gangster wore shined shoes, not schoolboy footwear. He set the galoshes in the nasty green puddle that had leaked from the heater.

He stepped out in polished brogans. Pat blessed himself, sign of the cross, for luck. He swaggered in the back door. As dull gray as it was outside, walking into the tavern was like being reborn into darkness.

Bess grabbed Pat's arm. She helped him shrug out of his

overcoat. She was Harry's Gal Friday, although her official job was running the coat room. She relieved the gangsters of their coats but more importantly their weapons, and Harry depended on Bess to keep gunfights out in the parking lot where they belonged.

Bess was thirty-plus years old, taller than Pat, with strong hands and arms, although she was not one of those, ahem, gymnastic females.

As Pat's eyes adjusted to the darkness he could see her better. She had fiery red hair, enflamed by regular appointments at the hairdresser. She wore a slit green dress, chosen to match her startling eyes, and show a flash of leg. Those eyes shone with a frightening intelligence.

Bess owned a high school diploma. And it hadn't been clipped out of no magazine, either.

"Crumley's at the bar," Bess whispered.

Pat was going to have to grow up someday, or so he'd often been told. If he was going to take over from Harry, he'd have to handle Inspector Crumley. Pat walked up to the bar and thrust a finger at the big man's ribs.

"Stick 'em up."

Pat didn't feel any actual ribs, due to layers of overcoat and fat. Crumley rattled the newspaper he'd been reading.

"What do you want?" Crumley groused.

To call Crumley fat was an insult to obese men everywhere. No shirt and certainly not his cheap seersucker suit could contain that massive gut. No matter the weather, salty rivulets ran down his spectacular jowls and soaked his frayed shirt collar. He overflowed his own personal barstool, which Harry had reinforced. Crumley had broken three stools meant for normal men.

"Where's Harry?" Crumley barked.

Pat lifted the bridge and passed behind the bar. Crumley bore the ashes of death on his forehead, but faintly. His wife had dragged him to sunrise Benediction.

"Harry ain't around," Pat said. He leaned in, confidential. "He's passing this tavern to me."

"Is that right?"

Pat rocked back, suit-coat open, thumbs hitched in the belt loops of his best trousers. Even indoors he wore his cap, protection against creeping baldness.

"Not everybody knows," Pat said, "Especially ..."

"Oh shit," said Crumley. "Bess? She knows everything, are you kidding me?"

Crumley lay the newspaper beside a cocktail glass that contained two melting ice cubes. He pushed said glass toward Pat.

Pat tossed the cubes into the sink, reached into an ice bucket for exactly two more, dropped them into the glass, flooded it with bourbon.

"Keep going," Crumley said.

Pat nearly overflowed the glass.

"You'll be treated right here, Jim," Pat said, and corked the bottle.

"I expect so," said Crumley.

"That ain't going to change."

Crumley bent to sip whiskey.

Pat set the bottle before the back-bar mirror. He caught the reflection of a frightened little fella. He straightened up tall. *Errand boy? Are you kidding me? Pat Reilly's the man to see nowadays.*

"Harry's at the farm or in town?" Crumley asked.

"He don't stay in town no more," Pat said. "G-men."

Crumley laughed. "This town been lousy with G-men before, and what happened?" He sipped. "Nothing."

Pat ran a damp rag along the bar. Drinkers needing after-church lubrication would soon push through the doors. Pat might hire a bartender tomorrow, but today he was master and slave in his own kingdom.

"If you need something from Harry," Pat said, "you go through me." He tossed the rag at the sink.

A hostile grin deformed Crumley's jowls. "Oh, well," he said. "If I need to talk to Harry direct, I suppose I can drive out to the farm."

Pat crossed his arms. "What do you need?"

"It's been an awful winter, ain't it?" Crumley said. "I could use a ton of coal."

"A ton of coal," Pat said. "I guess that could be arranged."

"You guess or you know?"

"I'll take it up with Harry."

"Who's the boss here?" Crumley asked.

"It's kind of split right now," Pat admitted. "Between me and Harry."

"And Bess," Crumley said.

"Not Bess," said Pat.

"Ain't what I heard," said Crumley. "You see the nails on that bitch? She'll scratch your eyes out."

Crumley fixed Pat with a stare. "Reilly, do you have any idea how many times I could have took an axe to this place? How many times I've gone to the chief and said leave Harry's joint alone?"

Pat picked up the Daily News.

"If the G-men ain't nothing," Pat said, and thrust the newspaper at Crumley. "Who brought Dillinger back from Tucson in handcuffs?"

Crumley waved that off.

"This time," Pat said, "Johnny gets the chair."

"Unless somebody deposits a fat sack of money in the sheriff's bank account."

"It's different now with the newsreels," Pat said. "They'll fry Dillinger and make a movie out of it."

Crumley pushed his massive sweating weight away from the bar. The stool dropped, thump, to the floor. Crumley would not, maybe could not, bend to pick up.

"So I'm gonna get my coal, right, partner?"

ST. PAUL POLICE
HUNT BANDIT DILLINGER,
SAID TO BE ON WAY TO THIS CITY

Crown Point Ind. (United Press) — Upward of 20,000 armed men engaged tonight in a gigantic search for John Dillinger, the nation's foremost desperado, who bluffed his way out of Crown Point jail today with a wooden pistol.

Dillinger commandeered the car of the woman sheriff who ruled the jail he broke out of and gaily drove off singing "Get Along Little Dogie, Get Along."

St. Paul Daily News
March 3, 1934.

Sunday evening, March 4, 1934

HARRY'S FARM

Almost three weeks had passed since Ash Wednesday, and in all that time, Pat had not run across Harry Sawyer, not in town, not at the tavern. This morning's one-word phone call had been the only communication. *Patrick.*

That's all Harry said, and then he hung up.

But it was Harry all right. His distinctive bark had given Harry his nickname: The Sea Lion.

Now freezing rain spattered the windshield of Pat's Essex as he bumped along Harry's long muddy driveway. Harry swore G-men were watching his farm, but Pat wondered if those federal spies existed only in Harry's imagination. There was nowhere to hide on this frozen prairie except for the occasional barn, farmhouse or slushy snow bank. G-men? Pat had mixed their drinks at the Green Lantern. They drank like sissies, talked like college boys and dressed like insurance salesmen. They could only operate from somewhere comfortable, Pat figured, like a warm office, or a fancy car.

Pat felt cheerful despite the murky weather. He imagined a ceremony at the kitchen table, where so many legendary deals had gone down. The names were bronze in the gangster hall of fame:

Pretty Boy Floyd, Harvey Bailey, Machine Gun Kelly. Hell, Harry's gangsters had ruined more banks than President Roosevelt.

Strong drink would be served after the handover of Harry's keys, payoff for Pat's years of faithful service. Now would be a great time for Pat's promotion. It would give him more than a week to prepare the Green Lantern for St. Patrick's Day. Pat had worked out a name change: The Saint Patrick Tavern. He'd celebrate by firing Bess. For her replacement, maybe Harry's maid, the hot little flirt Opal.

Pat's fantasy ended in a groan when he saw, parked at the farmhouse, a Chevy with Illinois plates. He yanked the hand brake, killed the engine. "Same old errand boy crap," he muttered.

Ever since Harry had arranged a certain kidnapping, he'd been laying low. But the man couldn't help it, he was a born fixer. It wasn't just the money. Harry was like the manager of a ball club. Too old and fat to play, he got a kick out of writing out the lineup and watching his boys swing the bats.

Pat pronounced himself a fool for driving up with dreamy expectations. With raindrops pelting him like tiny stinging ice bombs, he barged into the kitchen. Nobody seemed to be home. The kitchen smelled of pork sausage and maple syrup. Said aromas penetrated Pat's hangover and rang the breakfast bell in his brain.

He pushed open a swinging door for a peek into the dining room. The kitchen was gangster domain, but Gladys ruled the rest of the house like a clawed beast. She had forced Harry to move out to this farm, wanting a country atmosphere for their newly-adopted daughter.

But neither Gladys nor the little girl seemed to be home.

Pat lit a Lucky with his gold-plated lighter. The cast-iron stove radiated heat and Pat backed up to enjoy it.

Footsteps sounded on the porch. Harry burst through the door, swaying with drink. He bellowed like a sea lion: "Opal!" Then he muttered: "Gotta get a handle on that girl.

"Opal!"

Harry, with a nod to Pat, pushed through the swinging door and into the forbidden interior.

A thin, pale fellow entered from the porch, whistling a carefree show tune. He'd left his boots out there, walked in stocking feet. He had dark intense eyes and a pencil mustache. His trousers were too loose and long, like he'd borrowed them from a bigger man. He shook off a wet Navy pea jacket and hung it on a chair back. He smoothed his plaid shirt.

"How are you, sluggo?" he said. "I'm Johnny."

Pat shook and released his chilled hand.

Through the door walked a stocky, young, dark woman with an acne-scarred face. Her eyes avoided Pat. He figured she hated him on sight.

"Harry tells me," said Johnny, "you played for the Saints."

"Couple of games," said Pat.

"I played short myself," Johnny said, and mimicked a throwing motion. "Might've made the majors. Hurt my arm."

Johnny lifted a speckled blue enamel coffee pot from the stove, set it back in disappointment.

"Rained all the way up," said Johnny. "Miserable drive. Slippery. Usually I like a good long drive."

An alcove contained a secretary desk and wooden chair. Johnny's girlfriend huddled there, holding her purse against her coat, a dark one with gold buttons. She sat forward on the chair as if hoping for an excuse to leave.

"And this shy creature," said Johnny, "is Billie."

Her lips were painted garish red, which drew attention from her pancaked, pockmarked cheeks. Said lips moved in a silent, reluctant greeting.

"Harry says..." Johnny began, but the man himself appeared.

"Opal quit me again," Harry said. "How do you like that?"
He looked over his shoulder. "I can't afford to let her go."

Even before Harry had bought a farm, he was the butter-
and-eggs man. His farm hands, his wife, his downtown employees,
his gangster buddies, all clung to Harry because he understood the
magic of cash. Pat had learned this little poem from Harry:

The man with the dough,
not the man with the gun,
is the fella
who gets things done.

"No Gladys either," grumbled Harry when he too discovered
the coffee pot was empty.

Where had Gladys gone? Pat did not ask. Only cops and
rubes asked questions. A level guy would rather not know.
Knowledge was danger. If you knew something, and things went
wrong, somebody might call you a stool pigeon. And if somebody
called you a stool pigeon, you should chirp out your Last
Confession.

Gladys, Pat guessed, had gone crazy, cooped up all winter
drinking with Harry. Maybe she had taken little Francine on the
train to Florida. Everybody was abandoning Harry now, so it was
more important than ever that Pat stay loyal.

"Pat, I got something for you out in the car," Harry said, and
held open the kitchen door. He and Pat in shirtsleeves hustled
through frosty rain for a few sloshy steps and entered Harry's
Packard convertible, Harry behind the wheel.

In nicer weather, this car would have gleamed like a
showpiece, with cream paint job, leather seats and chrome
dashboard. But now it was just cold steel, glass and leaky canvas.
The breath of two chilled humans fogged the windows.

Harry took a nip from a flask, did not offer a drink to Pat and said: "I want these fucking people off my property. Pronto!"

He pulled his wad out of a trouser pocket, peeled off twenties and fifties and jammed them into Pat's shirt pocket. "Keep them away from me. They bring heat from Chicago, that's all they do."

"The regular?" Pat asked.

"The deluxe," Harry said. "The car, the cash, the backup. These people are level, I guarantee you."

The kitchen door slammed and out rushed Opal, in yellow rubber coat, holding a kerchief to her head, bounding over puddles. Like so many of Harry's people, she was Irish. Jew and Irish, somehow they got along good. The St. Paul gang was Irish all the way, except for a few no-nonsense Jews who had survived the bootleg wars.

Opal cranked up her jalopy. It smoked like it was on fire.

"Miserable dyke," Harry muttered. He watched as she mud-spun out of the driveway. "She'll be back when she needs to steal something."

Pat lit a Lucky. "You in love with her, Harry?"

Harry sputtered, smacked Pat with a friendly backhand. "You asshole Irishman," he said.

Pat and Harry trooped dripping into the kitchen, where Johnny sat at the table shuffling cards, Billie looking over his shoulder.

"It's arranged," Harry announced. "Pat's your man in this town. He's dependable like a gold watch."

Harry's praise tunneled warm into Pat's heart.

"Go ahead," Harry told Johnny, "tell him what you need."

Pat sat at the kitchen table and Johnny dealt him a poker hand. Pat got a whiff of Billie's perfume, nauseous sweet.

"For starters, a clean car," Johnny said. "Big, fast, reliable.

I'm not afraid of stylish."

"No jalopies," barked Harry. "Good Minnesota plates. All the lights working. Top class tires and battery."

"An apartment," said Johnny. "Nice part of town. Furnished. Two beds. Ground floor. Out where the swells live, not downtown. Away from the dives and gambling joints."

Harry pointed his thumb to his own chest, meaning he, not Pat, would arrange the apartment.

Pat glanced at Billie, who stood silent and glum. Suddenly Pat was overcome by the notion that this was the moment he'd been waiting for all his life. He became aware of his own breathing and all things around him. An orange cat in the alcove sat suspicious, swishing its tail. A brass clock ticked over the doorway. The riffle of Johnny's cards. The cloying of Billie's perfume mixed with the scent of sausage and scalded coffee. The bread crumbs and syrup rings on the checkered table cloth. The rain beating against the windows. The tight feeling in his throat, as if he might never swallow again.

Billie broke the spell, her voice so low Pat had to replay it in his mind: "Polished wood floors."

"She likes," said Johnny, "nice floors. I don't know why, since she covers 'em up with those Oriental carpets."

Johnny pushed back from the table, stood behind Pat whistling, and slapped him on the back. Pat wasn't sure he liked that slap. It was the kind of thing you did to an errand boy.

Harry, at the cupboard, poured whiskey into a coffee cup and swigged from it. Then he brought out three more cups and laid them on the table.

The best arrangers kept it simple and told each person only what they needed to know. Johnny would be safe from the cops now, and in return Harry would get a piece of his haul. Nothing was put in writing or said on the telephone. A sip of whiskey was a contract. A nod was a deal. A shrug, and maybe someone was going off level, and would never be seen again. Pat had learned much from Harry, the best arranger in outlaw history, as far as Pat was concerned.

"Billie?" Harry said and handed her a cup of whiskey.

"She don't drink," said Johnny. "She's an Injun."

"I do so drink." Billie put her lips to the cup and blew a little storm into the whiskey.

If Whistling Johnny's last name was Dillinger, as Pat strongly suspected, he was a cheerful fellow hooked up with a moody female. Pat knew what that was like. Where had all the fun girls gone off to?

Johnny wandered to the sink. He washed his hands with a rough bar of Cascade soap. He wasn't a striking fellow, not big, not impressive, not movie star handsome as the newspapers said. He seemed fussy about hand washing. Drying his hands with a red checkered towel, he sauntered to the table as Harry lifted a toast.

"Around here," Harry said, "we call St. Paul the Holy City. There are things we hold sacred."

Pat raised his cup.

"Like silence," Harry said. "Like loyalty."

"To the Holy City," said Johnny and the three men drank.

Billie picked up her cup. "Shiny floors," she said. "That's all I ask, John, shiny fucking floors."

"You heard the little woman," Johnny said.

CHICAGO AREA COMBED FOR DILLINGER DEN

St. Paul Daily News
March 5, 1934

Monday,
March 5, 1934

FILBEN

Pat hustled past the display windows of Emerald Radio Electronics. Said windows held displays in the truest sense. Outlandish prices taped to the radios insured that no rube would disturb the management, seeking to purchase a Philco.

Pat walked down a cold brick alley and pushed open a rotting wooden door. He entered a dark warehouse, flicked a brass toggle and a dull light revealed a riot of slot machines. Some were shiny, sitting high on tables. Others, like wounded soldiers, lay on the floor, bleeding out their innards.

"Tommy?" Pat called.

"In here, me boy."

Pat tiptoed over a floor scattered with gears, whirl-a-gigs, half-opened boxes. He bumped into dusty pinball machines, passed dusty safes, their doors gaping.

In the office, lit feebly by an occluded sun, stood Tom Filben, dressed like a nightclub emcee. He held some little red device in the palm of his hand. Tom devoted his spare time, and he had plenty of it, to magic tricks.

"By Christ, it's good to see you," said Filben.

"I've been busy at Harry's."

"Sit down," Filben said, and kicked a heavy oak chair. "How is our young reprobate, anyway?"

Pat zipped open his leather jacket, fished out a pack of Luckies.

"Harry is retiring," said Pat.

"Christ almighty!"

"He's dealing through me now."

Pat lit that Lucky and tried to figure, through the smoke screen, whether Filben took him serious.

"Well now," said Filben. "What about Big Ryan?"

"Harry will fix me up." Pat rocked in the chair, felt a thrill run through him.

"When you shake hands with Big Joe Ryan," Filben said, "Red Letter day indeed. Feast of the Assumption."

"Tommy, I need a clean car."

"Try the Lowry Garage."

"I'm not joking. High class, reliable, legit plates, not a speck of dirt on it. I've got an Illinois Chevy to trade, plus make-up cash. This is for a level guy and I mean level."

He tapped his cigarette. Ashes fell to the concrete floor. Filben shuffled a glass ashtray along the desk.

"I need it today," Pat said.

In the ensuing silence, a radiator whistled.

"That's quite an order," Filben said. "I don't suppose it's accompanied by the relevant bundle of cash."

"Harry pays."

"But he's retiring, you say."

Filben dropped that red object from his hand. The little ball, or whatever it was, reached the end of the string and zipped back into his hand.

"Ever seen one?" Filben asked.

Pat shook his head.

"Defies every known law of physics," Filben claimed. He shot the little ball toward Pat's face. Pat ducked, but the thing returned to Filben's hand.

"Direct from the Philippines," Filben said. "I've ordered a thousand." He threw the thing and Pat caught it. It wasn't a ball at all, but a red wooden disk, with string wound into a crack.

"By Christ, kids love these things. I can't get them away from my nephews. Try it. Wrap the loop around your finger, then let it go. Comes back to you every time."

Pat let the disk drop. It hung dead, like a man swinging from the gallows.

"Takes a bit of skill," said Filben, and snatched the thing from Pat, demonstrating the drop and retrieve. "They call it a yo-yo. Fantastic toy. I met a fellow last night could do all sorts of tricks. These fellows from Manila are going all across the country demonstrating them."

"Tommy, no joke about that car."

"See the thing is Patrick, I'm attempting a graceful exit myself." Filben whirled the yo-yo out. "The days of easy money and bathtub gin are gone."

Filben's game was feigned reluctance, which had the effect of raising his price. During Prohibition, he had made a fortune by "financing" bootleggers' automobiles. When cops confiscated a bootlegger's vehicle, Filben dug out the title and sent his lackey to the impound lot to reclaim it. Said vehicle was returned to said bootlegger for a considerable fee.

Pat smashed his Lucky into the ashtray. "You can't say no to Harry."

"I'll see what Herb's got in the garage," Filben said. He dropped the yo-yo, clonk, onto his wooden desk. That desk was the least cluttered surface Pat had ever seen, holding only an ashtray, a calculating machine, and now a yo-yo.

"Somebody's in town?" Filben asked.

"You might have read about him, that's all I can say."

"You want one car," Filben said, "so it can't be the two Shorties coming back to haunt us. No, those boys would never share anything. I have the feeling we'll never see the Barker lads, their friend Karpis, or their ugly mother in our gloomy Irish city again. Dragging their poor mother along on bank jobs and snatches. Those hillbillies should be ashamed of themselves. No Irish gangster would treat his mother like that."

"This ain't nothing to do with the Barkers," Pat said.

Filben sat on his desk. "What is it about our race, Patrick? Why do we gravitate to the cold and gloom?" He looked out the window. The sun in its heaven may have been a mighty orb, but it gave pitiful illumination to Filben's cobblestone alley.

"I'll bet you," Filben said, "there's not one Irishman in all of Arizona. Our tribe seeks gloomy misery and avoids sunshine and pleasure. If you'd ever visited the Emerald Island, Paddy boy, you would understand. Christ have mercy on that cold, gray lump of rock. It never stops raining there, never. A glimpse of sunshine, why in Ireland, that's a miracle. Equal to the loaves and fishes! It's the climate that made us a cruel people."

Filben shook his head.

"And a corrupt people, Patrick. Once you behold that accursed potato-loving island, you understand why we're a race of drinkers."

A stray pulse of sunshine flooded Filben's office, and Pat blinked.

"Tell me this," Filben said. "Why in all the world has no

Irishman ever emigrated to the Philippines? Is it the sunshine that offends the Irishman? The warm weather? The cheerful natives? By Christ, we find grimy Liverpool attractive enough. We're thrilled to clean the toilets of the hostile Yankees of Boston. We embrace the cockroach slums of the Bronx. And St. Paul! Christ almighty, how did we find this igloo? It's the one city in the world with worse weather than Dublin. By Christ, I've half a mind to settle in Manila and start exporting yo-yos. Think of it Patrick, the sunny beaches, the beautiful girls, an Irishman sipping from a sweet coconut instead of a pint of bitter stout."

Filben was beginning to sweat into his starched collar.

"But all you want is one car," he said, and his flush ebbed. "I suppose I can find you one spiffy car. But then I'm out of this game forever, tell Harry that. Don't come around looking for the old Filben, for I'm a new man tomorrow. Enough of these gangsters. Yo-yos, Patrick, yo-yos are the future."

Out on busy Wabasha Street, Pat wound his wristwatch. It was a gold Longines Harry had given him, traded in by a Chicago gangster in return for a month's protection. Said watch informed Pat that it was Opal's quitting time.

The day after Opal quit Harry, she took up her former trade, waiting tables at the Town Talk. Soft-hearted Harry had arranged that job for her, imagine that. Harry couldn't help himself, gruff gangster with a big sloppy heart.

Pat waited in the alley beside the Town Talk and when Opal emerged, he took her arm, hustled along Wabasha, a mad mix of cars, pedestrians, trolleys and even horse-drawn wagons.

HAMM'S

That neon beer sign was like a magnet. Pat opened the door

to the brass-and-marble lobby of the St. Paul Recreation Lounge.

Which was a fancy name for a pool hall.

"Is it clean, Patrick?" Opal asked, but stepped in.

Opal, unbuttoning her coat, seemed mesmerized by the Selectophone. She looked tiny before this massive machine. She ran her bright fingernails down the list of song titles. "You got a dime?" she asked Pat.

That was good for two songs. The first one Pat had never heard before: *Blame it on My Youth*. When it started playing, she said: "They got no dancing in here?"

"Unless you dance on a pool table," Pat said.

He hung up her coat, escorted her to the bar. Her uniform bore the grease marks of a double shift. She ripped a paper napkin from a dispenser, wet it with her tongue, dabbed at her uniform.

A kid bartender seemed irritated by their presence, although he had no other drinkers to take care of.

"A draw for me," said Pat. He flopped his cap on the bar. "Coke for the lady."

"Never too early," said the bartender, an Italian kid. He dressed in white, like he was working a hamburger stand. Bartenders, in Pat's opinion, should never wear white.

"You remind me, kid, so don't remind me," said Pat.

"Huh?"

"Of my humble beginnings," said Pat. "I used to be with the Saints, you know."

Pat looked to Opal for approval, but she only groomed her uniform.

The kid set the beer before Pat, who ducked his head for a look over the rim.

"Bad pour," Pat said.

"What do you want?" said the kid.

"A head," said Pat. "Tilt the glass. Don't you know nothing?"

The kid snatched the glass, poured the beer into the sink.

"Clean glass," said Pat. "Don't use that one."

The kid picked up a clean glass. "I know how to pour beer," he muttered.

"There's three people in this town who know something," Pat said, "and you ain't one of them."

"What's that supposed to mean?"

The bartender delivered a beer with a head, and Pat sipped through the foam. "I said Coke for the lady, didn't you hear me?"

The kid glared, but fetched a bottle of Coke and a glass loaded with ice cubes.

"Some day, kid." Pat fished in his suit-coat pocket for a Lucky and his lighter. "Comes a time when you stop taking orders and start giving 'em. That's when you know you're a man."

"Is that so," said the kid, lips curled.

Pat tapped his Lucky on the bar. He held that cigarette up, unlit, and stared at it. It seemed important, not just another cigarette. He lit it with his gold lighter, which was shaped like the Statue of Liberty. The flame came out the torch end.

"She don't smoke and she don't drink," Pat said, indicating Opal with a tilt of his head. "Good kid. I got this lighter at the World's Fair."

He lit his cigarette. "In Chicago. Now there's a city. I'm going there this summer. To see the Fair. Sally Rand, that's what I want to see."

Opal sipped her Coke. Her head nodded in time to a fading song.

"You play ball, kid?" Pat asked the bartender. "I played second for the Saints, like I was telling you."

"You did not," Opal challenged him.

"Before your time," Pat insisted.

Opal shook her head with an amused smile.

"You don't look like no ballplayer to me," said the barkeep. "You want another Hamm's?"

Pat hadn't been aware that he'd drained his beer. It had bum-rushed his throat without pestering his taste buds.

"Yeah," said Pat.

As soon as it was delivered, he sucked off the foam, set down the glass, swiveled to face Opal. He put one elbow on the bar, supported his head, stared into her blue eyes. He grabbed her hand and held it.

"Opal, it's really something to look at you."

She cast her eyes down to her greasy uniform.

Without lifting her eyes, Opal said, "You're a married man."

Pat let her hand go. She swiveled away to put both elbows on the bar, lips poised above lipstick-marked soda glass.

"I'm scared of you," she said.

"Of me?"

"I kind of like you but I'm scared of you."

Pat realized he'd been breathing heavy. From what? Sitting on a barstool?

"Look, kid, this is business, you see?" Pat said. "I ain't one of them romantic rubes. I'm a happy married man, my wife, you know, everybody in town knows her and me. So look, what I want from you, it's pure business. Guys like to look at you. You're cute like a pixie doll. You're what I need up front when the rubes walk in."

"I had my heart set on better things," pleaded Opal. "I want to go to secretarial school."

"Great! Ambition, you see? Nothing like it. You work at my tavern nights, daytimes, you go in for your shorthand and typing."

"The Green Lantern?" Opal said. "I'm scared of that place. It's such a rough crowd."

"We're going to class the joint up. Think it over. Take all

day." He swiveled off that barstool, stood, caressed Opal's shoulders and said, "I'll be right back."

As he padded toward for the restroom he glanced out the big windows and saw Bess. In black coat and high heels, she crossed Wabasha from the streetcar stop.

Pat spun around, returned to the bar, picked up his cap, fished a five-dollar bill from his wallet and threw it toward the bartender.

"I got business," he whispered to Opal. "Be right back."

{Pat challenges Bess}

Out the revolving doors Pat pushed, and stumbled onto the street to watch Bess Green duck down Filben's alley. He lit a Lucky and paced amid the streetcar rubes. The Como streetcar went by. The Randolph car screeched to a halt and idled. He glanced backward, worried that Opal, inside the tavern, was amusing herself on his money, playing every song in that record machine. Pat had smoked three Luckies down to their nubs before Bess emerged from Filben's alley.

Pat hailed her underneath the Hamm's sign. She cast him a nasty look.

"Been shopping for a radio?" he said.

She eyed a streetcar like she wanted to hop aboard.

"You don't visit Tommy much," Pat said.

"He believes himself to be a very attractive man," Bess said. "I need to catch this car."

"You still ain't learned to drive?" Pat called as Bess hustled toward the departing streetcar. Something inside nagged at him, but he couldn't put the words to it.

Was it even possible that Harry might backstab him and give Bess the Green Lantern?

Impossible. Here she was getting onto a streetcar. The boss

of the Green Lantern was the most feared gangster in town. Never in a million years would gangsters take orders from a woman. Never in two million years would the boss of the underworld be caught dead on a streetcar.

Bess swung up on the rear step, lost herself in the crowd aboard, and Pat felt better.

Although as he watched the streetcar pull away, he felt disappointed that Harry had felt the need to use Bess at all.

Those Luckies had left a harsh taste in his mouth and he needed another beer. He walked into the taproom, where Opal, pouty, was working into her coat. Pouty or not, Pat had settled on Opal as the right choice to replace Bess in the coatroom. His coatroom. In his Green Lantern.

"How about we walk down and get a genuine Coney Dog?"

Opal looked him over. "You shouldn't abandon a girl in a tavern."

"Coney's got private booths," he said. "We could talk better."

He took Opal's arm. He had to admit it wasn't just business, it was kind of a cheap thrill, walking beside a gorgeous young girl. He addressed the stern judge who presided in his mind's courtroom:

I know what it looks like, your honor,
But I swear on the Bible it was a business decision.

S.D. BANDITS
KIDNAP 4 GIRLS
BANK RAIDERS
USE STOLEN ST. PAUL AUTO

St. Paul Daily News, March 6, 1934

Using a car stolen in St. Paul, six machine gun bandits lined up the police chief, a patrolman and 40 others in the Security National Bank, Sioux Falls, S.D., today, looted it of $15,000, kidnapped four girls and one man, critically wounded a motorcycle patrolman and then headed back toward St. Paul.

One of the bandits closely resembled John Dillinger, witnesses said.

Thursday, March 8, 1934

BOWLING WITH MICKEY

Pat had been a pin-boy once. Bat boy, pin boy, altar boy, delivery boy, he'd been every kind of boy. So when he edged into the German-American Club, the crash of pins and thud of rolling balls spiked his memory. Pin-boy, Pat had enjoyed. Good tips! But a fella got exhausted, jumping lane to lane, and it was so loud that next morning you answered every question with "huh?"

So Pat had worked his Irish-Catholic connections to become bat boy for the Saints. It was a thrilling promotion. Those boozy rowdy team bus rides were as much fun as the games.

Homer Van Meter was at lane 12, closest to the door. He had not warned Pat about the female. This girl was so small she rolled a child's light-grey 12-pounder. She stood at the foul line watching the ball thunk down the alley and crash with little effect into the pins. She danced back to Van Meter, who sat at the bench, spread-armed, laughing. She play-slapped him.

Van Meter waved Pat in with his long arms, like he was directing a boat into a dock.

"Hey, Mickey," he said to the girl. "Get us some fresh beer."

"Well, give me the money," said Mickey. "Stingy."

From his floppy trousers, Van Meter pulled a packet of bills that had a bank wrapper around it. "Don't flirt with the barkeep," he said, and slipped her two fives.

"Little bitch." He watched her trot off in knee sox, short skirt, white blouse. He sighed. "I believe I've found the love of my life."

Pat slipped onto the bench. "I didn't know this was going to be a ladies social," Pat said.

Van Meter cocked his head. "Want to bowl me? Ten cents a pin."

"Um," Pat said.

"You afraid of me, Reilly?"

In a way, Pat was. All the Dillinger gang was red hot now, and that South Dakota bank job had only fanned the flames.

Maybe it was dumb, but Pat was spooked because they looked mismatched sitting together, with Van Meter tall enough to play basketball for the Gophers. Maybe somebody would be staring at them and say hey, the tall goofy guy, I've seen his picture in the Daily News. Pat's gaze fixed on the bleached spot on Van Meter's forearm where a Chicago quack had tried to erase the tattooed word HOPE.

Pat couldn't stop his legs from twitching. "I just want to get out of here," he said. He peered over his shoulder. He was getting like Harry now, every stranger looked like a Fed.

"Relax," Van said. "Have a beer with us."

Pat's eyes fixed on a bowling bag, dark red leather, set underneath a scoring chair. Van Meter stood, snatched a ball from the return slot, and all gawky limbs, ambled to the foul line. He fired a ferocious rumbling rocket that sent pins flying and endangered some cowering pin boy.

"The pins are like cops," said Van Meter. "You never want to leave one standing." His eyes sparkled as Mickey approached balancing a tray. It held three schooners of beer and a bowl of popcorn.

"That's my girl," said Van, and handed Pat a flat, lifeless

Hamm's beer. Hamm's had brewed better beer during Prohibition. Nowadays, they were rushing the brew, and it tasted green.

"Want a tip?" said Van.

"Yeah," said Mickey.

"Nellie Bell in the fourth race."

"Ha ha," said Mickey. "Heard that a million times."

"You ain't heard nothing," said Van. "Hell, you were a five-and-dime girl when I swept you off your feet."

"I was tired. It was the end of a long day."

"Get me a pack of Old Golds."

"What am I, a dog? Fetch this, fetch that."

"I give you two tens," said Van.

"Two fives, asshole."

"Keep the change," Van said. "And take your time. We got men talk here."

Mickey flashed him the middle finger and, slowed by her own defiance, backed toward the concession stand. She taunted Van Meter, cupping hands at ears to mime eavesdropping.

"Crazy about that girl," said Van Meter. "I wanted you to meet her. Ain't she cute and sassy?"

"Is everything set? Because I want to leave."

"Aw, she's all right," said Van Meter.

"This dough is from South Dakota? They'll want to know. They don't want no ransom money mixed in."

Van Meter nodded.

"Pure bank," he said.

"How'd that job go?" asked Pat.

"It went stupid," said Van. "Don't you read the papers? But we got the dough. Little Jimmy went crazy and shot up the town, but we's all right."

By "little Jimmy" he meant the fellow that the newspapers called Baby Face Nelson. Little Jimmy was so brave it was stupid, always the first guy to let the bullets fly.

Van Meter gulped beer, snatched popcorn. "Got us a cop. One less prick in the world." He tilted his head and dribbled popcorn into his mouth.

"I'm going," said Pat.

"You just got here."

"If everything's all right, I'm going."

"It's all right, just like I said."

"Then I'm going."

Pat picked up the red bowling bag just as Mickey was retuning with a pack of Old Golds.

"Nice to meet you ma'am," said Pat.

"Well you ain't sociable," grumped Mickey, "but your mother taught you manners."

Pat slunk off. He tried to be the least memorable person at any meeting. That habit had kept him out of jail, so he wasn't worried about the opinion of a Chicago five-and-dime girl.

Pat Reilly, was he there?

I can't rightly remember, your honor.

As Pat lugged that bowling bag into the dark cold parking lot, he thought of his mother and father, and what a lifetime in the family laundry had done to them. Washed out! It had killed his old man. Only two fates awaited the Irish: death by drink, death by hard labor.

But maybe there was another way. Since 1900, the O'Connor brothers, God bless them, had showed that Irishmen with wit and courage could run a city from the backroom of a tavern. Politicians and cops begged for an audience like the O'Connors were Popes. Money, that's all it was. The O'Connors proved that a couple of sharp Irishmen could take over a city without firing a shot. When the O'Connors turned senile, it was Harry Sawyer and Big Joe Ryan who took over the grand tradition.

Pat sat behind the wheel of his Essex sucking down deep breaths, that bowling bag on the seat beside him. He'd bought this used Terraplane on credit from Filben. It had once belonged to a wise guy named Powers, who had mysteriously disappeared, to Cuba, or so people said. Pat hadn't been crazy about a used car, but the Essex company boasted that its Terraplane could reach 83 miles per hour.

Pat could get only 78, floored. Still, the Terraplane could outrun any police jalopy.

Pat started the car and gunned the engine, his gut gurgling out a warning of backroom police beatings and shackled walks down Leavenworth's corridors. With shaking hands he zipped open the bowling bag and lifted out one bundle of bills wrapped in a white cotton sock. Pat the altar boy imagined a cop's baton rapping on the windshield. He pinched out a few bills and stuffed them into the pocket of his flannel shirt. He zipped the bag shut, breathing like he'd just run down a dark alley.

Pat the pickpocket opened the bag again and pinched another wad of money.

I needed it to feed my starving family, your honor.

He zipped the bag closed and patted it firm. He slipped on leather driving gloves and drove away from the grimy neighborhood, past brick compounds belonging to Minnesota Mining and Hamm's Brewery. In ten minutes, he arrived at the swell-elegant Rice Park. The park, its fountains dry for the winter, was surrounded by the new library, the opera house, the Wilder Charity Building, the Hotel St. Paul and the Federal Courthouse. Pat parked in a shadowy alley behind the hotel. It gave him the creeps to do business under the nose of the G-men. He hustled along the alley as fast as he could without looking too guilty.

They were burning the lights late, the G-men men on the second floor.

At the hotel entrance Pat dodged the bell captain and mixed with the crowd: women in furs and swagger suits, and men whose fedoras cost more than Pat's wardrobe. Pat carried that bowling bag nonchalant through the marble lobby, across plush rugs and up fire stairs to the third floor. No guest rooms occupied this floor, only offices with pebbled glass doors. Said offices belonged to lawyers and dentists and accountants and gamblers. This last one, in a dark alcove, had been rented by Big Ryan. In black letters it said on the glass door:

ST. PAUL PROTECTIVE ASSOCIATION

Pat opened his wallet and removed a brass key from a leather hanger. Nobody lurked in the hallway, so he slipped the key into the lock and nudged the door with his foot. Without crossing the threshold, he slid the bowling bag into the dark office, pulled the door shut, locked it, made a quiet exit down the fire stairs.

Somehow, Pat had a thirst for a highball or maybe ten highballs. Deliveries to Big Ryan made him nervous. The danger was getting robbed or losing the bag. That would be your last appearance on this unholy earth until they dragged your bloated corpse out of the Mississippi.

A thousand people claimed to know Big Ryan, but he had no close friends. Harry and Filben and the late Serious Bobby had dealt straight with him, but everybody else kept their distance. Big Ryan rarely appeared at his office. Errand boys brought him cash, which was divided according to a secret formula, among cops, politicians, jailers, judges and prosecutors. Harry was the most important gangster, but still, ninety percent of the cash flowed to Big Ryan, who took it in, and dished it out.

Pat pushed through the revolving brass doors of the Grill Room. Oh this was a theater-mad town. The pretty people got plastered at the Grill Room and sometimes you'd even find Hollywood stars in town to flog their latest mule of a movie. Oyster stew and strong cocktails, starlets and stage hands all randy after the play, that was the Grill Room. But any so-called gangsters in here were pretenders who went home to mama at night.

Pat pushed past black curtains that glittered with tiny silvery stars. He took two steps toward the massive oak bar and then stopped. Sitting with her back to him was Dolly, in a lame' dress, hair in curls, talking to some sandy-haired guy in a cream-colored suit. Pat saw her through the haze of cigarette smoke, his heart beating like a racing engine, his lips moving to a tortured language no tongue could speak. His Irish temper was the exact reason he never carried a gun, even on money runs.

Again! Dolly, you two-timing, fat-ass tramp.

His teeth ground in rage and he hustled blind through the revolving doors and whoosh into the cold night.

This is the thanks you get, marrying a notorious Carey. Married by a priest and behaving like a whore! Pat rushed to his Essex and sat behind the wheel. You can't do nothing with beaten-down love, and Pat knew it. You can't drink it to death, cry it out, sing it away, punch it senseless. Maybe you could jump off the Empire State Building but nothing else worked to crush this horrible sick feeling.

Betrayed by the love of his life! Dolly and Pat were meant to be, here on earth and in heaven for eternity, except that Dolly ... Pat dug out a Lucky and lit it with his Statue of Liberty.

He started the Essex. The fan on the dashboard, supposedly a defroster, only drained the battery, so Pat pulled a bandana out of his side pocket. Scattering loose tobacco and small change, he wiped the foggy windows so he could see clear to drive. He was having no fight with Dolly in the Grill Room, where the swells would laugh at him.

He drove down Fort Road, a strip of dive bars, pawn shops and cheap hotels. In the mirror he saw the same car behind him once or twice, it had one flickering headlight. If the Feds were on his tail this would be the prefect rotten ending to an awful night. He made a quick turn and lost that car. He stayed parked for exactly one smoke, rolled down the window, tossed the Lucky, and resumed his journey of anger toward Swede Hollow.

They were renters, the Careys, of the last shabby house on Maria Avenue. Said domicile was clad in asphalt siding and was sagging toward its date with the wrecking ball. One rusty steel chair sat on its peeling porch. Directly across the street was a Lutheran Church, and beyond that a cul-de-sac servicing fine homes at the rocky ravine known as Swede Hollow Park.

No light shone from the Carey house, but his mother-in-law Nora was in there, squirming with the gut-knowledge that Dolly was out late in danger town. Was this what she wanted? A divorced Dolly, playing with strangers?

Pat parked in the moon-shadow of the Lutheran Church, yanked the handbrake, waited. Patience is a virtue, Pat's mother loved to say, although what good came of virtue she never explained. All Pat wanted now was to see Dolly's guilty face and hear bullshit excuses roll off her lying lips.

The moment Dolly sneaked home, Nora would be up in her tattered robe, so Pat readied a barrage of curses. His mother-in-law was always nagging her daughter to find a man, any man but Patrick. We're in love, Pat muttered as if Nora were there. We'd work it out if you'd leave us to hell alone.

His worries were interrupted by the shine of a single headlamp. Pat knew what he would see next: the face that wallpapered Hell's waiting room, Inspector James Crumley.

Crumley waddled to the passenger side, and Bulldog McMullen rapped with a heavy ring. Pat cranked the window down:

"Was I speeding, officer?"

"He's a funny guy," said Bulldog over the roof of the car to Crumley.

Crumley, gasping and sweating, fitted himself into the passenger side of the Essex. Pity the car springs as the Essex leaned to Crumley's side. Crumley's entrance knocked the hat off his head, and he fanned his sweating face although it was near freezing.

"Give the Inspector a fucking heart attack," said the Bulldog, "making us chase you all over town."

Crumley coughed into a handkerchief.

"What the Inspector means to say," McMullen said. "Is we're feeling left out."

He tweaked Pat's ear.

Crumley croaked: "I see the boys brung a piece of change back from South Dakota."

"It's my favorite state," said McMullen. "Especially this time of year. Don't you like it, Jim?"

"I ain't never been there."

"Still, you like it, right?"

McMullen hammered Pat's shoulder. Pat's head filled with squeaky music like from a $5 Philco. His shoulder stung, mule-kicked. Pat had been hit by a line drive once, but McMullen's punch packed more sting.

"Where's our piece?" said Crumley.

"You get yours from Big Ryan," Pat said.

"That's where you're wrong, partner," said Crumley.

From his overcoat pocket, McMullen drew a dull revolver and handed it to Pat. Too late, Pat realized he should not have touched it.

"Oh, no," said McMullen. "Are we looking at a gun charge, Jim?"

Crumley took the pistol out of Pat's hands, inserted three

brass ammo rounds and said, "Loaded, too."

He twirled the cylinders.

"You know we have to make it safe for the citizens of this fine municipality. Is that how you say it, Bulldog? Mew-nish-aw-pal-it-ee?"

"Nope," said Bulldog. "There's no pal in municipality."

"How do you say it then?"

"Ninety days and a hundred dollar fine."

"That's how you say it," said Crumley. "It's a crime. Deliver a fat bag to Big Ryan and you forget Jimbo and the Bulldog."

Crumley's jowls moved in waves.

"What do you guys want?" asked Pat.

"You know the city don't give us no clothing allowance, now," said Crumley. "We gotta pay out of pocket. That's hard to do when there's holes in your pockets. New wardrobe, overcoat and all, what's that go for Bill?"

"Hundred bucks easy," said McMullen. "Including shoes."

"Just a couple of bills out of Big Ryan's bag," said Crumley, "that's all it is. He'd never know it was missing."

"I'll see what I can do," said Pat.

"In the meantime, Bulldog, keep that pistol. Take it to Tierney, see if he can pick up some prints on 'er."

"Come on, Reilly," said Bulldog. "How much did you keep for yourself? Anything less than five hundred, you're a sucker."

Pat gripped the steering wheel with both hands and said: "I'll see you boys tomorrow."

"Damn right," said McMullen.

"One way or the other," said Crumley

Thanks for reading the beginning of *The Resurrection of Saint Johnny*. The book is available in electronic version for Kindle devices, and in print at Amazon.

www.ingramcontent.com/pod-product-compliance
Lightning Source LLC
Chambersburg PA
CBHW020235180626
46810CB00006B/2211